THEY HAVE CONQUERED

Part One

Herbert Wiens

Paperback ISBN 9798987879627
eBook ISBN 9798985408355

H.P. Waterhouse Publishing

CONTENTS

PROLOGUE

Every exhaled breath propelled the old man closer to his final fate. His frail body was giving up the fight. Legs that carried him through some of the most turbulent times in history lay uselessly still. Ears that were subjected to the explosive sounds of wartime munitions and the rhetoric of violent social change heard only his weakening pulses of blood. Hands that joyously welcomed new life into this world and mournfully held loved ones as they slipped from it, lay numb at his sides. Using eyes that refused to surrender to time, he spent his remaining earthly hours studying the water-stained, textured ceiling in the room which had become his prison cell. A lone spider made its way across the interconnecting mint green waves of plaster. Lint and dust clinging to the spider's burgeoning web amplified the illusion of foam riding on turbulent seas. The sight washed a tsunami of memories over him—memories he had spent his life compiling.

CHAPTER ONE
RETURN TO RUSSIA

Young Gerhardt Wiens clung to the heaving deck's railing, mesmerized by the turbulent October 1894 North Atlantic Ocean. Small for his age, he stood on the railing's lower rung to see over the edge. Having just turned seven in July, he was already an experienced traveler. His family had come to America in June of the previous year.

In that short time, they visited New York, Chicago, and Ottawa. He and his siblings—older brother Heinrich, younger brother Johann, and sister Helena—helped his parents build a house in Mountain Lake, Minnesota. When the relative who sold them the land couldn't produce its clear title, they rented out the house and left to stay with other relatives in Hillsboro, Kansas. There, his mother gave birth to a new sister, Maria.

Gerhardt and his siblings enjoyed living in the United States. The American culture was very different from their homeland, making it a grand adventure. Their father was from a wealthy German Mennonite family in the southern Ukraine region of Imperial Russia.

Since children were required by the Imperial State to learn High German and Russian in their private schools, his father and the older children were trilingual. His mother and the younger children were bilingual. None of those languages were English. At home, they used the earthy Plautdietsch that their community had spoken for generations.

Their mother, Helena Schmidt Wiens, had been born into a poor family and never learned to read and write. The language barrier in the United States wasn't a problem as long as they stayed in communities of their own ethnicity who had arrived in the Midwest two decades before.

The earlier immigrants left Russia when the Imperial government dictated that the Russian language be taught in the German settlers' private schools—no matter if they were Catholic, Lutheran, Mennonite, or Hutterite. Also revoked was the promised exemption to military conscription. Not wanting to comply, Hutterites and some of the more conservative Mennonite branches left for Canada and the United States.

After a Midwestern drought in 1873 and a locust invasion in the summer of 1874 drove many farmers into submission, the religiously conservative immigrants arrived with the resources to buy large tracts of land. Luckily for the American Midwest and the Canadian prairie provinces, they brought their Turkish Hard Red Winter Wheat with them. Immediately, the immigrants planted this new strain of winter wheat, tilling under the failed summer crop—transforming the American Prairie region into a grain juggernaut.

"Where have you been, Gerhardt? Mutta is worried."

Gerhardt's older brother, Heinrich, approached on his left, with their younger brother Johann in tow. Following close behind was their father, also named Heinrich, holding the hand of their little sister, Helena.

Not only did Heinrich and his father have the same first name, they also shared similar physical traits—tall, thin, with light brown straight hair, angular faces, and square cleft chins. Gerhardt took after his mother with darker skin, black hair, and a rounder face.

Stepping down from the railing's lower bar, he grinned. "I was watching the curl thrown up by the ship's bow. This boat's much nicer than the *Pennland*."

"Yes, boys, that ship was a real rust bucket," their father said. "The crew was incompetent and too busy being sick to do their jobs. So far, on this ship, we haven't had anything stolen like my watch and suit were on the *Pennland*. They were probably taken by the Turks or

Gypsies. They also gave us the lice which plagued us until we arrived in Minnesota. Mutta's wondering where you went. She's in the cabin feeding baby Maria and didn't want you causing trouble if she was unable to twist an ear off."

Gerhardt beamed back. "Oh, Foda, you know we're always good."

"Son, you're the worst offender," the elder man snorted. "There's a reason you're called the Little Devil. Not an hour goes by without you being in trouble for something." As he strolled over to a bench on the deck of the almost new *H.H. Meier,* their father smiled. "You boys weren't so brave when we arrived in New York."

The children gathered around their father on the slatted bench, and he continued, "I guess it wasn't your fault. None of us knew that the very next day they'd be celebrating the nation's independence. It took forever to pry you out from under the bed to watch the fireworks going off."

"Oh, Foda, we weren't that bad!" the eldest boy protested. "Didn't we help build the house in Mountain Lake? We really liked the relatives in Kansas."

"Yes, son," the father answered. "You boys were a real help. We probably would have stayed if that troublemaker, Eugene Debs, and his union hadn't started that railroad strike. I'm still amazed how the workers at the Pullman rail car factory can disrupt the whole railroad system. It got really bad when the *Harsha,* President Cleveland, had to put troops on the trains for guards. No, boys, America is too politically unstable and will probably come to another revolution. We'll be better off back in Russia where it's peaceful, stable, and safe. With the tsar leading the country, it'll be that way for a long time."

The boys solemnly nodded and looked ahead to their arrival in Bremerhaven.

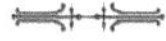

Gerhardt could barely keep his anxious feet still and his busy hands out of trouble during the family's long journey from Bremerhaven across Eastern Europe. They traveled by train, riverboat, and carriage until reaching their Ukrainian hometown of Karpovka in the Memrik colony. Immediately upon entering the village, the two older boys jumped from the wagon and ran ahead to their grandparents' house.

"Grootfoda, Grootmutta . . .Grootfoda, Grootmutta!"

Nearing the house, the boys remembered where they were and assumed a more solemn demeanor. Their grandfather came out from the barn end of the traditional house-barn building mandated by Johann Cornies decades before. The eldest Wiens was an imposing figure with his shirt buttoned clear to the top, his traditional cap and pitchfork in hand. The boys lined up in front of their grandfather for inspection as he turned to lean the tool up against the barn door.

"Well, boys, you've made it just in time to help your Grootmutta in the garden. If you wish to have supper this afternoon, you'd better hurry."

They took that to be an effusive greeting and joyfully ran around the house end of the building to find their grandmother. On the way, they took great care not to trample any of the flowers lining the path to the rear of the house—a sure way to receive a firm twist of the ear. Flowers were the only outward display of luxury she permitted herself.

It wasn't as if the house wasn't filled with nice things. The traditional Kroeger clock sat on the mantle in the winter living room, and high-quality furniture filled the immaculately kept home. But these fine things were also utilitarian and therefore not placed in the luxury category. There was a strong distinction placed between quality, which meant long lasting, and the merely frivolously fancy.

The family had standards to maintain. They were, after all, considered to be upper-middle class in their village. Gerhardt's namesake grandfather was the head elder in the church, which made him the village's de-facto mayor, and also the lead arbiter in local disputes. Having lived in the area for over a century, the family had always held a prominent position in the community.

The elder Gerhardt was the fourth generation. Fifty years before, *his* father had butted heads with the tsar's favorite Mennonite, Johann Cornies, over community discipline. To be on Cornies' bad side placed you in the tsar's disfavor. As a result, young Gerhardt's great-grandfather, Heinrich Wiens, had been forced into exile for more than a decade. Now revered within the community for defending his religious principles, almost all first-born sons in the clan were named after him.

Sneaking through the garden, the boys took care not to get too close to the long thorned gooseberry bushes. They quietly wound their way through the raspberries, under the grape arbors, and crept into the orchard of apple, cherry, plum, and fig trees. In the grove of white mulberry trees bordering the property, their grandmother was animatedly talking to a few Russian peasants.

The family employed Russian men as farmhands and a couple of women as household help. Since it was late fall and the field crops had been harvested, but it was still too early to butcher, she had commandeered a few spare fieldhands to help put the garden to bed for the winter. Her main concern at the moment seemed to be keeping the fieldhands from fraternizing with the peasant girls canning and pickling at the brick outdoor summer kitchen.

The pungent conflicting odors of wood smoke, boiling watermelon syrup, pickling crocks fermenting, and shredded cabbage being pressed into barrels for sauerkraut left the boys dizzy with nostalgic delight.

"*Grootmutta! Grootmutta!*"

The boys ran up to the prim lady with a high frilled collar on a white starched blouse and gathered around her welcoming apron. The normally staid Eva released her apron corners, dropping its cargo of late harvested potatoes, and grabbed the boys up in a joyous hug.

"Heinrich, Gerhardt! Where'd you come from? You've grown such."

After a rousing round of kisses to the foreheads, she grabbed Gerhardt's hand (Heinrich considered himself much too old for such a thing) and led them to the outdoor summer kitchen.

"Come, it's time to take the zwieback out of the oven. You're just in time for supper. Gerhardt, go get the butter out of the well. Heinrich, tell your Grootfoda and the workers it's time to eat."

Having not eaten since getting off of the train that morning, the boys didn't need to be told twice—even if that were an option in their family. As Heinrich ran off to gather the men, Gerhardt headed for the well.

Knowing her grandsons well, Eva had instinctively assigned each boy the task which they most desired. Heinrich got to associate with the older fieldhands and wedge in some much valued one-on-one time with his busy grandfather. And Gerhardt—well, Gerhardt was small for his age and had always fought for the privilege to do tasks normally assigned to a larger boy.

He was barely tall enough to see over the edge when he arrived at the well. Undaunted, he sourced out a nearby stool and pulled it up to the brick wall. Ignoring the water bucket rope, Gerhardt peered over the side into the well. After deciding which remaining rope was connected to the basket of dairy products on the cooling shelf near the water line, he hoisted it up.

Using the greatest of care not to bounce the basket against the wall of the well, unwilling to risk spilling its contents, he retrieved the butter and lowered the basket back down. Butter was a valuable commodity. Poorer families sold all of their butter in the market to get disposable income. Lard, in one form or another, was used for all of their household cooking needs and as a spread on bread.

After delivering the butter, Gerhardt was dispatched to get a couple of watermelons out of the house's attic. Since younger children were not usually allowed into the attic, this was another honor. Houses in the colony were designed for ultimate practicality. To reduce time outside during harsh winters, the barn was attached to the house, with an enclosed passage between. Just inside the indoor kitchen on the right, was the pantry. Inside the pantry were stairs leading down into the root cellar. Above the root cellar stairs were the stairs leading to the attic.

He ascended into the dark attic and made his way past the sacks of flour, oats, feed, and seed grain on his left. To his right, were sacks of dried apples and cherries, raisins, and plums. He was probably the only one in the family who didn't need to duck to make his way past the sacks of aging cheese hanging from the rafters. At the end of the attic, he carefully felt his way through a stall full of straw and retrieved two watermelons.

The very thought of the melons made him happy. These melons weren't like the large ones in America. They were small and round with juice so thick, sweet, and sticky, it was closer to syrup. Before leaving the attic, Gerhardt paused and inhaled. The assault of scents—dusty hay and grain mixed with pungent cheese and dried fruit—it smelled like . . .home.

Barely making it back to the large outdoor table the family shared with the laborers, Gerhardt's parents, grandfather, and younger siblings came around the house, heading toward the outdoor washing station. After washing off the day's soil, the eldest Wiens offered a prayer, and the men and older boys sat at the table. Eating separately didn't have as much in the way of cultural significance as practicality. In large gatherings, there usually weren't enough plates for everyone to eat at the same time.

The women served generous helpings of plumemooss with kjielke—a rich, hearty milk soup made with plums and raisins ladled over thick flour noodles. Sitting on the table were bowls of zweiback, the traditional double buns made with copious amounts of butter, a platter containing the last remnants of ham from a previous butchering, and jars of freshly made jam.

After sating themselves, the men retreated to the benches on the garden's edge to catch up on current events. They discussed the upcoming butchering day and Gerhardt's father's plan to buy back the farm he sold when they left for the United States. Now, it was the women and younger children's turn at the table to eat. Tickled to be included in the men's shift, Gerhardt and his older brother, Heinrich, did their best to sit still and emulate the adults in the waning mid-October sun.

It was Saturday. So, while the men chatted, the women set about preparing the next day's faspa, a traditional mid-afternoon cold meal requiring little preparation that farm families enjoyed on Sundays. A pre-prepared meal freed the women to enjoy a respite from hard work on at least that one day of the week. Life in turn-of-the-century Southern Russia was a peaceful existence filled with days of hard work, evenings of close family ties, and mental tranquility.

Gerhardt's father explained how America was too unstable for his taste. "The government seems unable to stop the labor strikes which upset daily life. The peasant class can band together and vote for anyone they choose to be in charge of the government. Newspapers openly criticize leadership's decisions. I admire the American's complete religious freedom but question how a country without an all-powerful centralized government can possibly survive."

Gerhardt's namesake grandfather mulled for a few moments. "I know what you mean. For a long time, the Narodniks have been spreading anti-government pamphlets, trying to foment unrest among the peasants. They just can't get it through their heads that peasants *can't read*. What good is a pamphlet? The peasants aren't dumb and see right through the act when rich, young agitators dress up in rags to fit in. They think those Narodniks are buffoons."

"Yes," Gerhardt's father added. "Now these Marxists are running around ranting into the wind. How in the world anyone would think that their crazy ideas will work is beyond me. Thank goodness our government doesn't put up with this nonsense."

The eldest Gerhardt said, "Remember when the Narodnaya Volya assassinated Tsar Alexander II back in '81? You were young then. In 1887, they were planning to do the same to Alexander III but he caught them, and they were hanged."

Heinrich senior asked, "Wasn't one of the ringleaders a fellow by the name of Alexander Ulyanov? Wasn't his younger brother kicked out of the university for rioting at about the same time? What was his name?"

"I think it was Vladimir. Yes, that's it. Vladimir Ilyich Ulyanov. I hear he's now a lawyer in Saint Petersburg working for the Marxists."

"It's too bad the tsar is so sick right now," Heinrich senior added. "If he wasn't expected to die any day now, he'd crack down on them again."

The eldest Gerhardt concluded the conversation, "We'll see how his son, Nicholas II, does when he takes over. He's young, smart, and will control the fringe elements."

Gerhardt and Heinrich didn't understand the politics their grandfather and father were discussing. What the boys *were* sure of was these were the two smartest men they knew.

Within two weeks, Gerhardt and his siblings were enrolled in the local community-run school, and his father had made arrangements to re-purchase their old farm. The family's possessions were temporarily stored in his grandparents' now empty ice house, awaiting their old home to become vacant.

Gerhardt's family of six made themselves comfortable in his grandparents' two spare bedrooms. Once their own children had come of age and moved out, the rooms were maintained for visiting relatives and dignitaries. The winter living room was opened up earlier in the season than usual to make room for the sudden influx of excess household occupants.

CHAPTER TWO

BUTCHERING DAY

Today was butchering day. The women had been up for hours preparing breakfast for the invited helpers. Before dawn, a horse had been hitched to an overhead snatch block for hoisting. Rendering vats were at the ready, and substantial fires were built in the outside summer hearth and under the scalding pots. All of this before the volunteers arrived, carrying their butchering aprons and favorite knives.

After a blessing was shared and a hearty breakfast, the first hog was led to the stunning station. Some preferred to shoot the animal before it was cut open. However, the local method was to stun the animal with a hammer, slit its rear hocks, and hoist it still alive. Hanging inverted over a blood vat, Gerhardt's grandfather took a sharp knife and thrust it into the base of the hog's neck. In one well-practiced upward curving motion, he inserted the blade into the chest cavity, slicing the aorta. It only took a few seconds for the animal's heart to pump virtually all of its blood into the vat. A couple of gurgling breaths, and it was done.

Fascinated, Gerhardt watched as the animal was placed into the scalding trough, then shaved. Hoisted again, the hog was eviscerated. The heart and liver were placed into a saline bath. Two women sat, inverting and cleaning the intestines by expertly drawing them between knitting needles. As the master butcher cut off large chunks, assistants caught the sections and placed them onto the cutting table. Knives seemed to blur.

It was now Gerhardt's turn to shine. Placing an empty bucket by the cutting table, he picked up a full bucket of fat trimmings with both hands. Carrying the bucket between his legs, he waddled to the summer hearth. A couple of the younger women placed the fat into the rendering pots to melt. Thinking of stealing the first cracklings being skimmed off when no one was looking, his mouth watered.

His older brother beat him to it. As Gerhardt was ferrying a bucket of fresh fat to the hearth, Heinrich passed him juggling a hot piece of the crispy pork delight, trying to cool it enough to devour. Gerhardt glared at his brother for stealing his thunder, but the size difference and the presence of the adults made it impossible to do anything about the affront. Angrily kicking an empty bucket, he received an immediate cuff to the back of the head by a passing matron when he used a cuss word.

Refrigeration didn't exist. Large estates and retail establishments might have an icehouse. All of the pork not consumed immediately had to be either cured or packed in salt. Cuts of meat were sorted into piles for hams, bacon, chops, or ribs. There were tubs filling up with scraps to be ground into sausage or wurst. Older boys cleaned the feet and hocks for pickling. Another boy cleaned the heads to be processed into head cheese, setting the brains aside for frying.

At lunchtime, neighborhood teenage girls served a meal they had prepared on their own. The girls beamed with pride as workers lustily wolfed down fried chicken and potatoes, traditional zwieback buns, washed down with hot coffee.

Gerhardt was so busy eating, he didn't notice the absurdity of enjoying the meal while surrounded by the smells and sights of their morning activity. Nearby, the dining table was a wheelbarrow filled with stomach and intestine contents not yet taken to the garden for fertilizer. Bloody aprons lay over a fence by the washing station, boiling fat, vats of blood, and piles of raw meat not yet processed. No, the food was just too good, and he was hungry.

After the butchering crew was fed, the girls loaded up a buggy with food for the field workers. Led by Gerhardt's father, the field workers needed every second of daylight and couldn't take the time to come to the food. It must go to them. It was late in the season, and the winter wheat needed to be planted. Due to the family's late arrival from America, they were getting the next year's crop planted instead of helping with the butchering.

The elder Heinrich assumed the task of planting not only his recently re-purchased fields but also his father's fields in exchange for his family's temporary shelter. The concept of free room and board didn't exist in their society. You worked as much as you could for your keep.

Before lunch, five hogs had been killed and roughly cut up. The rest of the day was dedicated to final butchering, cleaning entrails, rendering fat, and preparing for the curing process. Young Heinrich turned the handle of the meat grinder while his grandmother expertly handled the stuffing of the sausages. She shoved the largest section possible of cleaned intestines over the outlet of the grinder. As the meat forced itself out of the grinder into the casing, she would allow it to slip through her calloused fingers at a uniform rate.

Eva knew how to exactly maintain enough pressure to ensure firm sausages without tearing the delicate casing membrane. Each time a length of stuffed casing spanned the width of both her hands, she'd give it a twist, sealing that section and starting another one. Whether she was creating link chain sausage or a continuous rope, it was coiled into a basket at her feet.

Gerhardt and Heinrich each took a handle of the basket, placed it on a flat, wooden wheelbarrow, and carried it off to the smoking shed. Making good use of the boys' absence, Eva kneaded more of her special spice mix into the unground meat. Other boys carried the hams and slabs of bacon to the smokehouse for curing.

The boys' mother, Helena, supervised the lard rendering operation. It wasn't as simple as boiling a pot of water. As the fat melted and came up to just the right temperature, cuts of spare ribs were thrown in to boil. Cooked ribs needed to be removed, floating cracklings had to be skimmed, more cuts of fat added, and the clear lard ladled off.

Lard, a very important commodity, needed to be made properly for little waste. Clear lard was used for cooking and soap making.

Gray lard that settled to the bottom of the pot was saved as a spread for bread. Many times, the boys left for school with tasty lard sandwiches in their lunches.

At the end of a long day, the cleanup of the yard and tools was finished, and the volunteers left for home with their complementary bags of meat. After a light supper, the exhausted children headed off to their shared bedroom. The adults sat in the winter living room in front of a crackling fire, recapping the day and laying out the agenda for tomorrow.

The little girls were snuggled up together in a pile of bedding on the floor. Lying under the heavy quilt on the bed with his brothers, Gerhardt listened to the murmur of the adults' conversation through the walls. He'd been treated as an adult, and it made him feel important. It had been a good day. Unable to imagine a better life, Gerhardt knew that he wanted it to remain the same forever.

CHAPTER THREE
THINGS THAT MATTER

Christmas had come and gone. New Year's was at hand. Since the Russian Empire still ran under the old Julian calendar, it was mid-January by modern standards. A cold winter wind blew snow across the western Russian steppe. Gerhardt's mother had shooed him out of the kitchen where she was making a batch of portselkje—New Year's fritters.

Helping brother Heinrich with the chores, they heard their father talking to someone out at the lane. Leaning against a sturdy sleigh, loaded with ice blocks cut from the local lake, he was chatting with a wealthy Muslim trader from a neighboring village. The boys were fascinated by the animal hitched to the front of the sleigh, a camel sporting a heavy winter coat of fur. To them, it resembled a large, brown, unshorn sheep with a long neck and legs. Distracted by the uncommon animal, they forgot to close the pig pen gate. Before they could react, a hog trotted past them toward the road.

The ruckus raised trying to corral the pig interrupted the men's bartering. Seeing the Muslim merchant's distress over the hog heading their way, the boys' father grabbed the whip off of the front of the sleigh and used it to drive the hog back toward the barn. Even though Gerhardt knew that he and his brother were in trouble, he was amazed that the merchant wouldn't allow the ornate whip to be put back on the sleigh after it touched the pig.

Refusing payment for the defiled whip, the merchant was adamant that keeping the unclean animal away was more valuable than money. The merchant and the boys' father developed a trusted bartering relationship that lasted for many more years. Gerhardt never forgot the incident.

For the next decade, life was a simple, blissfully innocent progression of planting, harvesting, schooling, holidays, and family. It was the Golden Age for their ethnicity in the Russian empire. Gerhardt's beloved grootmutta, Eva, died November 1897. His grootfoda had just died in March of 1904. The family continued to grow.

Besides Gerhardt's twin, Conrad, who died at birth, his mother gave birth to David in 1890 who only lived three months, Jakob in 1895, Eva in 1897, Daniel in 1899, two-week-old Elisabeth died in 1900, Peter in 1901, and the second David and twin Katerina in 1902. The next two children, Abraham died at three months, and Anna died within a few hours on Christmas 1905. Gerhardt's mother would have one more child in 1908, the second Elisabeth.

His father took over his grandfather's land holdings. Now fairly wealthy by the area's standards, they built a large, red, brick house. Gerhardt had completed school and was preparing to go away for his mandatory service in the Russian Empire's forestry corp. Since being in the military would violate their beliefs, the corp was a concession by the government to communities of conscientious objectors, allowing them to still serve the Empire.

Before leaving, Gerhardt and some friends went to the picnic area along a stream through a grove of trees near the village, intending to kill some time without the elders' scrutiny. One of the boys passed around some alcohol purloined from his parents' pantry. Since some community members had problems with alcohol abuse, Gerhardt's parents kept it out of their house. When the bottle was passed, he took his first drink.

Never having grown past five foot three inches, he was short tempered and fiercely sensitive to teasing. Because of his diminutive size, it didn't take long for the alcohol to affect him. After only a couple of drinks, he became woozy and started to stumble. This new sensation alarmed Gerhardt. He'd seen drunkards make fools of themselves in the village.

"Please, God, don't let me become an alcoholic," he inadvertently prayed out loud in his stupor.

The teasing commenced. "Oh look, shorty is asking God to stop him from getting drunk!" A substantially larger, older boy, fueled with drink, started pushing him around.

As the teasing grew in intensity, Gerhardt aggressively defended himself, "Who are you to tease me? You don't even know how to read! You'll be just a lowly laborer all your life!"

The situation degenerated. "What? I'll show you who's lowly!"

A blindside punch knocked Gerhardt to the ground. The larger boy hovered over him, kicking him in the ribs. As the older boy pummeled him, Gerhardt pulled his utility knife out of its sheath and swung wildly, gashing the thug's cheek. Staggering back in disbelief, the drunken bully felt the blood dripping off of his face. The party was over, and everyone went home.

The incident would have been forgotten except that the older boy's wound became infected and he died a short time later. The village's elder council met and interviewed witnesses. Ruling it self-defense, Gerhardt was exonerated. The decision didn't alleviate his remorse. He'd killed someone. It would haunt him the rest of his life.

CHAPTER FOUR

GERHARDT'S GRAND ADVENTURE

By early spring 1910, Gerhardt was repairing imported harvesters for Mccormick Deering. He had worked for a while as a manager on a ranch when first released from the Forestry Corp, giving him the thirst to own his own land. With a single-minded obsession to accomplish whatever task he had set for himself, his tunnel vision and impatience meant anyone in his immediate sphere would have to have an equally strong personality, or be shoved aside.

Still diminutive with a quick temper, Gerhardt kept his thick, coal black hair trimmed short and combed to the side. Although not as prominent, he'd inherited the same cleft chin as most of the males in his family. He had his mother's dark skin, brown eyes, and rounder face, giving his chin a more blocked appearance. Hoping it would give him an air of gravitas to counter his 5'3" frame, he sported a shortly trimmed chevron mustache.

Gerhardt decided that to accomplish his desire of becoming a successful landowner, he needed to have a dependable, inexpensive labor force. That meant having children. To have children, he first needed to procure a wife. It was a logical progression which didn't need much mulling over. He announced that he wanted to marry.

Once his intent was made known, the matchmaker network was more than happy to pick up the gauntlet.

A wide net was cast for prospects. Following the established code of matchmaking meant that prospective candidates must be of similar ethnicity, social standing, and religious background. Most importantly, prospective mates should help elevate the economic status of both families. It didn't take long before a close relative narrowed the search to Kalinova in the Molotschna colony and the Dueckmann family's oldest daughter.

Maria met all the main parameters of a prospective bride. The fact that she was already in love with another man was of little concern to all involved—except her. There wasn't much she could do in the culture of the day, short of running away. She could possibly be shunned by the church and disowned by her family.

The wedding took place on September 7, 1910. Not varying even the slightest from his practicality, and still wearing coveralls, Gerhardt took time off from work just long enough for the wedding. He'd passed one more benchmark in his laid-out trajectory for a successful life.

The eldest of five surviving children in her family, and accustomed to being in charge, Maria had other ideas. She was strong-willed, vocal, and not used to being dictated to. An inch taller than Gerhardt with blonde hair and pale blue eyes that could spit fire, she was a presence which needed to be handled carefully.

Yes, she complied with her wifely duties in the bedroom and allowed her new husband leeway in managing the family finances. But, make no mistake, she would *not* cede any authority in household management. It didn't take long for Gerhardt's iron dreadnought to run aground on Maria's granite reef.

The relationship was cordial. For the most part, first names were used in polite exchanges. But, with winter approaching, the house was too small to contain two such strong personalities. Gerhardt decided it was unsafe to be confined in such close proximity for the winter with Maria's temper and strong throwing arm. The heavy ceramic statue of a royal lady adorned in a fine, flowing, turquoise gown left its perch on the mantle more than once, leaving a dent in a wall as he made a hasty retreat.

After only two months of marriage, and with winter coming, he announced, "It's time I go in search of land for our future home."

His brother, Heinrich, arrived with the carriage to take him to Zhelannaya Station. Maria watched Gerhardt loading his necessities from the kitchen window. Before leaving, he did a quick check to make sure that all was in order. With enough money for incidentals in his pocket, the rest he had safely stowed in a secure hiding spot. He packed warm clothes for the expected conditions. His attaché contained letters and maps relatives and other homesteaders had sent him, describing possible areas to investigate.

Maria went to the cottage's open front door as Heinrich urged the horse into motion. As an afterthought, Gerhardt turned and gave a farewell wave. Even though their relationship was strained, she'd half-heartedly hoped for a goodbye hug. She hadn't told him she was pregnant.

At the station, Gerhardt paid the agent 5.25 rubles for a Home Seeker's ticket to the East. Even though he was planning on venturing through primitive areas with limited amenities, he was dressed formally for travel, according to his status. Underneath his dark brown wool suit, he wore a black vest, starched white shirt, and tie. His hair was recently cut and combed to the side. His black mustache was trimmed short in length and ended at the corners of his mouth.

While waiting for the train, Gerhardt sat on a slatted bench against the station's wall to get out of the winter wind. With his possessions tucked safely between his legs, he watched other passengers gather on the platform. It seemed like he was looking at his potential travel-mates through a kaleidoscope

On his right, at the far end of the platform, were a couple of Turkish merchants with embroidered satchels. A little closer was a group of students heading to the Halbstadt Commerce School. To his left, a family of ethnic Ukrainian peasants chatted with an Eastern Orthodox priest. Curiously, Gerhardt noted the platform also contained a Roman Catholic priest and three nuns conversing in High German.

Above the din of the various dialects, and towering over the ethnic crowd, stood a large American. The man was gesturing animatedly, trying to make his wishes known to the ticket agent. Gerhardt smiled. Even though he worked on their imported machinery, this was the first American he'd seen since his childhood boat ride home.

As the eastbound train pulled into the station, Gerhardt was happy to find it pulled by a fairly new class "U" 4-6-0 oil fired locomotive. With the designation "U.127" on the front nameplate, it promised a brisk pace on his journey to Omsk.

Boarding the wooden passenger coach, he made his way down the aisle until finding an empty window seat. Looking around at his fellow passengers, he noted the doctor and nurse, mandated for all long-distance trains, sitting in the back of the car. He was pleased the seat beside him stayed empty as the car filled. Just before the trains started to move, the brash American from the platform descended beside him with a flourish.

Gerhardt stashed his belongings under his seat to make room for the large man and his high-quality leather valises with brass buckles on the gusset straps. Mangling the Russian word for hello, the American extended a large hand with an enormous golden ring. Gerhardt smiled and shook his hand. The man brought out a large map. Using broken Russian and gesturing, Gerhardt ascertained he was also going to Moscow. This was going to be a long trip.

About a half hour into the journey, the Roman Catholic priest came by on the way back from the bathroom. "Guten abend," the American greeted the priest in passable High German.

"Guten abend," the priest replied.

Surprised, Gerhardt turned and asked the American, "Sprechen sie Deutsch?"

"Doch!" the American replied.

Gerhardt thought this may not be such an arduous trip after all—until the American started talking.

"I'm a Singer Sewing Machine company executive on my way from Kiev, where we have one of our larger outlets, to the company's Russian factory in Podolsk to visit my old friend, Albert Flohr. I met Flohr in the Hamburg facility years ago. He's now the Manager of Kompaniya Singer in Russia. We're having a strategy meeting at the Podolsk factory with plant manager William Dixon. After the conference, I'm heading east checking out the hub outlets in Omsk then Vladivostok. After Vladivostok, I'm going to Yokohama to check out the Japanese operation."

Gerhardt nodded intently even though he felt his eyes glaze over as the American's monologue backtracked to his recent visit to the company's Kilbowie plant in Clydebank, Scotland.

"There needed to be some assembly line changes to increase efficiency, but the women in the cabinet polishing section weren't happy about it. I hope that the grumbling among the labor force quiets down and doesn't devolve into a labor strike."

This was turning out to be a long trip after all. Simply looking out the window quietly and examining how the passing farms were set up had become impossible. Gerhardt was interested in equipment and progress in productivity. He was also interested in the world at large and how varied it was compared to his homeland. But, by the time that the train arrived at the Yaroslavsky terminal in Moscow, he felt that he knew all of the workings of the Singer company there was to know. The American left the station to make his way to Podolsk, and Gerhardt switched to a train that ran on the actual Trans-Siberian rail route.

Time seemed to crawl during the multi-day journey to Omsk. Passing through the Ural Mountains, the ascent of the western slope was steepish, the eastern descent gradual, seemingly nonexistent. Western slope flora had been mostly dense coniferous trees but switched to a sparser forest on the east side with hardwoods mixed in. Passing through vast expanses of nothingness, every now and then he saw a distant Katorga camp in the middle of nowhere.

Sporadically, small groups of nomadic peasants eked out an existence. With not many actual farms, it seemed they were trying to survive by allowing their animals to dig through the snow for foliage while hunting to feed themselves. As the train drew closer to Omsk, the rolling Eurasian steppes were pockmarked with birch-laden swampy areas.

The long rail journey inevitably led to knowing everyone on the train and their life's history. During the trip, Gerhardt befriended two Russian boys.

"I'm Albert, and this is Vasily. We just completed our mandatory military service and are heading east to make our fortune."

"I know how that is," Gerhardt replied. "I finished mine a while back. Are you going home to see your families?"

Vasily snorted. "Hah! We're both orphans and grew up in the Russian peasant foster care system. I know the government meant well when they took us out of the orphanage and gave us to families to raise. But we ended up being used as slave labor."

"Yeah," Albert added. "We have absolutely no intention of returning to our home villages. Neither of us has fond memories of our childhoods. We're going to make our fortunes in Siberia. Omsk is a good place to start."

"How would you like to accompany me on my search for land?" Gerhardt asked. "I could use the company."

In Omsk, the second largest city in Siberia, he hailed a horse-drawn taxi in front of the station and instructed the driver to take him to a hotel a fellow train passenger had told him about. Even though it was the dead of winter, the city was filled with activity preparing for the upcoming Siberian Exposition of Agriculture and Industry. Originally scheduled for the previous fall, the exposition had been postponed due to unexpected exhibitor demand.

After passing a few ethnic Evenki tribesmen, peasant Slavs, and western European construction workers, the taxi pulled over long enough for a unit of Siberian Cossack cavalry to clatter by. The soldiers wore lofty fur hats, long wool coats designed for horseback, and tall boots without spurs. Rifles strung diagonally across their backs, shashkas—the Cossack version of a saber—at their sides, and the metal hardware on the bridles, the passing men made quite a cacophony.

It seemed every soldier had an identical bushy mustache drooping past the corners of his mouth. Gerhardt mulled over their choice of horses as the unit rode by. He was more familiar with the Russian Don the cavalry rode in his area. The Bashkirs these men rode were shorter and stouter.

Used to the plain churches he had grown up with, the giant Eastern Orthodox Church Dormition Cathedral with its four blue domes and large gold dome in the center left him awestruck. Near the hotel, he passed Dutch, German, and British embassies. After paying the desk clerk, he retired to his shared bachelor room with four other beds. He didn't care about the snoring. It was the first time in a week his bed didn't sway.

The next morning at breakfast, Albert and Vasily showed up. After eating, Gerhardt set about outfitting his expedition. His two companions found a mercantile to get bedding, a tent, and basic food-stuffs. He went in search of a horse and wagon.

Mid-morning, Gerhardt showed up at the mercantile with the droshky and a horse. The wagon wasn't in as good of shape as it could have been, and the horse was more of a green broken pony, but they were cheap. While his traveling companions loaded the droshky, he went into the store and dickered for a rifle and ammunition for protection and hunting. Being frugal, some would say cheap, Gerhardt settled for a used Berdan 10.75x58mm rifle and sixty rounds of ammunition.

They barely made it out of town the first night because the pony's deficiencies soon manifested themselves. It didn't like bridges. The first small bridge the pony encountered brought on a small circus for the local peasants to enjoy.

Gerhardt's short temper got the best of him. He reached for the rifle. "I'm going to shoot that unruly beast!"

"Wait!" Albert grabbed the harness and launched the pony down the embankment and across the shallow stream.

Any other time of the year, this maneuver would have been impossible. However, in mid-winter, the water level was extremely low. With very little snowfall so far, the ground was frozen and mostly easy to traverse. As they made their way southeast toward the Altai Mountains on the Mongolian-Kazakhstan-Siberian border, the men still had to be wary of soft spots in the swampy ground.

At the evening campfire, the young men's growing camaraderie manifested itself with all three taking on tasks each individual was most suited to without much discussion. Albert seemed to have the best rapport with the green broken horse, so he tended to it and the cart. Vasily took care of the camp setup and ensured a defensible perimeter. Since Gerhardt grew up helping his mother and grandmother in the kitchen, he prepared the evening meal.

While sitting around the fire recapping the day, Albert said, "I think we should post a guard tonight."

Vasily agreed, "That band of Gypsies we passed outside of Omsk seemed awfully interested in us."

Gerhardt took first watch.

Making their way southeast toward the Altai Mountains, they stopped in Slavgorod then Rubtsovsk to replenish supplies. Gerhardt had heard of settlements consisting of Mennonites and a few Roman Catholic villages with German descent in the Altai Krai area of Siberia. He wasn't satisfied with any of them and followed the Katun River toward the steep, snow-covered, northern slopes of the Altai Mountains and the Mongolian border.

Deciding the terrain was getting too mountainous, he turned his little expedition due south. Just before crossing into northeastern Kazakhstan, they reached a small ford over a Katun River tributary. The weather conditions being just right, the stream bed was frozen with the water flowing over the top of the ice.

"I don't like the idea of taking the wagon across this slippery crossing," Gerhardt grumbled even though both of his companions told him it'd be fine. "I don't want my feet getting wet in such cold weather."

Stubbornly insistent, he walked upstream to a deep pool in the river where the ice was on top. Confidently, he stood in the middle of the river and jumped on the ice to show his companions that his judgement was best.

"See? The ice is plenty thick."

"Quit jumping, you idiot!" Albert yelled at him. "You'll break through!"

"Nonsense," Gerhardt taunted. "It's fine."

He fell through the ice. The smallest of the three men, the others knew they couldn't get to him. Albert ran back to the droshky and pulled a rope out of their camping equipment. Vasily immediately lay on his belly and started inching out to where Gerhardt had disappeared. Albert threw the rope to Vasily while holding on to one end.

Vasily rolled onto his side on the cracking ice and tied the rope in a half hitch around one wrist, then continued crawling toward the hole.

Gerhardt surfaced, spitting ice water. Vasily tried handing him the rope, but Gerhardt was shivering badly and couldn't grasp it. As Vasily inched closer, the ice gave way under him as well. He kicked closer and grabbed Gerhardt before he also lost motor control. Albert pulled the two men toward shore through the collapsing ice until they could climb out.

Using violently shivering hands, Gerhardt and Vasily tried to get out of their wet clothes while Albert built a fire. Neither said anything to Gerhardt about how stupid he'd been. They just let him shiver and fester. Albert walked back upstream to retrieve the rope while his two companions warmed up.

When he returned, he simply stated, "There's an underwater spring in the pool. The warmer water's keeping the ice thinner there." Smiling, Albert then displayed a little of his ornery side. "Oh, and since you two already have wet boots, I'll let you lead the horse across the ford while I ride and keep my feet dry."

That was the end of the incident for Albert and Vasily. Everyone makes mistakes. Gerhardt earned a bruised chink in his bullheadedness. Continuing on between villages, they met hospitable nomadic locals living in yurts. Happy to accept any offer of hospitality, the travelers still kept the rifle within reach and a wary eye on their possessions.

A little over a month into their journey, the men camped on the eastern shore of still frozen Lake Zaysan. After Gerhardt's previous encounter with ice, he was adamant they go around the lake. However, local villagers told them it wasn't possible without backtracking for three days around the lake's basin.

"I don't really want to backtrack," Albert said.

Vasily suggested, "Why don't we hire a local guide to get us to the other side?"

"That costs money," Gerhardt protested, not wanting to admit he was still fearful after his ice water bath. "But I guess, if that's what it takes."

Vasily and Albert ice fished while Gerhardt searched for a trustworthy-appearing local to guide them across. By the time he'd returned, Vasily and Albert pulled four nice Lenok through the ice. Supper that night was an excellent change from the normal fare of borderline rancid meat the nomads offered, or whatever unlucky wild game stood still long enough to be dispatched by the Berdan.

The next morning, the guide led them across the frozen lake to the west side. Albert's patience with the horse paid off when it gave only minimal resistance during the crossing. Albert and Vasily were so busy watching the horse, they didn't notice Gerhardt's tentative walking behind them. Hiring the guide proved to be a wise choice. He didn't lead them directly across at the narrowest point the young men would have chosen. Instead, he took them in more of a southernly direction in a wide, sweeping S-shaped path.

On the way, the guide pointed north and simply said, "Thin ice."

This time, Gerhardt listened to the caution. If he'd learned nothing else on this trip, it was driven into him that sometimes it was best to heed the advice of someone more knowledgeable than himself.

The crossing took most of the day. Nearing the other side, they paralleled the shoreline far enough out; solid ground was barely visible through the ice fog. The guide finally became satisfied that the shoreline's grade was mild enough for their ascent onto dry land. With dirt beneath his feet, Gerhardt started to breathe normally again.

Once the guide was paid and he'd given them some vague directions on a course to get out of the lake's basin without too much hardship, they parted ways. The young men set out to find a campsite with a little more protection from the bitter wind. The guide went to spend the night with some of his kin.

For the next few days, they traveled west out of Lake Zaysan's basin and back onto the steppes. With little snow cover, the ground was windblown down to an ice crust layer. Getting out of the wagon to walk for a while, resting the horse and their bottoms, the three crunched across the frozen ground. Vasily stared pensively at his feet as they plodded along. After quite a while, he broke the silence with a simple, short sentence.

"Jute is coming."

Albert nodded in agreement.

Gerhardt, looking puzzled, asked, "What's Jute?"

"Jute's a time of poor grazing," Albert said.

"Yes, it can be brought on by a lot of different weather conditions," added Vasily.

"Oh, I see."

"Yes, it can be from drought or excess heat in the summer that kills the foliage," Albert said.

Vasily nodded. "Or it can be caused by snow that's too deep in the winter for the animals to dig through and graze."

"A late hard frost could kill the early spring foliage," Albert said.

"This year, there's not enough snow to insulate the ground." Vasily studied the ground. "The ice layer is too thick and hard for the animals to dig through."

Gerhardt summed up the conversation. "No matter what the cause is, I can see it'd be a severe problem for the nomadic people living in the area who depend on their herds finding enough food."

Another good reason, he thought, to tame the land and raise hay for the winter. He started paying more attention to the livestock they passed. Assuming it was normal for the local breeds, his tunnel vision kept him from paying too much attention to the emaciated animals. Until then, he focused mostly on soil, lay of the land, and water availability. He'd been trying to dovetail potential homestead sites into farm layouts and methods he grew up with. He started to factor this variable into his land hunt equation.

Traveling a large, clockwise arc through northeastern Kazakhstan, they arrived at Semipalatinsk on the Irtysh River. The area the most acceptable they'd seen so far, Gerhardt began seriously looking for a farm site. He and his companions went from settlement to settlement along the Irtysh River between Semipalatinsk and Pavlodar.

Narrowing the search to a few burgeoning Mennonite settlements east of Pavlodar, he finally found a village he considered a perfect match for his ambitions. It had the proper combination of available water, good soil conditions, acceptable neighbors, nearness to the market and, most importantly, an economical price. He made a down payment on the chosen parcel and completed the paperwork with the local authorities.

In Pavlodar, he sold the droshky and horse to Albert who'd become attached to his work in progress. Although Albert didn't have the money, Gerhardt didn't worry—he'd be back to collect. He gave the old Berdan, which had served them well, to Vasily. Gerhardt and his companions had roamed around South Central Siberia and Northeastern Kazakhstan for over two months, and he was impatient to be moving along at a faster pace.

Pavlodar's waterfront was stacked high with freight which had backed up through the winter. Because of the Irtysh River's recent ice breakup, the port was bustling. Not a very big town, Pavlodar was an important intersection of roadways with the river. Gerhardt got out of the barely serviceable spring carriage at the ticket office of the Western Siberian Steamship and Commercial Company. Purchasing a ticket, he grabbed his luggage and headed for the American style double-decker riverboat.

Deep in thought, he didn't look back at his close companions for the last months. Gerhardt had never developed too much sentimentality; he'd always concentrated on the task at hand and the immediate future. Still young, he assumed people he interacted with would always be there in the future.

Ending his fears that he might be wasting his time, he was relieved to find a good piece of land. Gerhardt was proud that he'd done it on his own without his family exerting undue influence on his decision. He'd been frugal with Maria's dowery, saving most of it for the future. Still, his self-satisfaction was tempered by uncertainty of future variables.

Beginning its three-hundred-mile trip downstream to Omsk, the riverboat cast off its mooring hawsers and moved into the current. Walking around the deck during the two-day journey, he was surprised when he read the vessel's nameplate. The boat had been fabricated in the United States. He mulled how such a flat-bottomed boat could have made it to Kazakhstan. If it had been completely built in America, it would have made the journey across the Bering Sea and then thousands of miles through the Arctic ocean to the mouth of the Ob River.

The other water route seemed even more implausible. It would have had to cross the North Atlantic, follow the coasts of Norway and

Russia through the Barents Sea to the mouth of the Ob River. Either route seemed unlikely to him. He decided it had been prefabricated in America, shipped by boat to St. Petersburg, then rail to Omsk for reassembly. No matter how it got here, Gerhardt was still amazed that American steamboats were mixed in with the Russian-made fleet.

Making its way down the river, the boat dodged slow barges working their way upstream against the current. By the next morning, the boat made Tatarski, a border station between Kazakhstan and the Omsk Oblast in Siberia. An important Cossack military post, it also had major road junctions. Gerhardt sat in his deckchair in the spring sun watching the sandy shoreline pass by. It wouldn't be long before he arrived in Omsk to start the week-long train trip home.

CHAPTER FIVE
A GRANITE REEF

As Gerhardt's wagon disappeared down the lane toward Zhelannaya Station, Maria turned and looked at her sister-in-law, Helena. A year younger than Maria, and without any marriage prospects lined up, she had come to stay while her brother was away. Having become good friends, she put her comforting arm through Maria's as they walked back into the cottage.

Also staying was Maria's eleven-year-old sister. This was Aganeta's first time away from home for an extended time, and she was looking forward to no older brothers bothering her. It was a huge adventure for her. When not in school, being in the presence of two outspoken and very strong-willed women instilled an anchor of personal resolve which would serve her well for the rest of her life.

"It's nice of you to keep me company while your brother is off exploring Siberia." Maria leaned against Helena.

Helena had ulterior motives for being there. "This is a good time to be out of my parents' house. Mutta and Foda are having difficulty since diphtheria took young Elisabeth two days before her second birthday in July. That makes six of Mutta's sixteen children already dead at less than two years of age, including the last three. My parents have been putting on brave faces, but it's obvious they're suffering."

"I don't know if this is a good time to tell you, but I'm with child." Even though Maria was usually plainspoken, she tried to temper her announcement considering the circumstances. "You're the only one who knows. I haven't even told your brother."

Helena hugged her. "Well that *does* give us something to look forward to, doesn't it?"

The rest of the winter was spent making needed necessities for a child's arrival. It would be the first grandchild for both sides of the family. Sitting by the fire visiting, they kept busy making doilies and tablecloths for the newlyweds' household. Booties, scarfs, bunting blankets, sweaters, and socks weren't going to knit themselves. Unfettered by males, neighborhood ladies met at Maria's house once a week for a quilting bee. With no men to create excessive laundry, and an ample supply of fuel for the fire, the winter passed pleasurably.

One late winter day, Gerhardt's parents stopped by to see how the young women were doing. The elder Heinrich tied the horse to the hitching post beside the entrance path gate and helped his wife out of the spring carriage. On the way up the path, he eyed the house critically, looking for signs of neglect. The second obviously pregnant Maria greeted them at the door, the frenzy began.

The elder Heinrich launched into overlooked repairs, storming around the house roaring, "You've been left alone in your condition! What was he thinking? Look at this loose baseboard! I'm going to fix it right *now*."

The gloom shrouding Helena's mother instantly transformed into joyful expectation of her first grandchild.

While his wife fawned over their daughter-in-law in the winter living room, Gerhardt's father took a break with a cup of coffee. Sitting at the kitchen table staring past the steam into the black ripples, he swirled the floral-accented porcelain cup pensively. He knew his son was strong-willed, driven to make a better life for himself and be respected within the community. A majority of the time, this drive was at the expense of those close about him. Gerhardt also tended to make quick decisions, and then, with the tenacity of a bulldog, stuck by them.

The elder Heinrich knew these qualities well since he and his son were cut from the same cloth. The only difference was that the elder had mellowed with age and learned through experience that mistakes are spawned in the whirlpools of haste.

The patriarch mulled over the situation. He knew his son needed land to make a living for his family. He also knew all of the local land allocations available to foreign settlers had been taken and weren't allowed to be split any further. The next closest area in Russia proper was in the lower Volga River. Those land plots weren't as large, and the settlers didn't fare as well financially.

Land allotments along the Kuban River in the northwestern Caucasus region were also almost filled. Many ethnic Germans had already dealt with this reality. His own sister, Katherina, and her husband, Franz Ewert, had moved to the Amur River region of Siberia just north of China. The last letter he'd received placed them in the Vladivostok area.

His son, Gerhardt, was at that very moment roaming around northeastern Kazakhstan exploring newly established settlements. Those settlements were just about dead center in the middle of the continent, in very close proximity to the same description of nowhere.

As he sat, mulling, it dawned on him that there was one more option—a fledgling colony being established along the western shoreline of the Caspian Sea. If he recalled properly, the villages were near the Sulak River at its confluence with the sea. There was a railroad close by, and he knew other families who had moved there. Only a couple of days travel by train to the Terek colony, it was a good solution.

He drank down the rest of his coffee, rose from his chair, and entered the winter living room. The women quit their conversation, looking at him in unison.

"This will not stand!" he declared. "Come, Mutta, we have plans to make."

A week later, Gerhardt's parents were on a train to the Dagestan Governorate. In two days, they disembarked in Petrovsk-Port. Waiting at the station was the elder Heinrich's old friend, Semih. They had met years before, negotiating for blocks of ice to fill his icehouse. He still possessed the Muslim man's ornate whip.

Now running a freight business out of the Caspian Sea port, Semih brought a horse and carriage for the Wiens to use while conducting business in the area. Gerhart's mother, Helena, rode in the back as he took them to his house for lunch and to catch up. While at his house, she was taken to the kitchen to eat with the women. It was the Muslim way.

The next day, the couple arrived at C.H Toews's house, the Oberschulze of the overall settlement. Each village had been given a name and a number. After a week of Toews taking them from village to village within the settlement, Heinrich found a parcel that suited him in Sulak, village number five. Money was exchanged, paperwork completed, a firm handshake, and the deal was done.

Gerhardt didn't know it yet, but he had a new home, and it wasn't in Kazakhstan. Instead, it was in the Caucasus beside the Caspian Sea.

The fruit trees were in full bloom when Gerhardt's hired carriage pulled in front of his Karpovka cottage. All the weary traveler could think about was sitting on a chair in his own kitchen to drink a hot cup of coffee. He'd been on the road for over four months and just wanted to be still for a while. After he unloaded his luggage and paid the driver, he turned to walk up the path.

The door opened. Maria's younger sister, Aganeta, turned and disappeared into the house, loudly announcing his arrival, slamming the door behind her. When Gerhardt sat one of his bags down to reach for the door latch, it opened again. There, blocking his path was his own sister wiping flour off of her hands onto a long apron.

"Where's Maria?" he asked, becoming concerned.

"She's coming. It just takes her a little longer," Helena answered.

Bending over to pick up his bag, he immediately dropped it when Helena stepped aside, revealing a very pregnant Maria. Unsure of each other's reaction, they didn't say anything for a few moments. Expecting to be treated as a returning hero from his successful land hunting trip, it took only a nanosecond for Gerhardt to realize his important news had been soundly trumped. He felt his time of triumph, with others fawning over him, rapidly draining into the fault line chasm created by this seismic event in his life.

"I see you've been busy," he said.

"Just preparing the house for your return," she replied.

That was it. His dreadnaught's iron keel had just been broken on her granite reef. After taking his own bags to the bedroom, he went into the kitchen and fetched his own coffee from the hot stove. It was Saturday, and Helena was busy making the next day's zweiback with Aganeta's help. He walked into the living room where Maria had resumed her spot on the couch amongst skeins of yarn, needles flying.

Gerhardt sat in an armchair beside the sofa and began filling her in on his trip. He went through the various settlements he had seen and why he rejected them. He described the settlement he'd decided on and told her it already had some distant relatives living nearby.

Proudly, he told her, "Thanks to my frugality with your dowry, the lion's share remains."

Nodding, she listened intently and waited for him to finish. "Your parents are coming for faspa tomorrow. My parents are here from Franzthal also."

Puzzled by her less than effusive demeanor, he left to put his belongings away and prepare his documentation to show his parents. Then, he went into the attached barn to take inventory of their equipment and what they needed. After supper, he spent the rest of the evening in the kitchen budgeting while the women visited in the living room.

Cherry and plum trees in full bloom, Sunday dawned in a glorious display of spring wonder. Maria's flower garden framed the front pathway as the couple and their sisters left for Sunday services. Only a short walk to the church, Gerhardt didn't bother to hitch up the carriage.

When they arrived, his parents were waiting with his siblings, eighteen-year-old Maria, fourteen-year-old Eva, and nine-year-old twins David and Katerina. In a separate wagon was Gerhardt's older brother Heinrich, twenty-six, twenty-year-old Johan, sixteen-year-old Jakob, twelve-year-old Daniel, and ten-year-old Peter. Having stayed the night with relatives, Maria's parents were already inside the church. With all of these people showing up to hear about his journey and celebrate his accomplishment, Gerhardt was in excellent spirits.

After the service, the families gathered at his house for faspa. The women went into the kitchen while younger children went fishing in a nearby stream. Gerhardt's and Maria's fathers, Heinrich and Martin, his brothers Heinrich, Johann, and Jakob went into the winter living room to chat.

Air in the room alive with anticipation, Gerhardt was prime for the telling of his adventures. With quiet, steely resolve, the elder Wiens and Dueckmann herded Gerhardt onto the couch and sat on either side of him. Knowing what was about to happen, his brothers could barely contain themselves, waiting for the impending explosion. Leaning forward with rapt attention, they sat in chairs facing the couch.

After his sister, Helena, served coffee and Aganeta had offered cream and left the room, Gerhardt started to tell his tale of adventure. His father sat his cup on an end table, taking care not to spill on the fine crochet doily. Twisting toward his son, he placed his hand on Gerhardt's knee. His brothers leaned forward in unison. Johann leaned far enough that his cup sloshed a bit on the floor.

As Johann dabbed up the coffee, the elder Wiens spoke. "Hold it, son. We have something to tell you."

No one drank their coffee. Johann's cup rattled a bit in its saucer. Gerhardt, somewhat miffed that his monologue had been interrupted before it had begun, asked, "What would that be, Foda?"

His father explained, "I've purchased an investment—a parcel of land in the Terek colony. The soil's acceptable, and rivers are nearby for irrigation. The weather is mild, and the transportation of goods is reasonably available. Relatives live nearby."

Gerhardt was getting very impatient with this interruption to his story. His father already had a significant amount of land. How was this more important than his adventure?

"I need someone to manage it for me."

Gerhardt's heart fell. It dawned on him what was happening. Not only had his dreadnaught broken its keel on Maria's reef, but now was taking on water and in the midst of capsizing.

His father continued, "Martin has offered to supply some livestock and machinery to be used in developing this property."

The room was spinning and closing in on him. His mind wouldn't focus. Incessant, indecipherable voices bombarded him. Leaning toward him, his brother's faces seemed larger than perigean moons. Doing his best to constrain his inner Vesuvius of emotion, Gerhardt uttered the only words his lips could formulate.

"That sounds like an excellent opportunity."

Maria saved him from an indiscreet explosion directed at his relatives when she announced the meal was ready. It had been a long time since he had a good home-cooked meal. The smoked ham, zwieback, plumemooss, kjielkje, and jam washed down with more hot coffee kept his mouth engaged long enough to allow his mind to digest what had just happened. When he did speak, he'd mustered up the ability to address the others more diplomatically. His brothers' expectations were deflated when the anticipated eruption didn't occur.

He mulled aloud, "I guess I need to figure out how to dispose of our Kazakhstan land and prepare for Dagestan."

After faspa, the men retired to the winter living room while the women and younger children ate. Gerhardt had finally settled down enough to relate the details of his trip, impressing his brothers with the grandness of the adventure. He showed a map of the path he'd traveled and the conditions found. Interested in the Mennonite and other German settlements he'd visited in Siberia north of the Altai Mountains, then in northeastern Kazakhstan, the elders were impressed at his research into the transportation of goods to marketing hubs.

His father was especially interested when Gerhardt mentioned he'd run into a fourth cousin. Peter Wiens was the village minister of Sabarovka. He'd also heard of a couple of other distant cousins nearby.

Spring went quickly. Gerhardt arranged to sell his Kazakhstan land. He and his father visited Sulak to survey the property and decide the best course for development. Too close to delivery, his wife stayed behind when he made another trip to start the house. In between trips,

Gerhardt tied up loose ends and impatiently treaded water, waiting for Maria. Both their families were adamant there would be no move until she gave birth.

CHAPTER SIX
THE ROAD TO DAGESTAN

The first grandchild for both sides of the family was born July 3, 1911. Out at his parents' farm keeping his hands busy, Gerhardt was interrupted by his sister, Eva.

"It's time! It's time!" she shouted.

Gerhardt hopped onto the wagon and whipped the team into action, Eva scrambling in before being left to walk back on her own. Built to haul heavy cargo at a staid pace, the utility wagon sped toward the village. Looking up from their tasks, his brothers watched their ride home disappear in a plume of dust.

Sustaining a large bruise on her hip and a long scrape on her shin, Eva bounced her way from the rear of the wagon and climbed over the back of the seat. There, she held on with both hands to prevent ejection. In front of the house, Gerhardt vaulted from the wagon while it was still moving. Eva had to scramble to grab the reins and bring the team to a halt before she ended up in the next village.

His mother and mother-in-law were tidying up the bedroom when he burst in. His sister, Maria, and sister-in-law, Aganeta, were picking up linen and putting them into a basket. His sister, Helena, was sitting on the bed blocking his view. Fighting his way through the crowded room, Gerhardt finally saw his wife, propped up with pillows against the headboard. Maria held a bundle with a wrinkly, purple, little, bald head sticking out, feeding.

Looking up and pulling back the blanket, she said, "It's a boy."

Knees shaking, he sat gently on the bed to admire the culmination of his wife's last nine months of preparation. It was his family's custom to name the firstborn son Heinrich after his iconic great-grandfather. Not breaking with tradition, they did, but always called him Henry. Gerhardt stroked his wife's sweat-soaked blonde hair and called her Mame, never addressing her as Maria again.

A month later, the small family was on a train bound for Petrovsk-Port. Since she had already said goodbye to her Kalinova family, they took a more direct rail route to the steel and coal industrial city of Yuzovka, then to the major transportation hub of Rostov-on-Don. Maria was used to the factories near the village she grew up in, but that port city overshadowed them all.

Located at the very northeast corner of the Sea of Azov, Rostov-on-Don was the closest major port to south-central Russia which had Atlantic Ocean access. The main railroad transporting the mineral wealth out of the Caucasus went through Rostov.

Even though he was impatient to get to Sulak, she made him stop for a layover visit with relatives along the Kuban River. Less than fifty years old, the German villages there consisted primarily of settlers just like Gerhardt and Maria, unable to find property in the Ukraine region. Keen on developing the area with what it viewed as a more desirable population, the Russian government made extensive concessions to the German settlers.

Semih met them at the Petrovsk-Port rail station with a couple of cargo wagons and a carriage. With their household items loaded into the cargo wagons and sent on their way, Gerhardt, Maria, and Henry went to Semih's house in the carriage. The rest of the day was spent settling up accounts. Gerhardt purchased one of the wagons and team from Semih. The next day, the small family left in Semih's carriage. Spending the day getting to Sulak, they entered the village not long after the slower cargo wagons.

News of their arrival preceding them, neighbors gathered in front of the house as the young family came down the road. Gerhardt didn't have to ask; men were already untying ropes and carrying the contents into the house. Not much supervision was required where the items needed to be placed. Since most settlement houses had similar floorplans, it was self-explanatory where everything went.

A couple village women had already tidied the house. When major events such as this took place, everyone chipped in without being asked. Reciprocal aid was also expected. As soon as the wagons were empty, the whole crew went across the lane for a meal at the Epp's house.

Later, Semih's two hired men unhitched the wagons and made sure the horses were fed, watered, and secured in the attached barn. Maria moved around the kitchen putting utensils away while waiting for Gerhardt and the men to set up the bed. Keeping her company, a neighbor woman fawned over Henry. Finally, after everyone had left and Semih's men were comfortable in the barn, the family collapsed into bed.

The next morning, Maria was up before dawn, feeding Henry and starting the wood cookstove. Gerhardt went to the barn and checked on Semih's men. After feeding the horses, hitching up the carriage and one of the wagons, they came into the kitchen for breakfast.

Maria had a hard time finding appropriate culturally sensitive fare to feed the men. Used to the pork-laden menu she'd been raised on, she settled on pancakes and watermelon syrup—until encountering the lard problem. She made do with butter in the pan. Once well fed and supplied with lunch, the two Muslim men left as the sun was rising for their return trip to Petrovsk-Port.

Gerhardt often made the trip to Petrovsk-Port for implements and hardware he couldn't source locally. Semih showed him around and introduced him to reputable merchants. It was a full day's trip each way, so he usually stayed at the Muslim man's house overnight. Gerhardt could see why his father and Semih were friends.

The next few years went smoothly. The ceramic statue of the royal lady left her perch on the mantle for quick airborne journeys across the room on fewer occasions. With pleasant neighbors, their fledgling farm progressed nicely. It was a short ride to the Caspian Sea shoreline for picnics. A good day trip took them to the top of a local mountain where, if skies were clear, they could make out what they had been told was Mt. Ararat in the distant southwest.

Just south of the village was the Sylak River, and the Aktash River wasn't far north. The village's community water well had a problem with venting gas, so a capturing system fed an eternal flame to burn off the explosive gases. An irrigation canal was dug for the community's gardens.

Local Nogai tribesmen, who still hadn't fully accepted the settlers, would sneak into a village every now and then for a little light larceny. Patrols from the large Cossack military barracks not too far north of the settlement kept the raids minimal.

In September 1912, fourteen months after Henry, a second son, named Martin after Maria's father, was born. Two years later, in July 1914, the couple's first daughter arrived and was named after Gerhard's mother, Helena. A week after her birth, while the village sat in Sunday church, a horse galloped up to the building.

The door burst open. "Russia declared war on Germany yesterday!"

All pacifists, the village men had been exempted from military service in treaties with the government. The exemption had eroded in recent years, but the men were allowed to serve in the government's forestry corp as an alternative. Having already served, Gerhardt wasn't overly concerned.

Early spring, 1915, with the couple's fourth child due in May, a letter arrived from the government. Gerhardt had been conscripted. He immediately rode to the governmental offices in Petrovsk-Port to protest the letter. The war wasn't going well, and his petition was rejected. He had to report soon. Dejected, he went to a mercantile and bought each of the children a pair of felt boots and a felt hat as gifts before returning to Sulak.

When he got home, his two excited boys ran out to meet him. Very pregnant Maria stood in the doorway with the recently standing Helena holding onto her leg. Smiling, he handed the gifts to the children before giving her the bad news.

"Mame," Gerhardt said. "I have news."

Henry and Martin inherited both of their parents' temperaments and their father's knack of finding trouble. They thought the felt hats gave them a jaunty air, making them look like Kuban Cossack Cavalry. Galloping around the yard on stick horses, they jousted with wooden shashkas. Soon, they mounted a full-on cavalry charge into a village of rebellious chickens, scattering the feathered villains.

Collecting their booty of avian doubloons in their new felt hats, they accidentally broke an egg. Looking into the hat, wondering how they were going to explain the mess, Henry remembered a story about Mongol hordes tenderizing their meat by riding with it under their saddles. How much different was meat under saddles than eggs in hats? It didn't take long before they'd filled their new hats with eggs from the barn and dirt from the garden to make a batch of dough.

Their mother stood in the kitchen, trying to tamp down an inner firestorm and maintain a stoic exterior. Gerhardt's news didn't find a welcome reception within her house. She would have to fend for herself and children while her husband was gone. A farm wasn't easy for two adults to run even with their hired help. By herself, it would be a daunting task. And, what if he didn't make it back? Barely holding back her tears, Maria blankly stared out of the kitchen window at the boys' activities in the garden—until the situation sank in. Consequences were swiftly paid.

Gerhardt packed a few meager belongings and a sack of toasted Zwieback to eat on the way. After tousling the boys' hair and kissing his daughter, he gave Maria a lingering hug. In front of the house, one of the other village families' carriage waited with an elderly man holding the reins. Two other young draftees were already sitting in the back as Gerhardt hopped into the empty front seat.

On the way to the station in Petrovsk-Port, the conversation mood was mixed. The men hated to leave their families with less protection, concerned that the war was close to home. Russians and Turks had been battling in the south near Kars since last winter. One of the men pointed out that surely the government would send them to the closest front. They would be close to home if sent to the Turkish front. The carriage reached Petrovsk-Port late in the day, and the reporting station was closed. Gerhardt imposed on Semih one more time before he left for war.

CHAPTER SEVEN
THE HOME FRONT WAR

The winter of 1914 and 1915 was a time of change on the home front. When the war broke out, most of their peasant Russian workers were conscripted, leaving the family shorthanded. But they made do. The oldest son, Heinrich, had to report for service early in December, 1914. The family was thankful that at least the harvest was done before he had to leave. The third oldest son, Johann, was away in Halbstadt attending business school.

Jakob, the fourth son, not quite twenty, was ineligible. He'd been limping for quite some time and, just before the war broke out, discovered his leg was cancerous. By the time Heinrich needed to leave, Jakob was using a crutch. Heinrich placed his bags by the door and went into Jakob's room. Their sister, Helena, who'd moved back into the house after Gerhardt and Maria left for the Caucasus, was tending to Jakob's leg.

"Might I have a few words with Broder, you old spinster?"

Twenty-five and still unmarried, Helena was in no hurry to be shackled to a man. Perfectly happy having to answer only to herself, the family's constant teasing about being an old maid still bothered her. Glowering at her oldest brother, she gave him a shove on her way out of the room. Heinrich sat beside Jakob on the edge of the bed and patted his arm.

"Are you going to be able to keep her in line while I'm gone?" he asked.

"Yeah, but every now and then, I get the urge to give her a swift kick," Jakob answered. "The only thing holding me back is that it hurts too much to kick her with my bad leg. If I try to kick her with my good leg, I fall over!"

The brothers shared a good laugh. Then, after a few moments of uncomfortable silence, Heinrich got up to leave.

"I'll see you in a few months when I get back, Broder." Heinrich headed for the door.

"I'll keep the family in line for you until you come back, Broder," Jakob answered.

Heinrich paused at the door and looked back for a moment. It seemed like much more needed to be said, but he couldn't get it to come out. Turning, he went down the stairs to war.

Since the oldest remaining able-bodied son at home was sixteen, the next spring was difficult for the family. Everyone, even the girls, went into the fields to seed, then again in late summer to thresh. Jakob was becoming less of a help. Doing the best he could while seated, he monitored an engine his father bought to power the threshing machine. By the first part of October, 1915, he'd become bedridden.

As the winter winds blew in, Jakob propped himself up and watched the family tend the farm through the frost-coated window beside his bed. When soldiers came and force purchased the farm's best horses for the war effort, Jakob wished someone would have left a rifle in his room. Then he came around, knowing shooting out of the window to scare the soldiers away would only escalate the situation.

With three younger brothers, two older sisters, and two younger sisters in the house to keep him company, loneliness wasn't a problem. Now and then, especially after returning from Sunday services, the family gathered in his room and sang to him. His school chums stopped in to visit from time to time, but the conversation was always stilted and awkward. As it became harder to hide the pain, he feared an inadvertent moan slipping out would make them uncomfortable.

Jakob never told his family, but he looked forward to the few private moments when no one was around. He spent the quiet time reading his Bible. It was never brought up in conversation, and the family did their best to avoid any mention of it, but he knew what was coming.

As winter thawed into early spring, the pain was constant, becoming unbearable. Jakob's younger brother would come in and sing his favorite song to distract him from the agony. With the sweetest voice of the whole family, thirteen-year-old Peter sang a song they learned just before the war from a traveling East Prussian Baptist evangelist. Always willing to give his best for his brother, Peter sang the new song, "How Great Thou Art," in German,

> "Du Groszer Gott, Wenn ich die Welt betrachte,
> die du geschaffen auf dein Allmachtswort.
> Wenn ich auf alle jene Wesen achte,
> die du regierst und nahrest fort und fort.
>
> Dann jauchzt mein Herz dir, groszer Herrscher zu:
> Wie grosz bist du! Wie grosz bist du!
> Dann jauchzt mein Herz dir, groszer Herrscher zu:
> Wie grosz bist du! Wie grosz bist du!
>
> Blick' ich empor zu jenen lichten Welten
> und seh' der Sterne unzahlbare Schar,
> wie Sonn' und Mond im lichten Ather zelten,
> gleich gold'nen Schiffen hehr und wunderbar
>
> Dann jauchzt mein Herz dir, groszer Herrscher zu:
> Wie grosz bist du! Wie grosz bist du!
> Dann jauchzt mein Herz dir, groszer Herrscher zu:
> Wie grosz bist du! Wie grosz bist du!"

Peter kept singing all six verses he knew, not stopping until his brother could sleep. February 28, 1916, Jakob was barely lucid enough to pat his mother's hand as she tended to him.

"Happy birthday, Mutta," he weakly murmured.

His mother smiled softly and squeezed his hand. Jakob died three days later, the seventh child she had lost.

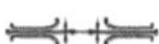

Life for Maria was busy after Gerhardt headed to war in April 1915. He left her alone with four children under five years old. Their youngest daughter was born shortly after he left. Maria needed to tend the garden, keep the house, and nurture the baby while trying to prevent the two oldest boys from destroying the village.

The Epp family who lived across the street, and others in the village, would lend assistance when they could, but they had their own chores. It could be a real adventure going to the town community water well with its gas venting flame. Keeping the boys out of the flame while getting water required more appendages than she was born with.

At least money wasn't too much of a concern. With the day-to-day operations of the farm leased to another village family, she received a small income from sharing in the harvest profit. Both her and Gerhardt's families were well to do and forwarded funds frequently. He sent home money whenever the government saw fit to pay him. Every few months, Semih would come from Petrovsk-Port bringing not locally available supplies.

Early fall 1915, when she arrived at the well, there was a group of government engineers surveying the area. Not saying much to the villagers in their month-long stay, the engineers were spotted taking soil and water samples. Every now and then, they hammered a location monument into the ground. Speculative rumors were a favorite topic whenever a group of villagers congregated.

On his next trip to Sulak, Semih told her he'd seen similar crews all over the area. "They've known for a while that there's oil in the Caucasus. The government's trying to figure out how much oil there actually is, where it is, and how to get it. Now that we're at war, petroleum is needed more than ever."

"We've always assumed the gas venting out of the town's artesian well was methane from nearby swamps," Maria answered. "This revelation has the village in turmoil."

A favorite topic of conversation for the next two years was whether to keep farming the fields and digging irrigation canals. Or, would the government take back the land to sell mineral rights to oil companies? It all seemed a moot point as the war drug on. The government was too occupied with other concerns. Oil companies were reluctant to move into the area with the Central Powers desperately trying to drive the front across the Caucasus to the Caspian Sea. It would be a definite boon to the Central Powers to deprive Russia of the oil and acquire it for themselves.

With more immediate problems, it was just too vague of an issue for Maria to worry over. She had more immediate challenges to deal with. Henry and Martin were two of the most pressing of those. One summer 1916 day, she'd entrusted the boys to watch their little sister, Helen, while she washed clothes. She placed baby Katherine on a blanket near her washing station. Pausing to check on the infant, she realized things were a little too quiet in the yard.

Leaving her wash station behind the house, she spied the boys indulging in roughhouse play while toddler Helen sat quietly off to the side. Suspicious, Maria walked over to see why her daughter was so quiet. When Helen looked up with distress in her eyes and tears running down her face, Maria shrieked. The boys had filled their sister's mouth with onion peelings to keep her quiet. Consequences were again swiftly paid.

Across the lane, the Epp family grandfather sat in his chair, bemusedly watching events unfold. After the cacophony quieted sufficiently, he slowly put his coffee cup down, laboriously rose out of his chair, and sauntered over to the Wiens' cottage. Coming around the house, he saw Maria fervently working out her aggressions on a white blouse in the washtub. He paused for a moment, unsure if he wanted to risk interrupting her stress relief exercise.

The young woman's normally tightly tied bun had come loose, and a shock of hair hung down in her face, sticking to her sweaty forehead. The ground around her was covered in a layer of white froth flung into the air with every angry backstroke on the washboard. He was unsure if the steam coming off of the hot water kettle was the result of the fire underneath or the heat of her proximity to it.

"I don't suppose the boys could use a fishing excursion tomorrow, could they?"

It took a moment for Maria to realize she was being addressed. Looking up, she wiped the lather off of her hands onto her already soaked apron, and replied, "That would be a blessing, Grandfather Epp. They need something to burn off their energy."

"I'll pick them up in the morning," the old man said, then turned and ambled home.

Maria wiped the sweat off of her brow with her forearm. Looking after him, she felt her appreciation of the promised respite relaxing the furrows on her face. Sighing heavily, she sat in a chair beside the blanket she'd spread in the shade for one-year-old Katherine. It felt like she watched the child play for an hour before shaking herself back to reality and returned to finish washing and hanging the laundry.

Grandfather Epp picked up the boys the next morning in his carriage and headed northwest of the village to the Richart Canal. It was quite a ride for the young boys, and even more so for the old man. Resting up for the journey back, he managed to catch a few fish while the overly energetic boys vented excess steam from their boilers. Running up and down the bank with their cane poles, Henry managed to bring two fish onto the shore. Martin hooked a few but lost all but one before landing them. The first time the boys felt the pole dance in their hands, they became hooked.

The tactic seemed to work for a while. After only one trip to the water, the boys became instant self-proclaimed experts, arguing theories of proper bait presentation all the way back to the village. Maria was forced into preparing the three six-inch-long Moby Dicks for supper. The way that the boys described their day, Jonah landed the whale with a cane pole instead of being swallowed.

Anticipation of the old man taking them to either the canal or farther out to the river south of the village brought out their inner angels. It was too good to last. Late in the fall, he left to visit his other children in the Kuban River region along the Black Sea.

Accustomed to her sons' newfound model behavior, Maria mistakenly let her guard down. Surely, they could now be trusted long enough for her to make a quick trip to the well and back. An unanticipated variable arose when an elderly woman from church descended while Maria filled her containers.

The inquisitive woman kept chatting, filling her own mental cistern with the affairs of the other villagers. The longer the old woman chatted, the more an unease welled up in Maria. She couldn't identify the unease or the source, but Maria knew she couldn't stand there any longer. Breaking off the conversation in a borderline rude manner, she headed for home. The closer she got to the house, the more urgent her walk became.

When she turned into the house's front path, the boys' loud laughter and Helen's shrieks caused her to drop her pails and break into a run. Bursting through the door, Maria's worst fears were confirmed.

The boys had dumped a pail of whey on the kitchen floor. Each boy had one of Helen's ankles, pulling her across the wooden floor on her bare bottom. When they reached the far end of the kitchen and swirled around for another trip, their mother's crimson face brought them to an abrupt halt. They looked at her for a moment, still holding their sister's legs in the air. In unison, they dropped Helen's legs and quickly wiped their hands on their trousers as if nothing had been going on.

Maria stood quivering, surveying the kitchen. The whey had splashed up onto the papered walls above the broad, wooden baseboards. It was on the chairs, table legs, and wood-fired cookstove. Helen's hair and dress were soaked, her bottom cherry red from the friction. Helen's bottom soon wasn't the lone occupant of that end of the color spectrum. Severe consequences were *vigorously* dealt out.

CHAPTER EIGHT

THE NORTHERN FRONT

Stationed near St. Petersburg, a disappointed Gerhardt had to get used to its new name of Petrograd. Because the original name had Germanic roots, the government changed the name shortly after the beginning of the war. Russia's capital was on the opposite end of the continent from the Turkish front, where he had assumed he would be stationed. He'd never been this far north before. Even in his youth, when his family went to America, they used ports in Germany.

There were many governmental buildings in Petrograd along with the emperor's winter palace. Although it was an impressive place, he'd only be able to visit it twice during his time there. Even though most of the Russian aristocracy spoke German, his ethnicity made rank and file soldiers nervous. Suspicions over his loyalty kept him close to his posting. In spite of the scrutiny, he ventured into town with comrades and wandered the streets admiring the city's opulence.

Gerhardt sat at the granite base of the statue of the Bronze Horseman and tried to figure out the mechanics involved in casting such a magnificent tribute to Peter the Great. In front of him was the giant Admiralty building. In another direction, sat the golden-domed St. Isaac's Cathedral. Everywhere the men went, stood another statue.

The soldiers walked across a bridge over the Neva River and stopped at a small cafe near the Senatskaia Ploschad. Gerhardt enjoyed the best Borscht he'd tasted since eating supper in the home of a child-hood Russian friend. They boarded an electric tram back to their barracks during the setting sun's blinding reflection off St. Isaac's Dome.

Fluent in German, Gerhardt was assigned to guard prisoners of war brought from the front in cattle cars. He helped transfer prisoners to other trains heading to whatever Siberian camp had room. Usually, inbound prisoner trains also carried wounded Russian soldiers.

February through August of 1915 was dismal tactically for the Russian army. The whole Polish front was collapsing. All initial gains the Empire made in the opening days of the war were evaporating. The few rail cars containing Central Powers prisoners of war had become far outpaced by the flow of medical evacuation cars. Without enough hospital transport ambulances, the wounded stayed on the station platform when the train pulled out. Often, the backlog was cleaned up just in time for another train to arrive.

He'd become used to seeing bandaged wounds from explosions and other traumas, but his first casualties from chemical attacks were different. Men got off the trains, their uniforms stained with coughed up blood. Soldiers with traditional wounds also suffered secondary chemical injuries when the chlorine gas entered the trenches. Unable to get off of their stretchers, trapped at ground level in the heavy gas, the pain from their wounds was multiplied every time they convulsively coughed up blood.

Gerhardt hadn't been there for the thousands of chemical casualties in late May. He'd just arrived in Petrograd and was too busy with prisoners to see the thousands more in mid-June. However, he was on the station platform for the chlorine casualties in the first part of July. The chemical casualties seemed to dissipate for the rest of the month.

In early August, POWs from the northern campaign, near the East Prussian border, were even more hollow-eyed and confused-looking than usual. They weren't visibly injured on the exterior, but didn't look or act as he expected. Breaking protocol, he engaged one of the prisoners with a blood-splatter-stained tunic, in conversation.

"What brought you here?"

"We were attacked by the dead," the dazed German soldier replied. "The devil set his spawn upon us."

Used to fantastic tall tales coming from the front, this was really hard to believe. Once he'd secured the prisoners and his shift was over, Gerhardt sought out a nurse on the other end of the station platform who knew what the prisoners were talking about.

She gestured toward a few not yet picked up walking wounded Russians, "See those men?"

"Yes."

"They're from the 226th Zemlyansk Regiment which has been defending the Osowiec Fortress on the Biebrza River."

"I know where that is. What happened?"

"The Germans have been attacking the fortress for months. On August 6th, they launched a massive artillery attack, then sent chlorine gas across the front."

"It must have been horrible to endure that," Gerhardt said.

"Yes. The Germans thought everyone in the fortress must already be dead so they sent thousands of their troops in a direct frontal assault. They were surprised when sixty Russians were still alive."

"Sixty? That isn't very many."

"No, it isn't. But, those sixty half-dead men had machine guns and mowed down many attackers," the nurse said proudly. "Then, they counter-attacked with coughed up blood from the gas attack all over their faces and uniforms. The sight of the blood-covered men attacking out of the fortress spooked the Germans. They turned and retreated."

"Really?"

"Yes. The fortress still had five operational artillery pieces and cut the retreating Germans to pieces."

"That's inspiring. So, those wounded men are from the fortress?"

"Yes. They're among the very few survivors from our side, but the fortress didn't fall."

Gerhardt later heard the soldiers' sacrifices had been in vain. Russia abandoned the fort before the end of the month.

Letters from family kept him informed of the locations of his brothers. Conscripted Heinrich was somewhere in Poland. Johann had volunteered and was stationed in the southern Caucasus.

In January 1915, Heinrich was assigned to Russia's 20th Army Corp in the Augustow Forest. He settled into his role as an unarmed ambulance teamster ferrying wounded to a hospital train. Growing up in a community where blood and exposed meat was commonplace, he thought he was well steeled for his assigned job. He was wrong.

When slaughtering farm animals and wild game for consumption, the goal was to dispatch the animal quickly, drain their blood into a container, and move on. In war, his job was to keep horribly wounded and suffering men alive as long as possible, hoping they could be saved. Their blood covered every surface in the ambulance.

The oldest child in his family, Heinrich grew up as the responsible one. Quite a bit taller than Gerhardt, he was also substantially more restrained in temperament. Of all of the children in the family, he most closely physically resembled their father. He was tall and lanky with a chiseled face and a deeply cleft chin. His blue eyes formed a divider between his unruly, windblown, light brown hair and ruddy, sun-blushed cheeks.

As the eldest, it was his duty to be the family patriarch's right-hand helper. If any of the children misbehaved, it was him who was brought to task to explain. As a result, Heinrich became the slowest to react to a situation. He would always stop and ponder before taking action. Even though he was older than Gerhardt, his role as their father's responsible helper had kept him from taking time to get married.

From the first day in his new unit, Heinrich was appalled not only by the volume of injured soldiers but also the magnitude of their injuries. Each trip, he listened to constant cries of pain from the wounded. Every pothole jolt induced wails in the ambulance. Doing his best to avoid rough spots in the road, he navigated a fine line between passenger comfort and expedient treatment of the injuries.

After a winter storm the first week of February, the thundering roar of exploding German ordinance broke through the peace of the softly falling snow. Heinrich hitched his team, pointing them toward the front lines for the flood of casualties he knew was coming. Through the blinding white of the morning snow collecting on his face, he ran into officer-filled vehicles heading in the opposite direction, moving their command headquarters farther rearward. The roads became a confused traffic quagmire with reinforcements moving forward and command staff retreating.

After loading the shivering wounded in his wagon, Heinrich headed for the hospital train. It was slow going down the traffic-laden forest road. Passengers delivered, he returned for more. For the next week, each trip to the front became shorter, and his return leg farther. The hospital train moved so far back, he couldn't reach it in less than four hours.

Once the German Army broke through, it made major headway with a two-pronged assault. The front had moved over forty miles and was closing in around his unit on all sides. It was getting harder to find a path through the closing gap, but Heinrich kept up his transports.

Early on February 20, the artillery was landing close enough that rounds sprayed the wagon with dirt. He was exhausted. His clothes were soaked, and he was shivering from the cold. After unloading his latest batch of wounded, he staggered back to the wagon. When he wheeled the team around to head back for more wounded, the left horse staggered. A passing officer grabbed the horse's harness and stopped the ambulance.

With a quick look at the team and driver, the officer ordered, "Unhitch, and give the horses and yourself a rest. You're not capable of another trip today."

Heinrich protested vociferously, "There's still wounded to evacuate."

"I don't care. You're not going out again today." The officer wouldn't budge.

"But if I don't go, more wounded may not survive."

"You're not going out again today!"

"But, sir, I'm all right."

"Let me put it this way, soldier, it's not you I care about. There are plenty of men to take your place holding the reins of horses. It's the team I'm concerned with. They're harder to replace."

Shocked, he looked at the officer, speechless.

"Now, soldier, go put your team away so they can work another day."

That confrontation saved Heinrich from being killed or captured. The gap closed that night, leaving no way in or out. To prevent complete annihilation, the entire 20th Corps surrendered the 21st of February.

The battle raged on as the 12th Army counterattacked. Heinrich hitched the team and headed east, chasing the hospital train. When he finally caught up, there was no unit to report to. They'd almost all been captured or killed. A doctor pointed him in the direction of a command tent. After a few days, the stragglers who had escaped the encirclement were assigned to other units. Heinrich was sent south to flesh out a unit near Warsaw.

By May, he'd settled in with his new unit a few miles west of Zakrzew, a little village southwest of Warsaw. It was a fairly defensible position, with the steep banks of the Rawka River on one side and marshes on the other. With fewer forests in the area, roads were also better. In a futile attempt to bring beauty to a bleak world, spring's blooms were fighting their way up through the war-torn landscape.

Even though his trip to the stationary hospital near Warsaw was farther than chasing the mobile train, he still used a team of horses instead of a motorized ambulance. With the supply deficit a growing concern, there wasn't enough fuel to operate many mechanized ambulances. Bothering Heinrich most was the units of new soldiers marching toward the front without weapons. With the shortages, they were expected to pick up and use the weapons of fallen comrades.

When the sun came up on May 31st, Heinrich was filled with apprehension but wasn't sure why. He'd learned westerly winds just might hold poisonous gas within their grasp. Today's wind seemed too strong for such an attack. The enemy preferred a light breeze to effectively spread the gas yet allow it to linger over the trenches. He checked on his team, then went to breakfast.

Either his assumption was wrong or the Germans miscalculated. The gas attack alarm rippled through the medical corp. Heinrich quickly tied cloths soaked with water around his team's noses. It wouldn't completely keep the gas out, but it was better than nothing. A dead horse was of no use to anyone. He made sure he had plenty of cloth left for himself. Considered rear echelon, he hadn't been issued an as yet rare gas mask.

Headed toward the front, Heinrich heard fighting in the distance. He hadn't even made it to the secondary lines before he saw the dead lying seemingly everywhere. Overcome by the gas, wounded soldiers were sitting along the road, waiting for pick up. The gas had blown completely over the front lines and settled into the trenches of secondary units. Heinrich could transport more of these men faster sitting up in the ambulance than normal casualties.

As the day wore on, he was astonished by the staggering amount of dead and wounded piling up. This new gas—phosgene—worked faster and more efficiently than chlorine. However, because the gas had overblown the front line, the German assault was driven back. Even though the front lines held, it still took Heinrich and his cohorts days to clear up the eleven hundred killed and nine thousand wounded.

Less than two weeks later, the Germans sent another cloud of gas across the front on the other side of the village. Another thousand were killed and over two thousand wounded. Morosely watching green reinforcements pouring into the area, he wondered if these optimistic young men would have the same bravado if they knew they were marching toward a slow, suffocating phosgene death. The first week of July, another attack killed or wounded five thousand more. Heinrich's horses were becoming worn out from the pace. By mid-July, the Russian high command ordered a tactical withdrawal.

The frontline troops began pulling back, but the Germans weren't letting up the pressure. Their artillery rained down all around, harassing the retreating troops. Heinrich had no intention of venturing too close to the front to pick up wounded. The front kept venturing too close to him.

On the last transport of the day before his team's scheduled rest break, he could hear bullets whistling by while he loaded wounded in the dark. He'd only made it about four hundred yards when a blinding light and ear-shattering explosion vaporized the team and launched the wagon over backward. Heinrich landed on his stomach, and the wagon came crashing down on top of him. The world turned crimson, then black and silent.

CHAPTER NINE
WARTIME LOVE

Spring 1915, Johann graduated from the Kommerzschule, the school of commerce, in Halbstadt. Two of his brothers had already been conscripted. As a college graduate, he had some control over his destiny. He joined the Army and was sent, as an orderly, to the Caucasus front against the Ottoman Empire.

A perfect melding of his parents' physical traits, he cut quite a dashing figure in his uniform with black, wavy hair combed straight back. His mother's pleasantly oval face combined with his father's piercing blue eyes, cleft chin, and height, made him unquestionably the handsomest brother.

The third son and fourth child, Johann grew with a freedom his older siblings didn't enjoy. He wasn't burdened with the responsibilities Heinrich and Helena had. He didn't have the chip on his shoulder the second child and shortest in the family, Gerhardt, had. He was smart, witty, and liked by all.

Following major fighting the previous winter, the Russian army was on the move south. The Ottoman Empire's third army was almost completely destroyed. Russians had surrounded and captured the 17th, 28th, and 29th Divisions. Ottoman corps commander, Ali Ihsan Bey, and his command staff had been taken prisoner. By the time Johann arrived at his posting near Kars in mid-May, the Turkish prisoner backlog was just about wrapped up. The last trainloads of prisoners were leaving for the Varnavino POW camp east of Moscow.

Moving around the rear staging areas, Johann marveled at the military units' diversity. There were Armenian volunteers, Cossack cavalry, and even Muslim units from the Caspian Sea region. All of southwestern Caucasus was awash with activity as Johann walked about.

Trains ferrying cargo from the port of Batumi were being unloaded. Truckloads of supplies moving from the railway to various depots splashed mud on his boots. Wherever there was a large enough flat area, a sea of conical white troop tents took up residence.

Russia's military medical services, being woefully inadequate, leaned heavily on the Red Cross. Johann was assigned to be a liaison between the local command staff and the Red Cross. In Russia, nurses were called Sisters of Mercy. On the fairly stable Western Front, they were in medical units in stationary facilities. Nurses on the mobile Eastern Front sometimes found themselves in frontline trenches as the battlefield rapidly shifted.

The first time Johann went to the hospital complex, he wondered how the derelict structures were still capable of standing on their own. As the war wound on, the buildings became familiar. The hospital, currently far enough back from the front, was used for long-term treatment of wounded deemed able to eventually return to combat. Soldiers who would never be able to fight again were stabilized and transported to Russia proper.

In late August, Johann entered the hospital for the daily casualty report. Field reports tended to be wildly inaccurate. Every day, he made the trip so headquarters could reconcile the numbers from field reports with wounded actually received at the hospital. With the way the war was progressing in Poland, the government was loathe to send replacements south unless absolutely needed.

As Johann rounded a corner in the administrative wing, a Red Cross nurse running with a box of bandages collided with him. The collision sent the box sliding down the corridor and pushed her to a sitting position against the wall. Johann and the nurse traded effusive apologies as he helped her to her feet. He picked up her box without looking up. When he handed her the box, he froze.

Wearing the traditional Russian Red Cross uniform of a dark dress and white apron with a red cross on the bodice, she was the most breathtakingly beautiful girl he'd ever seen. Having been outside, she had an elbow-length cape matching the dress, clasped at the neck. Tied under her chin, framing her delicately featured face, a white lace head covering hung to her shoulders. Golden waves of curly locks fought to free themselves of the lace and emulated rays of sunlight radiating from the late afternoon summer sky. Her blue eyes bore into his core.

Unlocking their gazes, he stammered another apology and turned to go. They both looked back after a few steps. Johann ran into a table loaded with supplies along the corridor's wall and almost knocked more boxes to the floor. Grabbing wildly to keep the boxes on the table, he cursed himself for being so clumsy. Susanna smiled the rest of the way to the ward.

For two weeks, Johann looked for the nurse every time he made his daily trip to the hospital, but didn't see her. He'd just about given up meeting her again when one Sunday morning, as he walked up the hospital's front steps, he saw her pushing a wheelchair-bound patient into the sun at the end of the building.

She looked in his direction, but he wasn't sure if she'd seen him. If she had, she made no indication of recognition. Dejected, he turned to walk into the building and promptly bumped into an officer walking out the door. His profuse apologies didn't save him from a thorough loud dressing down by the indignant superior.

There were no new casualties admitted or patients who died in the hospital. It was a good day. As Johann exited the front of the hospital, he paused and looked in the direction he'd last seen the nurse, but she wasn't there. Putting on his hat, he started down the stairs.

"Do you make a habit of running people over?" Johann heard behind him.

Turning, he saw the nurse standing beside the stairs opposite to where he'd last seen her.

"No," he sheepishly replied. "I've just been distracted lately."

She asked, "Where are you going?"

"Not anyplace special. There are no new reports to take back to headquarters," he replied. "What about you?"

"Me either," she answered. "It's my day off. Now that I've wheeled that patient into the sun, I was thinking of going to the cafe and getting a cup of coffee and some pie."

Even Johann's thick skull could tell that he'd possibly . . . maybe . . . been invited along.

"That sounds like a good way to enjoy a sunny day off. Would you mind if I walked with you?"

"Not at all." She smiled at the ground. "It would be good to talk to someone I'm either wheeling around or changing their dressings."

They strolled down the street toward the village, the opposite direction from headquarters. Her name was Susanna. She was from a Volga River region Lutheran German settlement near Saratov. *At least she's a Protestant*, he thought, although he really didn't care. Her soft voice soothed him like a brook in the forest, her laughter the bubbling water flitting over a gravel shallow.

His face was warm. He didn't think the sun would be so hot this early in the day. Both of Johann's legs were feeling the tingle of falling asleep yet still functioned as he strolled beside Susanna. His heart pounded, his hands trembled, and his stomach cartwheeled in his abdomen. He was smitten. Much to his amazement, she was too.

From that first luncheon, every free moment the two could spare at the same time was spent with each other. If they weren't together, Johann found it hard to not fidget. He'd walk around restlessly in the Orderly Room trying to keep himself busy. Susanna didn't have that problem. When she was on duty, the wounded relentlessly commanded her attention. Though, when off duty, she wistfully stared out a window, pining for his presence.

January 1916 brought conflict into the two lovestruck youths' lives. General Yudenich ordered an attack on the winter headquarters of the rebuilt Ottoman 3rd Army near the mountain town of Erzurum. The winter campaign took the Ottoman command by surprise and, in short order, the Russian Army captured the town. With the front now so far south, Johann's unit was ordered forward.

Once the area around Erzurum had been stabilized, General Yudenich ordered another two-pronged attack. One branch attacked northwest toward the port city of Trabzon, and the other headed east.

Johann was struck with the fervor and cruelty of the Armenian volunteers. Decades of ethnic purging of the mostly Christian Armenians by the Islamic Ottoman Empire left them with a revengeful bloodlust. To make it even worse for the Ottomans, Armenian resistance units, sensing they now had the upper hand, rose up in the south and attacked from behind. That summer and fall, Russia made its greatest incursion into Turkey.

Johann wrote letters to Susanna and kept himself busy with his duties during an especially bitter winter. It was impossible to fight, so both sides dug in and waited. Days seemingly drug on forever. He spent a lot of time in his tent with comrades, trying to stay warm, fending off boredom by playing cards.

Life at the hospital wasn't much better for Susanna. Since there hadn't been much nearby fighting, there weren't many new wounded to take care of. However, the usual casualties from cold and disease still needed to be dealt with. Typhus epidemics always followed on the heels of military campaigns. Lack of decent nutrition and close quarter living in squalid trenches were main ingredients in creating such an outbreak.

But at least these patients didn't bleed so much. As spring approached, Susanna received disturbing letters from home describing increasing political unrest in the country. Even though she wasn't a political person, instability in the government didn't sound good for the war effort. Murmurs around the hospital became open discussion and speculation of what was happening in Petrograd. Then came March, 1917.

CHAPTER TEN

DISASTER AT LAKE NAROCH

Late summer 1915 losses in Poland, and the continuing retreat by the Russian forces, meant fewer German prisoners. Gerhardt's job of guarding prisoners became less necessary. The Russian Army had been suffering from the lack of supplies, and troop morale was falling. He was transferred to a transport unit ferrying munitions to the much closer front.

Being of German background, he wasn't completely trusted, and his religious exemption still kept him from bearing arms. That exemption didn't prevent his superiors from parading him in front of enemy fire to deliver wagonloads of munitions. Slowly, the stores of supplies built up through the winter, and the shortages didn't seem so severe. While Gerhardt chatted with the soldiers unloading his cargo, it didn't seem that morale was getting any better since the previous fall's massive exodus out of Poland.

He'd heard his brother, Heinrich, was somewhere along this front driving ambulances. Every new unit Gerhardt ran across, he asked if anyone had seen his brother. In February, as he delivered supplies to a field hospital, he met an ambulance driver with a burn-scarred face and a patch over his left eye. When Gerhardt described his brother, the man thought for a moment.

"Oh, yeah, I think I met him. If he's the fellow I'm thinking of, he was a German teamster delivering wounded to the same hospital I was at the time." The man continued, "I haven't seen him since August south of Warsaw. The whole front had collapsed, and the hospital was evacuating. We were scrambling to get the last gas victims out before being overrun. Most of our unit was either killed or captured. I barely made it out myself. That's where I received these souvenirs."

The man pointed at his face, then turned to walk away, bringing the conversation to an end. It wasn't good, but at least it was news.

By March, the spring thaw was in full force. Gerhardt's wagon constantly fought early morning frozen ruts and afternoon mud to deliver cargo near Lake Naroch. Since the entire area was swampy, he didn't dare venture far from the road.

By mid-March, he was certain something was about to happen. New reinforcements were flooding into the area, slogging down the muddy roads. It seemed that he'd done little else other than delivering rounds to artillery batteries near the front for quite some time. He wondered why anyone would have so many defensive positions in such a marshy area. It would be lunacy for the enemy to attack across the marshes when it was so difficult to just walk from battery to battery in the spring mud. He didn't have to wait long.

Russian artillery opened up on March 16, maintaining constant fire for two days. His sole duty delivering more rounds to the batteries, Gerhardt hated going near the guns while they were firing. Although the constant roar and nighttime flashes were exciting, it hurt his ears and spooked the horses. Looking across the frontier, it was hard to imagine being on the receiving end of such violence. He paused and whispered a small prayer for everyone involved, then turned back toward the depot for another load.

He hadn't made it a half mile down the heavily rutted, muddy road when thunderous explosions erupted behind him. Looking back, he saw explosions all around the batteries he'd just delivered munitions to. The Germans were firing back. He urged his team to put distance between himself and the carnage. Sleeping uneasily that night, he wondered what morning would bring.

Before dawn the next day, Gerhardt was at the depot loading up for his first trip to the front, dreading what he might find there.

Winding his way through the artillery craters to the same batteries where he'd been the day before proved an arduous affair. It was as bad as he'd feared. With deadly return fire accuracy, the Germans reduced about a fourth of the batteries on the low ridge into smoldering piles of rubble. Body parts not yet policed up and disposed of lay scattered in the mud.

With Russian cannons silent, waiting to be re-supplied with munitions, the German artillery concentrated its fire on Russian infantry wading across the swamps. While the battery crew was unloading the shells. Gerhardt struck up a conversation with a passing forward observer.

"Have you been to the assault area yet?"

"No, for the moment, that's useless," the observer replied. "The signal corp didn't have time to lay phone lines between the various command posts before the attack began. Every time we try to lay one across the frontier, the swamp swallows it, and someone trips over the wire, breaking it. The fog is barely above ground, so the aerial spotters can't see to direct fire. No, for the time being, we're spotting from that building."

The observer pointed toward the top of the ridge. To call it a building was using quite a bit of poetic license. Nothing but a pile of rubble, it had one section of a remaining corner wall to the second floor still standing. The engineers had constructed a scaffold behind the wall with an access ladder.

"We can't fire for a while, so you can go up there and have a look for yourself."

Gerhardt shrugged. With his curiosity getting the best of him, he headed for the wall.

The spotter yelled after him, "Hey, keep your head down while you're up there. It's a high spot, so the Germans take pot shots at it."

Approaching the wall, Gerhardt kept to the back of the ridge. Stumbling across the rubble, he made his way to the ladder. On the platform, the largest pair of binoculars he'd ever seen lay on a table with a map. Picking up the binoculars, he peered over the wall. He wished that he hadn't. But now that he had, he couldn't stop looking.

A couple of hundred yards in front of him, Russian front-line trenches were full of troops waiting to make another assault wave.

Beyond the trenches lay a vast swamp. Soldiers wading up to their waists in frigid, mucky water were trying to hold their weapons above the surface. Sprays of water were churned up by German machine gun rounds raking the poor devils.

Soldiers crouched behind fallen comrades, using the corpses as protection and platforms to rest their rifles on. When possible, they'd float the corpse in front of them to make a mobile barricade. Geysers of mucky water laden with blood and body parts thrown up by German artillery reminded Gerhardt of the splash a heavy ladle makes when accidently dropped into a kettle of beet borscht.

Far in the distance, he saw muzzle flashes of German machine guns decimating the hapless Russians. Even as far back as he was from the actual fighting, the continual din of the battle sent pressure waves of pain radiating from his ears. It felt as if his head was trying to explode while at the same time being squeezed in a vice. He laid the binoculars down and quickly descended the ladder. At the bottom of the ladder, he met the observer.

Gerhardt said, "That's sheer lunacy."

"Yep," the observer answered. "But that's what high command ordered."

Gerhardt headed his wagon to the rear for more supplies down a road clogged with reinforcements slogging toward the front. It was a complete logjam of ambulances, supply wagons, and couriers going both ways, and fresh troops heading toward the front.

The carnage continued for weeks. What he didn't see were troops marching to the rear for rest and recuperation. Apparently, the only way an infantryman came back from the assault was in an ambulance or as a corpse stacked up on a wagon like cordwood.

March 26, the weather changed to heavy snow and bitter cold. Gerhardt heard that the Russians had, indeed, made some headway pushing the Germans back, but soon lost whatever gains they'd made. His wagon did double duty, hauling supplies to the front, and bodies back to the rear every trip. There seemed to be no lack of cargo for return trips. While mud-coated troops piled bodies on his wagon, Gerhardt saw what he thought was a familiar face. Stopping the loading, he wiped the frozen mud off the face of the last body loaded. It was the artillery observer he'd befriended.

"Where did this happen?" Gerhardt asked.

"We found them on the far side of the frontier," one of the shivering, muddy soldiers answered. "They'd been pinned down in the swamp and froze to death. We had to chop the whole unit out of the ice. Some of them made it, but they're in bad shape."

"They were frozen in the ice?"

"Yes, the swamp freezes over every night. Whoever ordered an attack through a swamp, much less this time of year, ought to be shot."

One of the other soldiers chimed in quietly, looking around to be sure no superior officer was in earshot. "I heard it was the tsar himself who ordered this attack. He doesn't give a single thought to us. He thinks we're just cattle to be herded to slaughter."

Other soldiers nodded solemnly. Gerhardt, not wanting to get tied up in what would seem to be a treasonous discussion, quickly departed. With his load of sludge-encrusted, half-frozen, corpses shifting behind him, he mulled over the discussion. The men weren't wrong. This battle was complete folly. He wasn't a military person. Having been raised a pacifist, he'd never considered such matters. Surely, this offensive was a mistake. No one in their right mind would have ordered such a thing if they'd known the conditions.

The ill-conceived attempted assault continued on. Discussions within the lower ranks became more open and disgruntled. When Gerhardt was a child in America, he remembered his father worrying about a revolution there. That was just a railroad strike with only a few injured. This was an incompetently managed war with many thousands of men dying from inept leadership. He couldn't see how morale could sink any lower without open mutiny.

The offensive came to a merciful end on April 14. Whatever gains the Russians might have had were lost with the lines returning to their original positions. Few reserve troops were left able to be transferred to other theaters. Gerhardt continued forwarding supplies to the front lines, but now, at least, there weren't so many bodies to bring back.

CHAPTER ELEVEN
BEHIND THE LINES

"This is a real mess, Unteroffizier. What do we do with them?"

"It doesn't look as if any of them are going to make it. We can't take the time to carry them back, anyway. Just stick them with your bayonets, and let's keep advancing."

Barely conscious, Heinrich thought he was hallucinating. The voices in his head were German. Regaining some of his faculties, he realized he couldn't move. Everything around him was moist, and something was holding him down. Slowly becoming clearer, the voices were definitely German.

Coherent now, he lay still. Frozen in fear, he heard boots shuffling above among moans of wounded men. He recognized the sound of blades sinking up to their hilts in flesh. He'd heard it many times growing up at slaughter time. Each stick was followed by the gurgling sounds of life leaving a body. The moans of the wounded quickly died down. All he heard was boots shuffling and men talking above him.

"Hey, Unteroffizier, I don't need to go down into the ditch and stick that one, do I? It looks like he's been blown completely in two. I don't want to get any more blood on my boots than necessary."

Heinrich lay absolutely still as the boots walked around above him.

"No, I don't even think he's all there. From what I can see, he must have taken the full force of the blast."

Heinrich lay there, listening to the soldiers move on, waiting for quite a while before trying to free himself. He had no idea how long he'd been unconscious, but it was now daytime. Finally, he wiggled his head free a bit and could feel slime slipping off of his ear. With his sense of smell returning, he knew the scent well.

Freeing one arm, he slowly brought it up and wiped his eyes. Held down by a large piece of liver, he was laying in, and covered by, the contents of a horse's belly. His head rested in a puddle of half-digested hay from the ruptured stomach and intestines. Slowly, he pushed away the rancid goo, pausing frequently to listen for approaching soldiers.

Finally, Heinrich worked his head free enough to survey his surroundings. He was underneath the overturned wagon. Fate had smiled on him, and he was in the cavity just behind the seat. When the shell landed, the horses shielded him from the major force of the blast. Their shredded carcasses absorbed the weight of the wagon as it came down on him. It was nightfall again before he finally was able to crawl out and survey his situation.

Slowly, he crawled up out of the ditch. Around the wagon lay the wounded he'd been carrying to the hospital, all dead. Seeing muzzle flashes and hearing shooting to the east, knowing he was now behind enemy lines, he hid behind the wagon until the moonless night fully enveloped the battlefield. He would never make it back across the lines by going down the road. To his north, on the other side of a mile-wide field, was a canal that flowed west to east out of the Rawka River. When the night was as dark as it was going to get, he headed across the field.

Heinrich forced himself to walk slowly in a crouched position, fighting every instinct to run. Near midnight, he heard approaching German voices. Quickly dropping to the ground, he lay still in the dark. The patrol stopped less than ten yards away in the tall weeds. One of the soldiers struck a match and lit a cigarette.

"Put that thing out, you fool," a sergeant barked at the man. "There could still be snipers around."

Pausing only long enough to drink from their canteens, the soldiers moved along. Heinrich let out a long breath and spent a few minutes composing himself. Crawling quietly, he hoped to make the canal by daylight.

He arrived on the canal's bank when morning twilight was creeping into the sky. After studying the shoreline, he swam across the canal to a defunct irrigation gate. The structure around the gate had collapsed, allowing him some semblance of concealment during the coming day. Soaked and cold, he would crawl out of the gate and sun himself for a while. When soldiers approached, he'd slip back into the water.

Heinrich believed his best chance of making it back across the lines was to stay in the canal as long as possible. At dark, he heard fighting and saw the flashes a few miles to the east. Tying his boots around his neck, he slipped into the canal and slowly started paddling with the current. Every few hundred yards, he found a convenient place to pull himself up the bank to survey his surroundings. It became obvious the front line had moved too far for him to cross by morning. The current started to pick up. Before he realized it, the current was going too fast to swim against.

Winding its way along the side of a ridge, the water's current pulled him toward the side. An artillery round had struck the canal wall and blasted the bank out. Water gushed out the gaping hole into a broad field. Coughing and choking, Heinrich tumbled with the rushing water into the newly created swamp.

Previously, this had been a grain field. He figured this new development had both positive and negative aspects. Beyond the breach in its bank, the dry canal was useless for concealment. On the other hand, the field-turned-swamp was too soft for military maneuvering.

In the final phases of a grain harvest, the threshing machine still sat in the far southeast corner of the field, sinking into the mud. Not yet removed stacks of straw dotted the entire expanse. These haystacks could be used for concealment and a dry place to rest during daylight hours. For the rest of the night, Heinrich cautiously worked his way from one haystack to another. When dawn was about to break, he climbed up into one and covered himself up to rest.

In between catnaps, he scanned the battlefield in front of him. From what he could see, the Germans hadn't bothered to bring forward and set up much artillery. In fact, it didn't seem there was much fighting being done at all. It appeared the Russians were retreating to more defensible positions, only offering delaying skirmishes to slow the German advance. That didn't bode well for him. The front could possibly outrun his ability to overtake and cross it.

Laying back in the hay, Heinrich mulled his options. Pulling up a mental map of the area, he tried to place himself in the shoes of a field commander. From his trips between the front and the hospital in his ambulance, he knew a small river wound its way east toward the Vistula River. He was now just south of that river. Warsaw was north by quite a distance.

Surely, the Russians would defend Warsaw, and it seemed probable they'd use the river as a defense point. For the moment, the Germans were probably south of that river and west of the Vistula River. There weren't that many crossing points, and fewer bridges, on the small river. The Vistula River seemed even more unlikely to be crossed in a short amount of time.

Heinrich made his decision. When he was first washed into the field, he'd worked his way northeast. Now, he'd head more northerly until reaching the river. As soon as it was dark enough, he climbed out of the haystack and waded north.

The new moon had passed, and a sliver illuminated the early evening, just the right amount of light to make his way without worrying about being seen from long distances. Considering the circumstances, he made good headway. Shortly after midnight, he saw the tree line along the river. Heinrich couldn't believe his luck that the breached canal water was making it all the way to the river.

Germans were on both sides of the flooded field, firing an occasional round. But he couldn't see anyone willing to be in the muck between him and the river. He slipped into the tree line above the riverbank and stopped to mull his options again. He now had a major decision to make.

If he crossed in the dark, friendly troops might shoot at anything making a noise. If he waited until light, he might be seen by Germans and shot while he crossed. He decided to wait. He was more confident with his ability to avoid being seen by the Germans than he was with the ill-trained Russian troops not shooting him in the dark.

Wanting all concerned to recognize his uniform, Heinrich waited until full light before tying his boots across his neck and slipping into the water. Paddling across the slow-moving current, he fervently hoped to make it across before the current pulled him in front of a more active section of the front.

Just as he was about to drag himself out of the water, a Russian yelled, "There's one. Shoot him!"

"Don't shoot, you fool, I'm Russian!" Heinrich hissed, trying to be loud enough to be heard by the soldier but not loud enough to attract the attention of the Germans.

"Put the gun down, he's wearing one of our uniforms."

Seeing partial faces peeking from behind trees on top of the bank, he put his hands up and ran toward them. About ten yards from the trees, he heard Germans yelling, and the air filled with gunfire. Making it into the trees and launching himself onto his face in the brush, Heinrich promptly found a rifle barrel pressed up against the back of his head.

"I'm Russian, I'm Russian, I'm Russian!" he insisted.

The rifle barrel was lifted, and he crawled farther back into better cover.

"Boy, you sure are lucky we didn't shoot you," one of the soldiers said. "Come on! We have to get out of here!"

A squad of soldiers materialized out of the trees and ran for cover behind a rise, where a truck waited.

"Our unit is being outflanked, and we have to pull back," a corporal yelled as they climbed into the back of the truck.

Artillery rounds started landing in the tree line with the explosions walking toward them. Pulling onto a rutted road, the truck wound its way through the low hills above the river. The hard rubber wheels in the ruts tortured Heinrich's already thoroughly bruised body, but he smiled. He was just happy to be on his own side of the line and relatively safe for the moment.

Germany had broken through both north and south of Warsaw. The front was collapsing. Russian army in full retreat, Warsaw close to becoming completely surrounded, the whole area was in disarray.

The corporal explained, "The Germans have crossed the Vistula River south of here and captured the Ivangorod fortress. Now, they're heading north on the other side."

The squad's truck fell into a convoy heading north, passing through defensive fallback lines manned by other units. The torch had been passed to those units to slow the Germans.

Warsaw was in full panic as the convoy moved through the suburbs. Leaning over the side, Heinrich saw their truck was toward the tail end of a line of military vehicles heading for the Vistula River. Panicked civilians were everywhere, trying to evacuate the city.

When the truck crossed the Poniatowski Bridge, demolition troops were scurrying up and down both sides, packing explosives. The slow convoy had only been across for about a half an hour when explosions arose behind them. Heinrich looked back, wondering if the bridge had been cleared of people before it was blown up.

The rest of August was spent with the Russians retreating eastward. In the confusion, unable to find any substantial command structure to report to, he attached himself informally with his rescuers' unit, driving one of the trucks. By the end of September, the German advance lost steam, but not before Russia had pulled almost completely out of Poland.

CHAPTER TWELVE

BRUSILOV'S BRUISING

When the front calmed down for the winter, Heinrich had been reassigned south to a unit near Rovno. Fighting had been sporadic, and there were relatively few casualties needing transport to the rear. With his experience and ability to read, his superiors finally trusted him with a motorized ambulance.

Slack time left him with more opportunity to socialize with the other troops. Morale hitting bottom as the war dragged on, rumbling around the mess tent got louder. In May, when the influx of new troops from other areas reported conditions elsewhere weren't any better, it only added fuel to the discontent. The upper echelons didn't seem to care what the lower ranks thought as long as they followed orders.

June 4, 1916, Aleksei Brusilov's Russian artillery opened fire along the southern front with the Austro-Hungarians. The Brusilov Offensive began. By June 8, the front was on the move. The Russians actually seemed to be pushing the Austrians back. By the tenth of June, Russians had overrun Lutsk and were heading toward the Carpathian Mountains.

These gains not without massive costs, Heinrich suddenly was overloaded with wounded. By mid-month, German units started showing up on the other side of the front, but gains were still being made. Thousands of Austro-Hungarian POWs marched past daily to be loaded into Siberian-bound boxcars.

The front kept grinding west until mid-July, when it slowed to a crawl. Heinrich worked day and night transporting the wounded. At least he didn't have to fight the columns of POWs clogging the roads anymore. The front had moved sixty miles west and stopped. There were no more reserves.

General Evert, the Russian army commander in the north, had been instructed to relieve pressure in Heinrich's area by mounting a second prong of assaults. Instead, the general just shuffled his troops along the line without ever committing them. The Germans were able to pull their troops from that sector and slow Brusilov's advance long enough for reinforcements to be transferred from the Western Front.

By the end of September, the advance ground to a halt and was losing ground. The Russian Army couldn't continue the attack. It had run out of both material and men. Hundreds of thousands were killed on both sides. Heinrich watched the troops' morale drop through the floor and wondered what the future held.

Things only got worse through the winter with soldiers openly disregarding orders from superiors. In February, 1917, Petrograd erupted into riots. Troops strained to glean any political information that might work its way to the front.

In March, there was a universal shock when the tsar abdicated. Rumors of units in open revolt and officers being murdered were rampant. The army held its collective breath. Later in the spring, Alexander Kerensky was named Minister of War.

Kerensky toured the front, talking to the troops. The soldiers cheered when he addressed Heinrich's unit and announced that officer oversight committees were being formed within the ranks. Morale seemed to improve, but Heinrich wondered how the officer corps being supervised by underlings could possibly work.

The boost in spirits was short lived. Kerensky, thinking a major military victory would raise morale and calm unrest in the country, ordered General Brusilov to go on the offensive again. The offensive began on the first of July, 1917. Kerensky became Prime Minister the next day.

Things looked up when the offensive first started. Regrouped since the previous fall, the army had loyal elite troops formed into shock battalions. Heinrich watched hopefully as Austrian resistance appeared to fall apart when Russian infantry and cavalry poured through a gap in the lines. His optimism was crushed when the advance again ran up against better German units. Heinrich's job of carrying wounded was shortly in full demand.

While unloading wounded at an aid station, he overheard a courier arguing with an officer. "Sir, the general needs you to immediately attack west on your side of the Dniester River."

"I can't yet." The officer shrugged. "I have to wait until the Soldiers' Committee approves the operation."

The courier, now red-faced, responded, "Sir, the general ordered an immediate attack!"

"Listen, sergeant, see that group over there watching us?" the officer replied, pointing at the committee.

"Yes."

"I can't make that order," the exasperated officer continued. "*You* go tell them to hurry with their decision. If I push them too hard, they'll simply shoot me. In any case, by the time they decide to comply—if they decide to comply—it'll be too late to accomplish what the general wanted."

The courier stared at the officer for a moment, then walked disgustedly back to his motorcycle. Starting it with an aggressive kick, he headed back to headquarters in a cloud of dust to face the general's wrath. The officer dejectedly watched after the courier, then turned and walked slowly back to his command tent, head down and shoulders slumped. Heinrich quickly ducked behind his ambulance so the officer wouldn't know the conversation had been overheard.

It didn't take long before the offensive disintegrated. July 19, the Central Powers mounted a massive counterattack. A doctor ran out of the hospital tent and ordered Heinrich to load as many of the wounded as he could fit into his ambulance. Grabbing him by the collar, the doctor looked intently into his eyes.

"Fill up your tank with fuel. Take the wounded and head east as quickly as you can without attracting attention. The front has collapsed, and we're about to be overrun. Do *not* alert the Soldiers' Council! They'll commandeer your vehicle for themselves."

Rattled, he did as told, and headed east through the camp. As he neared the compound's eastern perimeter, a Soldier Committee member tried to flag him down. Heinrich moved the ambulance's throttle lever to the wide-open position. The committee member reached for his pistol as the ambulance drove past. Heinrich was safely past before the Committee member could fumble the gun out of its holster. Shooting erupted, and three other ambulances, filled with wounded and nurses, converged behind him. The little convoy put as many miles possible behind them.

After about an hour, they'd made it thirteen miles down the road. Heinrich saw the driver behind him waving to pull over. Looking behind the convoy as it was going around a right-hand corner and seeing no pursuit within sight, he pulled over. He walked back to the second ambulance, and the group gathered for a conference.

He asked, "Are we clear?"

"I think so," the second driver replied.

"Is this all of us?" another driver asked.

"Yes. I had another ambulance in front of me, but the driver was shot and he crashed," the second driver said.

"Where's the doctor?" Heinrich asked.

"He stayed behind to care for the wounded who couldn't be moved," a nurse replied.

"God help him." Heinrich shook his head. "I hope the Germans aren't savages when they take the camp."

"What do we do now?" the second driver chimed in. "If the committee catches us, they'll probably shoot us."

We're heading toward the Podolia Governorate." Heinrich shrugged. "If we keep heading east, we're bound to run into some sort of military support unit."

"We're all from Latvia or Lithuania." the other drivers looked at each other. "Aren't you from around here?"

"Yes, but I came from quite a ways east of here in Yekaterinoslav Governorate. I'm completely unfamiliar with this area."

"Well, at least you know something about which way the rivers flow and have a vague idea where the villages are," the second driver answered. "That's more than the rest of us know. I say you get to be the leader for a while."

"I guess," Heinrich acquiesced. "Whatever we do, we'd better get started before they catch up with us."

A nurse got into Heinrich's ambulance, and the small caravan headed east. The one problem the group didn't encounter was traffic heading west. Since the camp they had fled was a rear staging area, there weren't many combat units this far back. From what he had seen, even if there were combat units, they'd also be retreating eastward. Nobody seemed to have the stomach for fighting anymore. As night neared, the little convoy entered an abandoned supply depot next to a railroad and searched for more fuel.

Rummaging through the camp, the drivers found enough fuel to fill the trucks and cans to strap more to the sides. Nurses tended to the wounded, trying to make them comfortable. The day's jostling down the rough road hadn't been easy on anyone. After fueling the ambulances, the drivers searched the camp for food.

The mess tent had already been ravaged. Heinrich entered a junior officers' tent and kicked open some abandoned footlockers with a little bread and a few tins of fancy meats inside. Another driver let out a yelp to come help. Quickly tying the rations into a blanket, Heinrich headed toward the sounds of joy.

The driver found the commander's tent. One of the lockers was full of cheeses, tins of meat, and two bottles of vodka. Heinrich took the bottles of vodka and was about to break them when a nurse grabbed his arm.

"What are you doing?" she asked.

"I'm going to break these to prevent distractions," he replied.

"Don't. The alcohol can be used as a disinfectant. We don't have much in the way of supplies with us, and we might need these bottles in case someone's wounds become infected."

"Then you better hide them," he said. "We don't need anyone getting drunk until we're somewhere safe."

"I'll put them in my bag."

"Don't let anyone see you hide them."

She nodded and discreetly disappeared. Soon, everyone was fed, and the wounded were made comfortable. Holding a conference, the drivers and nurses decided to layover for the night but would take shifts on watch in case the situation changed. None of them had a weapon, but at least the guard could raise an alarm. Heinrich was assigned a predawn shift, then turned in for the night.

"Wake up. Wake up! Vehicles are coming!" He was aroused early.

Leaping to his feet and stumbling outside, he saw distant headlights coming from the west. The nurses started loading the wounded into the ambulances as fast as they could, but it was apparent they wouldn't make it in time. While loading the last of the injured, a motorcycle pulled up to the group.

Heinrich recognized the courier he'd overheard having a confrontation with his commanding officer. A quick discussion revealed that the oncoming vehicles were the command staff of their division redeploying further east. The courier suggested the small convoy fall in behind the motorcade for protection. They gratefully complied.

For two more days, the motorcade drove east, pausing frequently to send messages behind and wait for updates to catch up. The group entered Ternopil and stopped in the center of town. They heard fighting behind them, but it didn't seem to be getting any closer. Once they found a hospital, the nurses and patients were transferred to more comfortable conditions. Heinrich and the other drivers went to a makeshift motor pool near where the command convoy had set up camp.

The courier walked by and, seeing the curious looks on the drivers' faces, told them, "Well, it appears they've stopped . . .although it seems they just outran their supply train rather than us keeping them back."

Heinrich studied a map and thought that it was about time. The Central Powers had just chased them more than one hundred fifty miles across Ukraine in less than a week. The surviving Russian units which escaped, straggled past for weeks. It was obvious the Russian army was done for. If the Germans weren't so occupied on the Western Front, they could have easily strolled into Moscow, whistling Die Fledermaus arias in the back of their transport trucks as they drove. Russia's command staff was no longer able to exercise enough authority to organize a dress parade.

The courier wasn't quite right. Once the Germans gathered enough reserves to attack the city, they did. Within two days, they drove the Russians out. Heinrich drove east again, withdrawing from Ternopil. He hadn't seen the nurses since they entered the hospital and hoped they had time to evacuate farther back with their wounded. It wasn't long before he was near the headwaters of the Southern Buh River in the Podolian Upland. It was August before the German advance finally stopped.

His former company no longer existing, the command unit which he and the other drivers attached themselves to informally adopted them. The government had been in a state of turmoil since before the withdrawal. Military units were in full revolt, and the news from Petrograd wasn't encouraging. It didn't appear that the Russian army in this area was going to be able to do anything substantial before winter.

He spent his time looking southeast longingly. He was so close to the Buh River; in no time at all, he could be in a boat floating down the river toward Odessa. The Buh River flowed into the Black Sea, only a short distance from the mouth of the Dnieper River—and the road home.

CHAPTER THIRTEEN
COMMAND CONFUSION

After Gerhardt's previous outfit was virtually wiped out attacking through half-frozen swamps in the ill-fated Lake Naroch offensive, he was reassigned north near the Gulf of Riga on the Baltic Sea. Now with the rebuilding Russian Twelve Army, his life had almost become tedious delivering munitions to the forward units.

Like his older brother, the attrition rate of native Russian drivers moved him into the driver's seat of a motorized vehicle. He smiled internally with a morbid sense of humor. Had he been promoted because he was the only one left standing to promote? Or was the promotion an acknowledgment of his ability to avoid being killed? He decided he was a driver by default because he was still breathing.

The war was doing that to the soldiers. Conversation in the trenches had regressed into levels not acceptable in civilized society. With little hope of living to the end, they prevented complete insanity by descending into ever lower forms of gallows humor. The gruesomeness of a comrade's death was no longer repulsive to the soldiers. To the contrary, the more spectacular a friend's demise was, the more it was celebrated.

It became almost a contest over who was blown higher into the air or how far a body part was found from its original possessor. No one expressed a desire, in front of the others, to meet their end in a mediocre manner. By universal consensus, being gassed was the most feared way to die.

It was almost common practice to use a recently deceased corpse as a bench to elevate yourself out of the trench bottom's mud. After a battle, a bleary-eyed, long-term combatant could be seen absent-mindedly having lunch or a smoke perched on a body that had been a breathing trench mate a few hours before.

This was now Gerhardt's world. Doing their best not to behave that way in public, it didn't take long for soldiers to slip back into the morass when sent back into action. Motoring along in the late summer sun, he mulled ever more extravagant euphemisms describing his ascension to the front seat throne of an ammo truck. In a rare good mood, he didn't mind having to wait for a detachment of Latvian riflemen marching across the road. Sunning himself, he started whistling a tune.

This, he thought, would be a much better time to launch an assault than the asinine Lake Naroch debacle. His good mood shifted slightly, but he quickly suppressed it. After all, the Germans were on the southwest side of the wide Daugava River. Russians and Latvians were on the northeast bank. A direct attack would be highly improbable. He shrugged and, putting his truck in gear, went merrily on his way delivering supplies.

Distant rumbling of artillery the morning of September 1, 1917 woke Gerhardt. He passed it off as just a harassment engagement. Both sides conducted bombardments frequently just to keep the opposition on their toes. While eating breakfast, it slowly dawned on him that the sounds of artillery were mostly incoming. Outgoing barrage sounds were dying off. That wouldn't be good. It meant the Germans' targeting was more accurate and the Russians were on the losing side of the exchange.

For three hours, the German artillery barrage continued. Activity in the supply depot became frenetic as Russian artillery fell completely silent. Gerhardt was still sure that the Daugava River was a mighty obstacle to swim. Then, clouds of dust rose off of the roads from the front as artillery pieces started passing, heading in the wrong direction.

His commander rounded up the drivers. "The Germans are building bridges. The depot has to be moved farther back."

Dividing up his trucks, the officer assigned half of them to continue resupplying the front. The other half would pack up the depot and move what they could out of harm's way. Gerhardt stayed to resupply the front. It was the first time he would see mustard gas casualties.

Retreating Russians clogged the road, making his trip toward the front difficult. Latvian units were to conduct a holding action while the Russians redeployed. But they couldn't hold out for long. Under the protection of the morning's artillery barrage, the Germans finished three pontoon bridges. Now, troops were pouring across. Having been amidst retreat chaos before, Gerhardt knew what to expect. It would be an arduous slog to and from the front.

Once unloaded, he volunteered to haul wounded back to the hospital. Mustard gas casualties looked almost the same as burn victims. An orderly warned him, "Don't touch the clothes of the wounded or walk around in the grass." The orderly needn't have bothered. Gerhardt had no intention of venturing this close to the front on his next trip.

The supply depot was virtually deserted when he arrived with the wounded. He managed to catch a lone ambulance relaying wounded farther to the rear. The one thing Gerhardt thought he didn't need was to disobey an order and have to abandon his assignment of delivering ammunition. His truck was loaded with high explosives meant for bridge demolition behind the retreating forces.

Driving toward the receding front, Gerhardt saw airplanes diving on the battle zone. Too busy concentrating on not running over retreating soldiers, he didn't have much time to watch the planes even though he hadn't seen that many. When the foot traffic parted in front of his truck, it allowed a momentary glance at the sky. He'd never seen an airplane that close before.

Transfixed, he stared at the plane as its wings bobbled in the turbulence. A technological wonder came toward him, fire spitting out the front. Little geysers of dust erupted out of the road; soldiers scrambled for the ditch. He absentmindedly thought of parallel rows of dominoes being knocked over. Realization slapped Gerhardt in the face. He was being strafed.

He launched out of the truck, joining the others in the deep ditch. He hadn't stopped sliding to the bottom, doing his best imitation of a cabbage worm squirming its way into concealment, when the truck exploded. He lay there for a few moments with his hands covering the back of his head. Hot pieces of the truck rained down all around. His ears were ringing so loudly, he couldn't hear the airplane turn and make another pass, strafing troops in the opposing ditch.

Dazed, Gerhardt wobbled and fell over a few times, crawling out of the ditch. Head throbbing, he tried to stand upright, but his head spun, and he became violently nauseous. Collapsing to his knees, he spent the next fifteen minutes displaying his breakfast choices on the side of the road for all to critique.

"Come on, buddy, we have to go! Come on, you have to get up and move."

Gerhardt looked up at the soldier pulling on his sleeve.

"Come on, the Germans are coming!"

He strained to get up with the Latvian's help. The soldier, his rifle in one hand, held Gerhardt's arm with the other, pulling him down the road. Regaining some equilibrium within a few yards, Gerhardt looked back at what little remained of his smoldering truck.

"Was that your truck?"

"Yes, it was," Gerhardt answered.

"You certainly made a mess in the middle of the road."

"That wasn't my intention. I was supposed to make a mess in the middle of a bridge."

"You missed."

"Yes . . .yes, I did. Now they'll probably take my truck away for not delivering the dynamite."

"Well, from what I saw back there, they won't be taking much."

Gerhardt started to chuckle, but his head hurt too much.

After about a mile, he didn't need the kindly soldier's intermittent stabilizations. Assuming the port was the Germans' objective, they didn't bother going north toward Riga. It would be safer heading in a different direction, so they kept trudging northeast through the night.

The Latvian 2nd Rifleman Brigade met them early the next morning, heading for the front. Gerhardt, along with the few other Russians in the group, were told how to find one of their own units. Latvians, including the young man that had taken Gerhardt under his wing, were scooped up for reunification with their units.

Trudging another four hours, dodging the westbound Latvians, he finally met a few Russian 12th Army artillery pieces heading to the rear. He was more than happy to accept a ride to a new staging area.

When he went to report that he was alive and ready to be sent back to his unit, wherever it was, the headquarters area was flooded by soldiers gossiping animatedly. Gerhardt joined a group of men waiting to report for reassignment. No one seemed to know exactly what was happening in Petrograd.

He asked, "What's going on?"

"General Lavr Kornilov has been arrested for treason."

"Wait a minute. Isn't he the Commander-in-Chief of the Army?"

"Yes, he was," a soldier replied.

"What did he do?" Gerhardt's curiosity was increasing.

"There's been a lot of unrest in Petrograd. You know, riots and the like."

"Yes, I've heard that."

"Well, Kornilov sent some troops to Petrograd to restore order. Kerensky had him arrested for attempting a coup," the soldier explained.

"Well, who's in charge then?" Now, Gerhardt was getting worried.

"No one is really sure."

Another soldier chimed in, "I heard they've brought back summary firing squads."

"What? I thought the firing squads were forbidden by Kerensky last year when he set up the Soldier Committees." This was getting to be too much for Gerhardt to believe.

"They claim there have been too many desertions, and too many soldiers are refusing to follow orders. The order was given in July but we're just now finding out about it."

Gerhardt shrugged. "I wondered how long asking the soldiers if they wanted to follow an order was going to last."

The instant the comment came out of his mouth, he realized he shouldn't have been so indiscreet. The mood of the soldiers was ugly. Excusing himself, he worked his way through the crowd. Making his way to the command tent, he was in conflict. He'd worked long and hard to be accepted on the same level of loyalty to Russia as the rest of the soldiers. Now, the other soldiers were openly turning their backs on the government.

Gerhardt did his best to keep his head down and mouth shut for the next month. Assuming the Germans were going to move up the coast out of Lithuania and try to take Petrograd, his unit was pulled back into Russia proper, just south of the capital. Making matters worse, riots and labor strikes in Petrograd throughout September and October were rumored.

The camp's mood was uncertain and tense. A common topic of discussion was about the conflicts going on in the Provisional Government. Matters came to a head the evening of October 25 when the Russian cruiser, Aurora, fired a signal shot while moored in the Petrograd harbor—starting the October Revolution.

Groups of soldiers gathered a few days later around the few newspapers that had made it into the camp. Since Gerhardt was one of the few literate soldiers in the lower ranks, he was delegated to read for the others. The first paper he picked up was the respected Novoe Vremia out of Petrograd. He read an article about a revolt which started in the morning when troops and workers stormed the government offices. The whole city was virtually in Bolshevik hands when the cruiser fired the signal shot at 9:45 in the evening. Vladimir Lenin himself led an assault on the Winter Palace.

The article continued, stating the palace was guarded only by cadets and one of the Women's Battalions. He was reading about the cadets being subdued and the women captured and subjected to atrocities, when a large soldier grabbed the paper out of Gerhardt's hands. The soldier, known to be one of the more rabid supporters for a change in the Empire, crumpled the paper and held it over his head.

He bellowed, "This is a Tsarist propaganda rag trying to suppress the will of the people! All it contains are lies trying to besmirch brother Lenin!" He flung a copy of the leftist Delo Naroda at Gerhardt. "Here, read this. It contains the truth."

Being half the man's size, Gerhardt complied. That paper's version of the previous days' events had a completely different slant. Government offices were liberated by brave patriots. The Winter Palace had been saved from destruction at the hands of hysterical women and misled cadets. All army units were encouraged to support the newly formed government led by the Central Executive Committee.

Gerhardt's narration was interrupted occasionally as the soldiers cheered in support of the one-sided article. By the time he'd stopped reading, the men were joyfully shaking hands and slapping each other on the backs.

He left to find a quiet spot to think. Walking away, he saw isolated small gatherings sitting sullenly in thought. The tsar and his family had been confined since the previous spring, but there were still substantial amounts of loyalists among the ranks. An equal number of men couldn't care less about who was in charge as long as they could go home from the war. Gerhardt grouped himself in with the latter, seeing absolutely no good that would come out of any of this. He ended up in his tent writing letters home to Maria and his parents. News from home had him troubled.

CHAPTER FOURTEEN

COLLAPSE IN THE CAUCASUS

Plagued with typhus and, because of the poor supply system, even scurvy in the lower ranks, the Russian Army in the Caucuses didn't have the will for further offenses. With the Ottomans not strong enough to attack, there had been only minimal fighting for months.

A Special Transcaucasian Committee was formed, including elected military representatives who had input on operations. The area's commanding general chose to retire instead of accepting a reassignment to another posting, basically a demotion. With the Russian command structure in the Caucasus in disarray, Johann just bided his time and went about his daily minimal duties.

Susanna's letters told a different story for her. The hospital had become extremely busy taking care of typhus cases. Morale was at rock bottom and gossip over the goings on in Petrograd rampant. It didn't get any better throughout the summer. Rank and file soldiers just didn't care anymore. Martial law over the local population had broken down, and villages were being raided by bandits. Johann's eternal optimism over the good in man had just about evaporated.

In September, 1917, the army started reorganizing the units in his area to include more Armenians outfits. Because of upheaval in Petrograd, the "Special Transcaucasian Committee" was replaced in November with the "Transcaucasian Sejim," a Socialist-leaning semi-independent state encompassing Georgia, Armenia, and Azerbaijan. With seemingly no one in charge, Johann wasn't surprised when, on December 5, Russia and the Ottoman Empire signed an armistice.

He suddenly became busy relaying messages to the smaller Russian commands in his sector. "Start preparing for a withdrawal from the front. Leave your infrastructure in place. The Armenians want to keep fighting, so all larger weapons will be transferred to their new army."

The professional officer class wasn't happy with the direction the country was going. Christmas day 1917, Johann sat in the front seat of his commanding officer's car headed back toward Kars. Leaving his unit's withdrawal to be supervised by subordinates, the general went ahead to headquarters. During the tense two-day journey, conversation inside the command car was subdued, almost nonexistent.

One side of the road was lined with ragged Russians marching northeast carrying few weapons. On the other side, Armenians marched southwest with newly supplied armament. Staring out the side window of the command car, the general's neck veins stuck out further the closer they got to Kars. Johann thought that he could hear the officer's teeth grinding over the noise of the engine.

When the command car pulled in front of the headquarters building, the general didn't wait for Johann to open his door. He was halfway up the walk before Johann could make it around the car. Running up the walk to open the building's door for the officer, Johann almost had to trot to keep up as they made their way down the halls.

Storming into the regional commander's office, the general made a beeline toward the door in the rear of the room. A clerk got up from behind his desk in the middle of the room to intercept, but the second they made eye contact, the clerk discreetly retreated.

Bursting through the door, the general slammed it behind him. Johann stood just inside the offices, trying to blend into the wallpaper. For over a half hour, loud, animated, garbled voices emanated from the next room. The general exited the back office, shutting the door hard. Before the door had closed, he said brusquely over his shoulder, "I'm done." He walked past Johann and said, "Come on."

Johann fell in behind as his commander headed toward the building's exit. When the officer pulled up short, Johann almost ran into his back. The general stood looking down for a few moments, then slowly turned and looked intently at Johann.

"How long have you been in my unit?" he asked softly.

"I've been assigned to your command for two and a half years, sir," Johann answered.

"Huh." The general stood, thinking. "Follow me."

Turning down another hall, they strode toward the rear of the building until coming to a door with "Records" stenciled on the glass.

"Wait here," his commander said and went into the room.

Johann stood in the hall for what seemed an eternity. Peeking through the glass infrequently, he felt sorry for the lowly clerk being terrorized by a general. The clerk ran to a row of file cabinets and pulled out some papers and then ran back to his desk. Johann watched as the officer hovered over the furiously typing clerk.

The clerk pulled out the paper and showed it to the general. Apparently, it wasn't good enough because he sheepishly started on a new sheet as the officer wadded up the first one. Finally satisfied, the general grabbed the paperwork and, with the clerk standing at attention on wobbling knees, headed out of the room.

"Here," the officer said softly, handing Johann the paperwork. "You've been here long enough."

Turning, the general headed toward the building's front door. Attempting to read the document as he hurried to keep up, Johann's eyes focused on the large printed word "Discharge" on the top of the form. Startled, he tripped on the uneven hardwood floor and fell into the general's back. Sure that he was going to get a dressing down, Johann snapped to attention when the officer stopped and turned to look at him.

"Is there something the matter, boy?" the general said kindly.

"No, sir," Johann stammered. "Uh, I mean I don't understand, sir."

"I cannot abide the way that this army is being managed anymore, so I've resigned my commission. I'm getting old, and I'm going home." The general reached around Johann's shoulders and led him toward the door. "As my last act as an officer, I'm giving you a discharge. Go home while you're still in one piece."

Offering his hand, the general gave Johann a firm shake, then turned and walked out the door with slumped shoulders. Thinking the man had aged quite a bit in the last few days and looked considerably shorter, Johann called after him.

"Sir!"

When the general turned to look back, Johann snapped to attention and delivered the sincerest salute he'd ever given. Smiling, the officer returned the salute, then got into his command car while the driver unloaded Johann's rucksack. Obscured by foggy exhaust in the brisk mid-winter air, the car disappeared down the road.

Johann watched until the car went around a corner, then looked at his paperwork. Amazed that his name was spelled correctly, he wasn't even aware the general knew his first name. The second page was a voucher for his back pay. Shrugging, he returned into the building and headed for the paymaster's office.

Susanna bent over a typhus patient's bed tending to his needs. It had been a long, dreary Christmas season, and she did her best to cheer the soldiers. Standing up and tucking her hair back into her scarf before moving to the next patient, she glanced out the ice-crystal-haloed second floor window at the late afternoon frost-coated landscape.

A lone, distant soldier walking toward the hospital struck an air of familiarity within her. She paused wistfully for a moment, wishing it could be Johann returning from the front. Slowly, realization flowed through her—the soldier's gait was more familiar than she had first thought. Her mouth tried to articulate his name, but it wouldn't come out. Spinning around, Susanna ran for the top of the stairs, emitting the only sound her body could manage—an ear-shattering scream.

The scream startled one of the other nurses who dropped a fully laden bedpan. Those patients who could, raised up on one elbow and stared after the running nurse. All in the ward at least looked after her. The scarf flew back off of her golden hair as she ran, dress flowing behind her.

One of the soldiers smiled and remarked after she disappeared, "That reminds me of an artillery shell exiting a cannon barrel, followed by the dark swirling cordite smoke."

Nurses gathered at the windows to see what the emergency was.

"Johann, Johann, Johann!" she screamed, running toward him.

Dropping his rucksack, Johann ran toward her. Susanna launched herself into his arms, almost knocking him over. He staggered back a bit as she kissed him all over his travel-grimed face. When she calmed down enough to put her back on her feet, he reached into his coat pocket and showed her his paperwork. Reading the documents, she looked inquisitively back up at him with misty eyes.

"I'm done," he said. "The war's over for us. Get your stuff, and let's get out of here."

Looking into his eyes for only a few moments, she broke free and ran back into the hospital. Johann retrieved his rucksack and found a place on the hospital's front steps to perch and wait for his love to return. Susanna flew up the stairs and back into the ward. Nurses were still pressed up against the windows, looking down to fully examine the young man on the steps—more than one dabbing at her eyes with a skirt hem. A happy reunion was a very uncommon event in this war.

Susanna went directly to her supervisor but could barely speak with the other women hugging and congratulating her. When the excitement subsided enough, she softly and apologetically asked the head nurse if she could tender her resignation. The other nurses gasped and then looked at their stern supervisor.

The head nurse looked at her for what seemed like an eternity, then straightened Susanna's hair and tucked it back into the errant scarf. Uncharacteristically, she then gently stroked Susanna's cheek with the back of her hand.

"Of course, dear. Go make a life for yourself."

The patients within hearing cheered as Susanna hugged the other nurses and headed for the dormitory to pack. At least someone was going to make it out of this hell-hole alive and happy.

Two days later, the couple was on a train out of Kars, on the first leg of a long journey to Susanna's hometown of Saratov along the Volga River.

CHAPTER FIFTEEN
ESCAPE FROM TEREK

"Quiet, children, quiet."

Huddling on the dark stairs, Maria held her children close. Hearing someone rummaging in the barn, she quickly gathered the children and shooed them into the cellar. Nogai tribesmen were getting bolder as the Russian military in the area collapsed. Thinking of the Caspian Sea shoreline German settlers as interlopers, the tribesmen came out of the Chechen mountains and raided the villages, stealing livestock and food.

The Imperial Government had never shown more than intermittent interest in protecting the settlements. Every now and then, a detachment of Cossack cavalry would come down from their barracks in the north. With the government degenerating, the settlers took to paying protection money to local thugs. Lately, that wasn't even working.

Maria did her best not to quiver as she tried to comfort the children and keep them quiet. Sitting silently in the dark, they apprehensively listened to footsteps moving through the house above them. Pottery crashed to the floor. The footsteps got closer, directly above their heads in the pantry. Shots rang out.

"Here now, what are you doing over there?"

An alert neighbor spotted the marauders and fired shots to wake the village. More shots rang out. The footsteps ran out of the house, and horses galloped out of the village. Maria kept the children quiet until she heard a familiar voice calling from the front door.

"Hello? Is everybody okay?" Grandfather Epp asked.

Maria shakily called back, "Yes, we're down here!"

The root cellar trap door creaked open, and the Epp family patriarch stood above, holding a lantern.

"They're gone now, but they sure have made a mess."

Maria's children scurried out of the cellar and hugged the elderly man. Even if the condition of the house wasn't too bad in spite of the recent break in, Maria was still shaken. The raids were becoming all too frequent. With a lot of discussion and soul searching, in spite of their non-violence creed, some of the local men had formed a protection militia. But they couldn't cover all the colony villages at once. A full-scale battle had already erupted nearby, and the Nogai were beaten back. The villagers lost one man, the tribesmen a half dozen.

Not knowing what to do, they met in the church often to discuss the situation and sent representatives to other settlement villages. The settlement couldn't withstand many more attacks—especially if the tribesmen banded together and formed a larger force. Scared, Maria had packed and hid the most important family belongings in case they had to flee at a moment's notice.

One night, the second week of January 1918, a knock came at the door. Maria peered out of a side window to see who would come in the middle of the night. It was Semih. When she opened the door, he quickly came in, and she shut the door behind him.

"Quick, get your things. We must go now. Gerhardt wired me that he was becoming concerned about your safety. He asked me to get you to Petrovsk-Port."

She only looked at him for a second before jumping into action. Gerhardt's family had known Semih for decades. They trusted him with all of their business. Now, she would entrust him with her children's lives. She quickly woke the boys and had them dress the little girls.

Going to her hiding spot, she gathered up the valuables and a few suitcases with clothes. Semih led the children out to the wagon. Not wanting them thinking she'd been kidnapped and place themselves at risk with a search party, Maria went across the street and told the Epp family she was leaving.

The large, stake-sided hay wagon had two large buffalo hitched to the front. Hay was piled high and hung over the sides. Maria gave Semih a curious look when she didn't see the children or a place to sit other than the driver's perch. Semih smiled and reached over the side of the wagon and pulled on the brake lever. Behind the bench, a trap door lifted the hay, revealing a false bottom in the wagon. Four little sets of eyes smiled up at Maria, delighted that they had fooled their mother. She looked back at Semih, and he smiled sheepishly.

"It comes in handy if you're carrying, uh, delicate cargo when there are thieves or government agents around. Not that there's much of a difference between the two."

He showed Maria how he could kick a hidden dog over to switch between engaging the brake and opening the trap door. He'd spread a quilt on the compartment's floor to make the wagon's rough ride a little more bearable.

"I'll leave the door open for as long as possible, but if I see someone coming, I'll close it."

It was dawn as the wagon cleared the village edge. Semih spoke quietly under his arm, "Keep below the back of the seat for a while. There are curious eyes watching from the woods."

"Okay," Maria whispered back. "Children, you heard him. Be still and quiet for a bit."

Lumbering along for most of the morning in the wagon, the children were getting very restless and unruly being cramped in such small confines. Taking turns, they squirmed toward the opening to get little peeks around. Suddenly, Semih grabbed Henry's head and shoved him down. The door slammed shut, giving Henry a smack on the back of his head. Henry squelched a yelp of protest when he heard horses approaching the wagon.

"Hold up there, Comrade. Where are you going this fine winter's day?"

Maria placed her hand gently over two-year-old Katherine's mouth. Henry and Martin held three-year-old Helen's hands as many horses gathered around the wagon. The rattling of bridles and clanking of sabers against stirrups was frightening.

"Oh, I'm just fetching some hay for my livestock," Semih answered.

"You're a long way from much of anywhere, aren't you, Comrade?"

"I go where there's the best price for the best hay that I can find," Semih confidently stated.

"Then you won't mind if we check it out, would you, Comrade?"

"Certainly not, as long as you don't eat any of it. I've paid too much for it to all be eaten by the likes of you." Semih smirked, then quickly regretted it, thinking he may have pushed his luck a little too far.

After the group leader waved for a few of his men to check out the wagon, horsemen rode around, probing the hay with their sabers. The children winced but didn't make a sound when they heard swords hitting the wooden false floor. Henry squeezed Helen's hand comfortingly when she started to cry quietly. Finally satisfied, the riders withdrew while the leader studied Semih.

"You should think about getting feed for your animals a little closer to home, Comrade."

Then the leader spun his horse and headed north down the road in the direction of the settlers' village, followed by the other riders. Semih urged the buffalo into movement. After a few minutes, he told the family they could breathe again.

Raising the trap door, he told Maria, "It's as I feared. That was a group of tribesmen heading toward your settlement. I fear the worst for your neighbors. These tribesmen weren't locals. They looked like they were going to join those who had been stealing from you. Soon their numbers will be too large to defend against."

Maria turned her head so that the children wouldn't see her wiping her eyes. The rest of the afternoon passed without any more excitement. Bouncing in the wagon had long since passed the tedium level and crossed into rib bruising torture territory. Each time Semih pulled off the road into some concealment trees for a bathroom break, it got harder to encourage the children back into the wagon.

Late in the afternoon, Semih shut the door as they entered a Muslim village. "We don't need any unwarranted gossip." Pulling the wagon in front of a barn, he said, "Keep quiet." He dismounted, opened the barn door, and pulled the wagon inside.

"You can get out now. We're at a friend's house who'll give us shelter for the night. We'll make it to Petrovsk-Port by noon tomorrow."

Semih took the boys into the house. A woman led Maria and the girls behind the house to a separate room. Ecstatic to be free of the wagon prison, the children were confused but Maria had become used to the local Muslim culture. The men and boys ate supper in the house while she waited with the other females. Henry and Martin slept inside the house that night with the men while Maria and the girls stayed in the little anteroom.

Before dawn, the little group was back on the road again. Semih said, "There's probably at least one more checkpoint manned by either Bolshevik soldiers or regional separatist militia. It depends on who's in charge today. I don't know much about either. The war's taken some strange twists. People who are allies today might be enemies tomorrow."

They were almost to the outskirts of Petrovsk-Port when the road was blocked. This checkpoint was more of a formal affair with a counterbalanced gate and a guard shack. Semih halted the buffalo team at the gate.

A bored, drunk guard came stumbling out of the shack. "Where're you going, this morning?"

Semih answered, "Into town. My stable is running low on feed."

"*Your* stable, huh? That sounds like you're a rich man. Are you a rich man, Comrade?"

"No . . .no, I'm not a rich man. I just have a few animals to take care of my meager needs," Scmih lied.

"You look like a rich man to me, Comrade. We'll have to check your cargo."

The guard waved over two more soldiers with bayonets attached to their rifles. The men started stabbing around into the hay. Another man stumbled over, throwing a recently emptied bottle on the ground.

"That's not how you check a haystack," he slurred.

The soldier fired a round into the hay. The children flinched, and Helen accidentally kicked the false floor. The Buffalo team jumped, and Semih fought to calm them. Laughing, the other two soldiers each fired a round into the hay.

Semih yelled at the men, "What do you think you're doing? I don't need my animals eating your lead and getting sick!"

The guards laughed and opened the gate.

"Be on your way, rich man."

Semih urged the nervous buffalo through the gate and down the road. Keeping the wagon moving steadily, he quelled every urge to look back at the checkpoint. When he finally couldn't restrain himself further, he lifted the trap door.

"Is everyone all right?"

Maria stuck her head up. "Yes, but the children are scared to death."

"It'll be just a little farther. Once in town, it won't look so out of place if the boys ride up front with me. You don't have the proper attire to be seen sitting beside me."

Maria nodded. "It's alright. I understand."

She may not have agreed with their culture but understood that they didn't comprehend hers either. All that mattered was her family's safety. Not getting to go to a city very often, the boys enjoyed riding up front. Once at his house, Semih pulled the wagon into his stable, and a servant closed the door behind them. Maria was overjoyed to be free of the wagon and have the opportunity to clean herself and the children up. She didn't even mind the separate eating and sleeping arrangements. Her family was safe.

The next morning, Maria and the children rode out of the stable sitting in the back of a carriage where all could see. One of Semih's servants guided the team. They looked like any other of the non-Muslim elite going through town. It wouldn't be long before that would be looked down upon in Russia even more than a Muslim man with a Christian woman sitting beside him.

Boarding a train, Maria and her family headed toward the Black Sea, through the Kuban, then home to her parents' house in Franzthal. The three-day trip with four young children didn't seem to be much of an ordeal compared to the two days they'd spent in the bowels of a smuggler's hay wagon.

Maria hadn't been at her parents' house for long when, in late February 1918, she heard the villages in the Terek colony had to be abandoned after a series of skirmishes. The settlers left in the middle of the night to avoid being wiped out by an army of tribesmen planning to attack the next night. Leaving everything they couldn't pack into a wagon, the colonists formed a two-mile-long convoy for the two-day trip to the town of Khasav-Yurt. There, they boarded trains for the trip across Chechnya to the relative safety of the Russian Kuban.

CHAPTER SIXTEEN

ABANDONING A LOST CAUSE

With the political scene drastically changing, Heinrich sat in his tent, mulling over his situation. In February 1918, the Ukrainian People's Republic was declared in Kiev. It had been largely ignored by Russia.

It seemed to Heinrich that, by the time front line units heard what their government was, it had already changed again in Kiev or Petrograd. Or was it Moscow? No one knew exactly which government they were supposed to be fighting for. Soldiers were throwing their rifles over their shoulders, grabbing their rucksacks, and simply walking off toward home.

Those who stayed appeared to all be Bolshevik agitators. The pressure from fellow soldiers to join them in open revolt became untenable. Heinrich became convinced that the government which conscripted him no longer existed. In late February, he threw his rucksack over his shoulder and headed east. He had never carried a weapon, so his load was only half that of other departing soldiers. Setting out across the wooded Podolian uplands, he hoped to make it home before the end of spring planting.

With all of the various militias forming in the region, it was hard to know which groups he could interact with on his journey. The Bolsheviks were always a risk. Would they encourage the departing soldiers for abandoning an institution that had propped up a Bourgeoisie system? Or would they shoot him on the premise that he deserted a unit which had converted to Bolshevism? Led by Nestor Makhno, there were even anarchist Ukrainian separatist militias forming. Makhno's men disarmed returning soldiers and kept the weapons for their own use.

Even the German settler villages were unknowns. Catholic, Lutheran, or Baptist settlements probably were armed and theoretically leaned toward the old Imperial Government. Mennonite settlements also had weapons. But since they were pacifists, they only had weapons for hunting and officially didn't care what the government was as long as they were left alone.

Heinrich plodded along through the early spring foliage. For most of its length, the Southern Buh River had too many rapids for a raft. He was going to have to walk most of the almost 500 miles home. Since he just quietly walked away from his disintegrating army unit, he had little money. Using what few funds he carried, he purchased food from local peasants. At night, he tried to find a concealed spot in the woods to sleep. The only friendly villages he was positive about were far to the east.

On the outskirts of Vinnytsia, Heinrich realized that this walk home was going to take a lot longer than he'd hoped. He was only a fourth of the way home, and summer was fast approaching. He decided to try and find a faster way home than following the Southern Buh River to the Baltic Sea and then taking a river boat up the Dnieper River. That was a long way to travel. Vinnytsia was a railroad hub. He changed his plan and would follow the railroad easterly cross country.

Spying an encampment of other deserters in the woods, he needed guidance and decided to take the risk. Larger camps brought undue attention by authorities and could result in capture. Unfamiliar with this part of Ukraine, Heinrich went against his better instincts and decided to make camp with them for the night.

Nervous as he entered the camp, it was obvious he was the only one who didn't have a weapon. Nevertheless, he walked up to the campfire where one of the other men offered him some coffee. Accepting the cup, he reached into his rucksack and gave them a loaf of bread he had bartered for earlier in the day. That gesture garnered him a warmer welcome from the others who hadn't fared as well of late.

It wasn't much of a meal, and Heinrich loathed to part with such a hard-earned prize. But the trade proved to be more fruitful than he'd hoped for. During the evening, he struck up a conversation with one of the other deserters.

He asked, "What did you do before the war?"

"Was there such a time? It's been so long, I'd just about forgotten I had a life before the war," the man replied.

"I know what you mean. I didn't get conscripted until 1915 and it seems like forever to me. You?"

"I was called up the summer of '14, in the beginning. I worked for the railroad before then."

"The railroad? What did you do for it?"

The deserter opened up, "Track maintenance mainly. I don't think there's a length of track I haven't worked on between Kiev and the Don River."

"Really? Where are you off to now?"

"I honestly don't know. I heard that my mother died a year ago. As far as I know, she was the only family I had to return to."

"That is too bad—not having anyone to go home to."

"What about you? Do you have a family?"

"Yes, a wife near Station Zhelannaya. Most of my family lives near there also."

"Station Zhelannaya? The rail lines go almost directly there from here. You should hitch a ride on the train."

"I thought about it, but I'm nervous about buying a ticket and getting arrested."

"Oh, no." The man shook his head. "You don't buy a ticket. You just hop into a car on a slow-moving train going in the general direction you want to go."

"That's a good idea. How do I know which train is heading where I want to go?"

"Well, the first thing is to avoid passenger trains. They move quite fast and only stop at major stations which contain authorities."

"That makes sense."

"Your best choices are freight trains. They usually move slower and tend to stop in industrial areas which have less police."

"Thanks, I'll keep that in mind."

Pulling out a scrap of paper, the other soldier continued, "Here, I'll draw you a crude map showing you the general layout of the tracks between here and Juskovka. That should get you home."

"Thank you. I wish I could repay you."

"Just knowing that someone here has a home they can return to is payment enough."

The next morning, Heinrich had two companion deserters when he left camp. The other men were on their way to Volgograd, twice the distance he had to travel. They spent most of the day skirting the town until finally finding a set of tracks heading northeast. His map showed that he had to zig-zag his way across the central Ukrainian steppes to get home. It was dusk when he spied an eastbound engine pulling empty coal cars.

Heinrich didn't hesitate as he ran toward the train. His two companions paused slightly then ran after him. Clambering up the ladder, he jumped into a car mid-train. His fellow deserters fell almost on top of him. When one of them started complaining about picking such a dirty car, he laughed and said, "These cars are heading back to the mines in the Donets Basin. For me, that's virtually home. We might get a little hungry if we hide inside this car for the two or more days it takes to get there, but I'm willing to make that sacrifice."

Heinrich curled up on the black floor of the swaying car, using his rucksack for a pillow, and smiled up at the late spring sky. He was going home.

CHAPTER SEVENTEEN
HEADING HOME

Stationed close to Petrograd, Gerhardt stayed near his tent through December 1917 and the first part of January 1918. The Army had ceased to exist from his perspective. However, leaving wasn't an option. Bolsheviks hovering over the unit, "encouraged" the men to join the new "democratic" army. When a new government was formed in Ukraine and had, by the end of January, broken ties with Russia, Gerhardt's unit was ordered to head toward Kiev.

He didn't want to get involved in another campaign, especially one as convoluted as this was shaping up to be. But, he reasoned while boarding the train, they were heading in the general direction of home. He might as well ride part way instead of walking the whole 1100 miles home. He also reasoned that he had not yet found an acceptable opening to walk safely away.

When Gerhardt's detachment arrived, the Red Guard had already taken Kiev. His unit barely had time to set up their encampment southeast of the city before the newly declared separatist Ukrainian Government asked to be made a protectorate of Germany and invited its army to occupy the country. The German Army rolled over the disorganized Red Guard as fast as its supply train would allow. By mid-March 1918, the Russians were hurriedly withdrawing.

He saw his chance as they gathered at a railhead to board a troop train back to Russia. In the crush to put equipment in the boxcars and personnel into the transport cars, Gerhardt felt the urgent need to step to the side of a building and urinate. To his feigned dismay, when he came back to the platform fastening his trousers, the train had already pulled out.

Before the Bolshevik political officer assigned to shepherd the troops onto the transports could corral him, Gerhardt faded into the crowd and disappeared casually. When he was sure that he was out of sight of the station, he broke into a run through the little village, ripping off all identifying insignias from his uniform.

Once he was clear of the village and into a nearby grove of trees, Gerhardt stopped to assess his situation. It was over 600 miles to his parent's home in Karpovka. He didn't know where his family was. He'd wired his father's old friend and asked him to try and get Maria and the children out of the embattled Terek colony but hadn't received news of Semih's success or failure.

If Gerhardt headed southeast toward home, he'd run into the Bolshevik army and surely be captured. Being returned to service was the best outcome of that scenario. He didn't want to think about the other possibilities. If he headed west and made it obvious that he was no longer a combatant, he just might make it into German controlled territory.

He knew what would happen if he was captured by the Bolsheviks. The Germans were an unknown. At this point, an unknown fate was preferable to a possible prison and probable firing squad. Under the cover of darkness, Gerhardt headed west toward Kiev. He'd planned ahead and, even though he only had the clothes on his back, he'd saved his pay and carried a pocket full of cash. Walking carefully down the road in the darkness, he spied a medium-sized village before dawn.

If he was going to be successful with his plan, he needed to change into civilian attire. Going into a village held the highly undesirable risk of running into unfriendly authorities, but he needed the clothing. Gerhardt surveilled the village before light. Farmers were already tending to their chores. Most farmers left travelers alone unless the stranger looked like a thief. He walked down the main lane through the village, trying to act like he didn't have a care in the world. Inside, he was in a state of turmoil.

Gerhardt found a general store with a selection of clothing visible through the window. He sat on the front stoop of the store and waited for the proprietor to arrive, hoping the owner was an early riser. Finding a small limb which fell from a nearby tree, he spent his time calming his nerves, whittling, and waiting.

Finally, in the crisp March dawn, a nicely dressed man strolled toward the store. The man's breath rose through the frosty air in puffs of mist, reminding Gerhardt of a steam engine chugging its way across the steppes of Siberia. It was obvious the man wasn't a farmer—unless this was Sunday and he was on his way to church. It wasn't Sunday. Or was it? He realized he was uncertain.

"Good morning," the man said as he reached for the door with keys in his hand. "What can I do for you today?"

Relieved, Gerhardt replied, "I was just discharged, and I need a new set of clothes to travel home in."

"Yes," the shopkeeper said. "Traveling in a uniform these days is an uncertain affair. It seems that no matter which uniform you are wearing, you will always meet someone who will take umbrage."

Gerhardt had found a sympathetic person in an era where few existed. He picked out a new suit and shoes from the merchant's wares. The store owner marked the outfit for tailoring and said, "If you can spare the time, my wife will make the alterations. There's an area in the back of the store you can clean up while you wait."

By mid-morning, a dapper Gerhardt stepped out of the shop, clean shaven with a new set of clothes and a valise. Against his nature, he hadn't even bartered with the storekeeper. He adjusted his new hat on his head and headed for the local inn where he would wait for the German forces' front line to pass.

From the conversations he overheard while eating at the inn, the new Kiev government had made a deal for Ukraine, clear to the Don River, to fall under a German protectorate. Gerhardt decided to simply follow the front, from a safe distance back, as it progressed eastward.

Germany had already captured Kiev on March 1 and were heading across western Ukraine. The village that he had holed up in was overrun within a few days of his desertion. When the cavalry rode into town, the villagers were terrified the army they had been at war with for four years would massacre them.

Gerhardt lined up with some other villagers near the inn to watch as the troops started kicking in doors, looking for supplies and possible belligerents. The captain of the unit headed for the mercantile with a small squad on his heels. Gerhardt saw the shopkeeper who'd shown him kindness was about to be roughed up. His guilt overrode his fear of the German Army.

"Hauptmann! Hauptmann!" he called out as he ran to intercede in the ransacking of the store.

The other villagers, hearing him speak fluent High German, stared at Gerhardt, wondering if there had been an enemy agent in their midst. He ran up to the captain and animatedly began reasoning with him.

"Captain, these people were kind and gave me shelter even though they knew I was of German lineage."

"How do I know that you're German?"

"I'm speaking to you in German, aren't I?" Gerhardt blustered.

"So? A lot of educated Russians speak German. Everybody knows it's a much more civilized language."

Gerhardt smiled. "Well, of course, that's true. Just don't tell these people that."

"What do you want?"

"These people opened their arms to me when I walked away from the Russian Army. I just want them to be treated kindly also."

"What were you doing in the Russian army fighting against your homeland?"

"I was born in Ukraine. My family settled here during more civil times. There are many, many more like me here. Unfortunately, when conscripted by the government, you don't have much of a chance to say no."

"Did you fight?"

"Actually, no. I'm Mennonite and therefore a pacifist. We have an exemption from carrying arms. I was an ambulance driver."

"An ambulance driver, huh? Are there any more like you?"

"Oh, you'll probably run into many German villages as you cross Southern Russia."

"So, these people knew who you were and were kind to you."

Gerhardt lied, "Yes, they knew."

The captain studied him for a moment, then turned to his detachment and yelled, "Seinlassen!"

The men mounted up and fell in behind the officer. The captain tilted his hat to the shopkeeper, nodded at Gerhardt, and waved his troop into motion. Thundering out of town, the cavalry headed southeast. Feeling his hands shaking, he put them into his coat pockets as he watched the horses clatter down the cobblestone street. The shopkeeper walked up behind Gerhardt and put his hand on his shoulder.

"Spasibo."

Gerhardt nodded at the man and, as he was turning to walk back to the inn replied, "No, thank you. You helped me when I needed it."

His legs shaking, he excused himself through the crowd of onlookers, blocking his retreat to the inn. Treated like royalty in the village for the next two days, he waited for the front to progress far enough to safely follow. He hitched a ride with a passing merchant the shopkeeper introduced him to. As Gerhardt climbed onto the wagon, the innkeeper's wife ran out and gave him a basket of baked goods to tide him over during the journey.

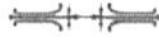

Maria managed to get the children back to her home village of Franzthal, just north of the Sea of Azov. She moved into her parents' house until Gerhardt could come home. As most wealthy families, they'd lost a lot of their money. The Revolutionary Government had nationalized the banks and confiscated savings accounts. If someone hadn't previously converted their wealth into gold or other tangible assets, they were left destitute.

The war left all of the farms strained, with the best horses requisitioned for the war effort. Now, with their bank accounts confiscated, the option of purchasing machinery to replace the horses was eliminated. Farming had become an onerous affair with more physical exertion needed to accomplish any task. That unpleasant reality funneled its way down from the landowner to the hired peasant laborers.

With civil unrest accompanying the collapse of the empire, looting was rampant. Maria's father, along with the rest of the villagers, hired armed guards to ensure that what belonged in the barn remained in the barn come morning. Rumors of a German army on its way to stabilize the situation was mostly anticipated with acceptance by German settlers, but dreaded by the native peasants.

The children were out playing in the yard, enjoying the spring air, when they heard approaching horses and the clanking of sabers. Seven-year-old Henry and six-year-old Martin ran to the edge of the road to watch the cavalry. Instead of passing through the village, the troop came to a halt. Dismounting, soldiers dispersed throughout the village. Two men pushed past the children and entered the house without knocking. The boys followed and peered in.

"Cook us a meal, mother," a man demanded.

Maria replied, "Sirs, we don't have enough food to cook you a decent meal."

"We'll see about that."

After rummaging through the pantry, they shoved her aside and went out the back door to the pig pen. They killed the lone, scrawny pig in the pen and gutted it in the yard. Martin and Henry watched from the corner of the house while the little girls ran to hide. The soldiers each took one leg of the pig and, dripping blood, carried the carcass into the house, throwing it on the kitchen table. When they grabbed Maria's arm and told her to cook it, young Martin became enraged.

In the confusion, he ran into the street where the horses were tethered and tried to climb up high enough on a horse to get a saber out of its scabbard. Try as he might, he couldn't jump high enough to retrieve the sword from where it was draped on the saddle. Finally, after extensive urging, Henry helped lift him up enough to get the saber while a group of bemused cavalrymen watched.

Intent on killing the soldiers and avenging his mother's honor, Martin ran into the house, dragging the saber on the ground. Henry followed behind to pick up what would remain of his brother. When Martin charged into the kitchen, the soldiers turned to see what the clatter was. He did his best to raise the sword but was too slow. One of the soldiers cuffed him alongside his head then, grabbing Martin in one hand and the saber in the other, headed into the backyard to beat him.

Maria ran along behind them, sobbing, "Leave him alone! Don't hurt him!"

The soldier stopped and studied the young mother momentarily. He nodded to his partner, and the men each grabbed an arm and a leg and threw the boy over the fence into the muddy pigsty, then walked back into the kitchen laughing.

"Now cook the pig, woman."

Still laughing, the men went to a bench in the yard and waited to be fed. Henry helped his brother out of the pen and steered him to the well to clean up. Martin kept glowering in the direction of the soldiers, but Henry managed to keep him contained. From that moment on, even though he was of German lineage, Martin despised the German army.

Mounting up the next day, the cavalry rode to their barracks outside of town where they would maintain a presence. The German army held the Russian Revolution at bay, keeping order in Ukraine, until the end of World War One. German settlers would be treated well as a whole, but that just led to more resentment by the Russian peasants.

Two weeks after the great porcine purge incident, Gerhardt rode into town in a carriage with his brother, Heinrich. The boys ran out and greeted their father, who handed down a couple of fuzzy puppies. The girls, who were too young when their father had left to remember him, held back, holding onto their mother's apron. They held back, that is, until they saw the puppies. Laughing, Maria gave Gerhardt a rare hug in public. The family was back together again.

It didn't take long for them to decide to move back to Karpovka. At the time, Gerhardt felt there was a better chance of finding employment there. He still hoped that the situation in the Caucasus would stabilize enough that they could return to their farm in the Terek

Colony. Within two days, they had said their farewells to Maria's parents and left in the carriage. What was left of their worldly possessions didn't take up too much room on the back luggage carrier.

CHAPTER EIGHTEEN
CAUCASUS TO KARPOVKA

Johann and Susanna sat holding hands on the train between Kars and Tiflis (Tbilisi). Before leaving, they had both purchased new civilian wardrobes. With the political landscape uncertain, it was best not to appear affiliated with any ideology. It was a certainty that, if you left an impression that you favored one side or the other, you'd run into someone who rabidly held an opposing view.

Politics in the 1918 Caucasus region had more than two sides—way more. There were Tsarists, Bolsheviks, and Anarchists. Every one of those groups was subdivided further into religious, ethnic, and tribal variations. Each sect would rather kill you than persuade you to their side.

The winter landscape flowing past the frosty windows was littered with abandoned, snow-covered, military machinery. Two men in the back of the car were having a heated argument. An Armenian and an Azerbaijani were accusing each other of one's great, great uncle's second cousin killing the other's great grandfather's sister's brother-in-law. Or, maybe it was a buffalo. Johann couldn't tell as far reaching as the argument had become. Susanna smiled and squeezed his hand.

Switching trains at Tiflis, the couple boarded the mainline train from Batumi, heading east toward Baku. Political posters all over the train station bragged that Lenin's right-hand man, Joseph Stalin, was born close by in Gori. As the couple watched out of their railcar's windows when it pulled out of the terminal, imperial loyalists were tearing down the posters. Before the train cleared the station, a riot had started.

The closer that they got to Baku, the more nervous Johann became. Susanna had only seen the resulting casualties of the conflicts. He had seen the volatility of the political alliances in times of war. One day, a group might be your military ally. The next day, your ally became your enemy. The allegiances since the October 2017 revolution were in constant flux. He didn't know what awaited them in the region's largest city of Baku and did his best to conceal his apprehension from Susanna.

The couple took a motorized taxi from the train station to the passenger port in Baku, a bustling oil boom town. With political posters on every surface flat enough to support one, tensions were high enough that it reminded Johann of an approaching thunderstorm. Both storms made the hair on the back of his neck stand at attention.

To his dismay, there wasn't an opening on a passenger ship headed north until early February. Susanna didn't seem to mind as long as they were together. Besides, she told him, this looked like a cosmopolitan city that could be explored. The couple checked into a hotel and spent the next few weeks enjoying each other's company. It had been a long time since either had eaten at a nice restaurant.

The new coalition government, based in Baku, ordered that all Russian troops be disarmed. When a large unit of militant Russian soldiers refused to give up their weapons near the Shamkhor railway station west of Baku, Azerbaijanis nationalist soldiers attacked and killed or wounded around a thousand men. Johann and Susanna had just passed through that station a few days before.

Baku's stability was falling apart. He heard the British were marching north out of Persia toward the city, trying to take possession of the oilfields. Johann, doing his best to insulate Susanna from the turmoil, fidgeted until they were walking up the steamship Skobelev's boarding plank.

A passing steward proudly informed them, "This is one of the revolutionary new oil-fired steamships. The coal fireboxes have been modified to burn the plentiful oil found in the Caucasus."

The acrid black cloud belching out of the ship stack's scent was completely different from the coal smoke he was used to. Johann was only mildly interested in the revolutionary propulsion system. Only caring that it moved the ship away from this God-forsaken place, he breathed a heavy sigh of relief as the Skobelev pulled out of the harbor into the open Caspian Sea heading north.

Relaxed during the 500-mile journey to the mouth of the Volga River, he and Susanna spent time walking the deck and watching the gulls hover over the ship. The rocking ship sucked over two years of war poison out of his veins. Susanna's glow replenished him, giving him a new zest for life.

Four days later, the ship dropped anchor off the mouth of the Volga River and waited until a smaller riverboat came alongside to transfer a river pilot on board. The *Skobelev* weighed anchor and slowly wove its way between the sandbars obstructing the 100-mile leg up the Volga to the port of Astrakhan. For a landlocked farm-boy like Johann, the upstream trip was nerve-wracking. Currents in the river were treacherous in water that wasn't very deep.

The Skobelev finally was pushed into her berth at Astrakhan, and the passengers started to disembark. He and Susanna strolled down the plank and headed for the ticket office to buy passage upriver to Saratov. Johann and the ticket agent didn't start off on good footing when he asked for tickets to Saratov.

"I'm sorry, sir, but there are no boats to Saratov until sometime in March."

"March! What do you mean there are no boats until March?" Johann yelled.

"There's still ice on the river. We can't get there until the ice clears."

"Well, when will that be?"

"No one knows for sure. Usually sometime in early March," the agent replied, starting to lose his patience.

"Sometime . . .!"

Susanna put her hand on his forearm and soothingly whispered into his ear, "It's not the man's fault Old Man Winter put ice on the river. It happens every year. We'll just wait until the ice breaks up."

"I'm getting tired of all of this travel. I want to get you home to your family."

"I understand that, but there isn't a thing we can do about it. We should have enough money left to get us by until the ice breakup finishes."

He smiled down at her and gave in to her optimism. After all, what was another couple of weeks as long as she was by his side? He gave up on his hastily conceived plan of pulling the man through the window and using the agent's body to break up the river ice.

Johann wondered how he had existed before Susanna. She seemed to wipe out any problems they encountered by just being near him. If a passing carriage splashed early spring mud their way, a simple tightening of her arm through his erased all consciousness the event ever occurred. Time flew, and he was almost disappointed when the spring thaw left the river ice free earlier than expected.

Red-Guard-manned armored river boats patrolling the Volga slowed the already lumbering pace of the passenger steamer against the current. At least once a day, the steamer was boarded and passengers' papers were thoroughly checked. In between checks, Johann wondered out loud to Susanna if the Bolsheviks suspected them of changing their political inclinations and identities within the last few hours. At the end of the 560-mile voyage, he was surprised his papers hadn't completely disintegrated.

Meeting Susanna's parents went as he'd expected. After all, he was Mennonite, and they were Lutheran. The fact that he was so intelligent, well educated, came from a relatively wealthy family and, above all, absolutely devoted to their daughter, quickly won them over. In less than a month after they arrived in Saratov, the couple was wed in a Lutheran ceremony.

Johann would have preferred a much simpler Mennonite wedding, but he would do anything to make Susanna happy. Besides, to have the simpler ceremony, they would have had to wait until they journeyed back to Ukraine. Neither of them wanted to wait that long.

In the month that it took to get the marriage out of the way, the political situation in Russia continued to decline. Lenin moved his government to Moscow just before Johann and Susanna arrived in Saratov.

Lenin sent Joseph Stalin to Tsaritsyn (later Stalingrad, then Volgograd), just 200 miles south of Saratov, to be in charge of food collection. Tsaritsin was almost halfway back down the Volga to Astrakhan. The couple had just passed through there on their trip from the Caucasus.

Because of the unrest in Russia proper, Susanna's family had been discussing relocating. Her family's accounts were confiscated when the Bolsheviks nationalized the banks. If anyone was nervous about Bolshevism, it was time to move on.

The Kuban region had been declared an independent country by the Don and Kuban Cossacks. Lithuania, Latvia, Finland, Georgia, and others had all declared independence or were just about to finalize the declaration. Since Ukraine was a German protectorate, it appeared to be the most stable.

After talking it over with Susanna's father, the couple decided to leave for Ukraine. Her father agreed and started to make plans to follow with his own family. There were Catholic and Lutheran settlements just north of Odessa where they could feel comfortable. The only other option was to move east to the Amur River region just north of China. Others were already heading toward the German settlements there, attempting to outrun Bolshevik expansion.

The day after the wedding, the couple left on a train south to Tsaritsyn on the Volga, the closest city to the Don River. The Cossacks had declared the Don River region an independent country on May 1. The German protectorate extended as far east as where the Don River emptied into the Black Sea. At the moment, that route appeared to be the least perilous for travelers.

Johann thought he felt everyone's eyes on them during the train ride to Tsaritsyn. Bolshevik sympathizers were constantly on the lookout for anyone who might endanger the movement. Suspicious looks from strangers the new norm in the country, he was becoming used to the scrutiny. Document checks were less frequent heading south on the train than traveling north on a riverboat. He assumed the Bolsheviks weren't concerned over "undesirables" heading *toward* the lion's den.

An Imperial loyalist would have to either be insane or brave beyond reason to go into Tsaritsyn. Johann wasn't sure which he was. There was no easy alternate route. Holding each other tightly, the couple kept their heads down and treaded lightly as they forged through the middle of a Bolshevist stronghold.

In Tsaritsyn, they boarded another train for the 70-mile trip west to Kolpachki, the closest city on the Don River. When the train stopped at the Novyy Rogachik station at the halfway point, Red Guards boarded and questioned the passengers. They began in the front of the coach and worked their way back toward where Johann and Susanna were seated. Military-aged men were singled out. After two young men were forcibly removed from the train, it became obvious that they were being unwillingly conscripted into the Red Army.

Susanna gripped Johann's arm tightly. Suddenly, she reached into her bag under the seat and pulled out her Sister of Mercy scarf and tied it over her head. She put her finger to her lips, signaling Johann to keep silent. He hadn't time to react when the lead Red Guardsman arrived beside their seat and demanded, "Papers please."

Susanna dug her nails into Johann's arm and replied for the both of them, "He's shell-shocked and has a bad leg. I'm escorting him home." She handed the guard her paperwork which still identified her as a nurse. "He has trouble speaking."

The guard eyed Johann suspiciously and asked, "Is this true?"

Johann did the best, slurred, stutter that he could manage, "I uh . . .uhh."

"Get up please," the soldier demanded

Johann, fearing their ruse was about to be discovered, struggled to rise into the aisle. Shots rang out on the other side of the train. The guard pivoted to look out the coach windows. Johann dropped back into his seat.

A company of Don Cossack cavalry was thundering down the village street toward the station. The Red Guards hurriedly retreated from the rail coach, loaded their prisoners into the back of a truck, and motored off in the opposite direction, firing back at the Cossacks through a billowing cloud of dust.

Passengers sat dazed, relieved that the Red Guards had left. One of the kidnapped men's young woman companion wept loudly.

Johann felt Susanna quivering beside him. He looked down, and she was crying softly, trying to not let anyone see her. He put his arm around her and held her tight.

"That was quick thinking. You were very brave."

"I was so scared that I'd lose you. A few more moments and they would have figured it out," she sobbed into his chest, staying cocooned under his arm for the remainder of the 30-mile trip to Kolpachki.

The river port town was filled with military hardware. Johann watched out of the coach window as the train passed armored cars, artillery batteries, and tent cities on its way to the port area. When the couple got off of the train, there were two German Army officers standing at the far end of the station platform, chatting with officers wearing Cossack uniforms. Johann hadn't yet seen a German uniform during the war. He assumed they were either attaches or strategic advisors. The couple hired a taxi at the rail-station to take them and their luggage the short distance to the port.

Johann was getting tired of boat travel as they walked up the gangplank to the riverboat for an uneventful trip downstream. Riverboats did have advantages over trains in that they allowed more room to move about and were quieter. However, trains covered distances faster. At the Black Sea port of Taganrog, they transferred to a seagoing ferry.

He promised Susanna that boat travel was almost over. The original plan had been to take a train from Taganrog to Donetsk but that route would take them across another military/political boundary. After the incident in Novyy Rogachik, they decided it was best to take the sea route to Mariupol before going cross country in the completely German-held territory.

The closer that Johann got to home, the more energy he needed to vent. The ferry offered a good opportunity to release that energy. When he'd exhausted Susanna from walking around the ship, he'd allow her to sit in a deck chair with a blanket on her lap. He leaned against the rail in front of her and watched the antics of the gulls. The cacophony of the birds swarming the boat was hypnotic and a welcome distraction. She peacefully smiled up from under her lap blanket, amused at how easily entertained her mate could be as he leaned over the rail.

They were in safe territory at last. Susanna laughed during the taxi ride to the train station in Mariupol when Johann kept muttering that he was glad to be rid of the sea. His newfound penchant for using colorful euphemisms about water transport made her think his inner sailor was exhibiting itself. Moving into her favorite position, she contentedly snuggled up against his arm.

Johann stopped ranting long enough to smile down at her. "Well, maybe when we're old, I could be talked into a cruise back to America or something."

"That would be wonderful. I've read so many nice things about America."

"It'll have to wait until our ten children are able to take care of our estate while we're away."

"Ten?!"

Johann laughed. "Well, maybe fifteen."

Susanna pushed him away, feigning outrage.

Like a salmon swimming upriver, the closer Johann got to where he was spawned, the stronger and more familiar the smells were which drove him on. Even the acrid scent of the coal-fired mills in Jusovka released imprinted childhood memories of home. In Jusovka, the couple switched trains and headed west to Zhelannaya Station, the closest rail stop to home.

It was too late in the day to start the journey south to Karpovka, so Johann wired his location home, and they checked into a hotel for the evening. He was a coiled spring waiting to be released. Susanna held on for the ride.

The next morning was Sunday. Unable to sleep, Johann was up at dawn and had cajoled Susanna into breakfast in the hotel's restaurant. By the time she arrived at the table, he was already on his second cup of coffee and had researched which livery would be open for carriage rental. Susanna had just spread the napkin on her lap when she saw, over Johann's shoulder, a short, dusty man walk into the dining room. He stood there looking around as if in search of something.

She leaned forward and whispered, "I think there may be something wrong with the fellow by the door. He's disheveled and looks confused."

Looking over his shoulder, Johann leaped to his feet, sending the chair skidding on its back.

"Gerhardt! Broder!"

Johann ran to his older brother and lifted him off of his feet with a hug. A cloud of road dust billowed into the restaurant as he slapped Gerhardt on the back with both arms and repeatedly hugged him. Susanna was shocked by Johann's unashamed show of affection. He usually tried to restrain himself in public, reserving his most enthusiastic emotional displays for when they were alone.

Johann grabbed Gerhardt's arm and led him to the table. "This is my wife, Susanna."

Gerhardt looked blankly at Susanna then back at Johann. "Your *wife?*"

Susanna stood up, and Gerhardt offered her his hand. She ignored the hand and went directly into a hug.

"What are you doing here, Gerhardt?" Johann asked.

"I was in Kalinova. Our sister, Maria, is marrying Ben Harder next Sunday. I came to his parent's house to pick him up and take him back to Karpovka. I received a message last night to pick you up also."

"You've already traveled ten miles from Kalinova this morning?"

"Anything to have the family all together for the first time in years."

"Sit, sit. Join us for breakfast."

"No, I'm fine."

"Nonsense. You've driven all of this way. I will not allow you to go all of the way back on an empty stomach."

After breakfast, Gerhardt helped Susanna with luggage while Johann settled the bill. During the ride to Kalinova and the Harder household, the two brothers exchanged war stories. Sitting in front beside the older brother, Susanna pumped Gerhardt for any of her husband's youthful indiscretions he might not have already disclosed to her.

Johann lost count of his brother saying, "*Then* there was the time that . . ."

Gerhardt would tell another embarrassing escapade Johann had been involved in, followed by Susanna's infectious laugh. She reached into her bag and retrieved a hanky to wipe laughter tears from her eyes. She put her arm through Gerhardt's and kept urging him on. Every now and then, she'd look back at Johann with a broad, loving smile. He sat in the back of the carriage, reveling in his wife and brother's instant camaraderie. Her incandescent personality had instantly won Gerhardt over.

At the Harder house, Ben was waiting for Gerhardt's return from the Zhelannaya Station. After loading Ben's luggage, they headed out again for the next ten-mile leg of their journey to Karpovka. Ben was relieved to have Susanna in the carriage. He'd been dreading being the new interloper in the large family. Her surprise appearance would take all of the oxygen out of the room and allow him to remain comfortably in the background. Ben, sitting in the front with Gerhardt, Johann and Susanna in the back, quickly joined into the merriment. The happy, anticipatory four were in Karpovka by Sunday afternoon faspa.

CHAPTER NINETEEN
CHAOS STRIKES A REUNITED FAMILY

When the carriage pulled into the yard between the large red brick house and barn, Henry and Martin were playing in the dust. They only recognized their dad. Knowing he was supposed to pick up their aunt's betrothed, the boys figured that Ben was in the front seat beside their father. They had absolutely no idea who the people in the back of the carriage were. Martin ran into the house to announce the arrival, and Henry ran to the carriage to lend assistance.

Gerhardt and Ben had barely dismounted the carriage and Johann stood up to aid Susanna when a shriek came out of the house. Martin ran back out, leading his mother Maria, his aunts Maria, Helena, Eva, Katrina, and Grandmother Helena. Family patriarch Heinrich came out of the barn, followed by sons Heinrich, David, Peter, and Daniel.

The brothers gathered around Johann, and the women descended on Susanna. When Johann introduced his wife, his sisters started hugging and kissing her. The normally gregarious Susanna, having never been the center of this much attention, looked pleadingly at Johann.

"All right, all right!" he said. "Give her some room to breathe!"

Gerhardt's wife, Maria, was overjoyed that she was no longer the only in-law. The crying women led Susanna into the house, leaving the men to give Johann congratulatory punches in the arm. Ben contentedly stood back a little. If it hadn't been for Susanna, it would have been him in the middle of that gabbing gaggle of girls. With the pressure relieved, he could just join in as one of the guys.

All ten surviving Wiens children were back together again under one roof. With all nineteen members of the family, including in-laws and grandchildren, gathered in the outside summer dining area for faspa, the family patriarch showed an uncharacteristic slip and choked up slightly while offering his prayer of thanks. All was good for this moment in time.

The next Sunday, the family hosted a double wedding in their large barn. Ben and Maria shared the day with another couple from the Karpovka church. The whole village and half of Kalinova showed up for the celebration. The after-wedding feast of sockatweeback, cherry mooss, borscht, and ham had been worked on for days by all of the sisters, sisters-in-law, and a few neighbor women. Susanna jumped right in learning the cuisine since the only two dishes she was even vaguely familiar with were the ham and borscht.

Johann jokingly chided Susanna, "It could have been a triple wedding if you hadn't been so impatient back in Saratov." She blushed and looked down at her lap, her hands fidgeting with the dress's lace.

After the wedding, life returned to a facsimile of normal. Gerhardt and family had previously moved into a small house across the street from his parents in Karpovka. Johann and Susanna moved to the other end of town, and he became an accountant for the large, coal-fired steam plant attempting to open back up after the war. Ben and Maria Harder returned to Kalinova where he worked in his family's business. Brother Heinrich worked on the family's farm along with the rest of the siblings.

Life under the German occupation was tense. Because their army treated German settlers with a preference over native Ukrainians, everyone saw the situation was being made worse. Most of the time, if there was a dispute, the German settler would be favored and the Ukrainian peasant would likely be hanged or shot by the army.

The Wiens family had lived locally for a long time. Having always treated their workers fairly, they had a good reputation. The children grew up playing with Russian friends. The same couldn't be said for some of the larger German estates.

After losing the war in the west, the German army started pulling out of Ukraine in mid-November, withdrawing back into their own borders. The Bolsheviks saw an opening and immediately attacked the German-backed separatist government. Within two weeks, the government was overthrown. Ukraine erupted into a civil war.

Sitting in the parlor of the large family home before faspa on Sunday, December 1, 1918, the Wiens men discussed life in general. The conversation turned to politics and what was happening with the withdrawal. The Bolsheviks were barking at the heels of the Germans, occupying unprotected territory.

"I hear the Don Cossacks have joined with the Kuban Cossacks to fight the Bolsheviks in the Caucasus," Johann broached the subject.

"That's what I heard also." The Patriarch Heinrich added, "There is a rumor that they're joining with General Denikin's White Army."

"It's getting hard to keep up with all of the different colored armies," Gerhardt said. "There's the Bolshevik Red Army, loyalist White Army, Kiev's Green Army, and now this Makhno character is taking a bunch of thieves and calling them the Black Army."

"Is that the Makhno who was supposed to hang? I remember his trial in Huliaipole before the war. I thought he'd be dead by now," brother Heinrich said. "I heard he's only thirty years old. The same age as Helena."

"It sure makes it a pain to travel to Maria's parents in Franzthal," Gerhardt replied. "His base around Huliaipole is directly between here and there."

"Wherever he's from," Johann said, "he seems to hate landowners a great deal, just like the Bolsheviks."

Gerhardt's wife, Maria, and Susanna came into the living room with coffee and a plate of siaroppskuake.

Maria looked slyly sideways at Susanna as they were setting the platters down on a side-table and asked, "Have you told him yet?"

"Tell me what?" Johann asked.

Susanna blushed, looking down. "Now isn't a good time."

"Any time is a good time." Maria grinned broadly.

"Tell me what?" Johann insisted.

Susanna looked down, blushing for a few more moments with all eyes centered on her. She finally said softly, "I'm pregnant."

"What? I didn't hear you." Johann leaned forward.

"I'm pregnant!" Susanna said loudly, standing upright, looking him in the eye.

Johann sat, mouth open for a second, digesting the news, then leaped to his feet. "Yahoo!"

He grabbed her in a hug, lifting her off of her feet. The rest of the men gathered around, slapping backs and shaking hands. This would be the first grandchild other than Gerhardt and Maria's children. Children were always a blessing in the Wiens family.

The alarm bell at the firehouse began clanging. Henry and Martin ran inside. "There's a crowd by the schoolhouse!"

Volunteers ran toward the firehouse next to the schoolhouse. The family joined in to lend a hand. At the firehouse, villagers just stood around making no attempt to pull out the firefighting wagon. Puzzled, Gerhardt ran up to a group of villagers gathered around a wagon in the street. Making his way past some sobbing women, he looked in the back. It contained the body of Johann Epp.

"I found him lying in the snow beside the road north of town," a Russian worker was explaining. "I didn't see his horse or carriage anywhere. He must have been robbed."

Gerhardt was shaken. Epp and his family lived two doors down from his house. The town had become used to theft, but thieves usually avoided contact. After a community meeting, the villagers decided it would be unwise to travel alone for a while. A guard was posted to watch the village at night.

December 10, Wilhelm Hamm and Nicholas Block left on horseback to get the village's mail at the Zhelannaya train station. They didn't come back. A few days later, the village heard that they'd been attacked and killed by a gang at the station. Their bodies were buried behind the station. Trains were being robbed.

Karpovka kept fairly quiet for the remainder of December. It didn't snow for the rest of the month, but the weather was very cold. The village gathered for minister Peter Warkentin's solemn Christmas service in the schoolhouse. After listening to the choir's final hymn, the congregation was filing out of the building when a rider galloped up.

"They've found three bodies by the river near Alexandrovka," he said.

New Year's Day 1919, the firehouse alarm sounded again. About twenty Cossack cavalrymen thundered through town. Pedestrians jumped out of the way as muddy clumps of snow were flung into the air by the horses' hooves. About an hour later, there were gunshots west of the village where some of Makhno's Black Army peripheral gangs had been sighted.

"That'll keep those thugs away," Gerhardt told Johann.

"I hope so," Johann replied.

Susanna took Johann's arm, and they strolled home, feeling safer with the White Army in the neighborhood. Friday morning, January 10, Johann kissed Susanna as he walked out the door to work.

"What are you doing today?" he asked.

"I'm going to the clinic this morning to help the doctor out. It isn't going to be long before I won't be much help, so I'm doing what I can now."

Johann hugged her and left for the mill. Late in the morning, he heard a group of horses coming into the village. He stood up with the others to look out the office window. It was about thirty of Makhno's Black Army mounted soldiers. They had a team of horses pulling a tachanka—a carriage-mounted machine gun. Immediately, the men started looting local businesses. It wasn't long before they'd found a good supply of alcohol and were well on their way to becoming drunk.

At lunch, Johann decided to check on Susanna at the clinic. Walking out the front of the mill office, he headed toward the clinic near the church, on the far side of the school. He heard a scream. Three of the soldiers had Susanna, grabbing at her body and ripping her clothes. They were dragging her behind a building across the street. Villagers looked on helplessly as the other soldiers blocked them from interfering. In the distance, Johann could see Gerhardt and Maria running from the other direction.

"Leave me alone! Leave me alone!" Then Susanna bit the hand of the soldier dragging her.

"You stupid witch!"

He flung her to the ground and kicked her in the stomach, delighting the cheering soldiers looking on. Bursting through the perimeter of thugs, Johann ran to her rescue and bellowed, "Leave her alone, you *huarebauljch!*"

When he bent to help Susanna up, a soldier hit him in the back of the head with a rifle butt, knocking him down. He rolled over and stood up to confront the leader. His coworker, David Block, ran in behind Johann to offer assistance. Susanna scrambled out of the street into Maria's arms. Johann and David stood back-to-back, staring down Susanna's assaulters. The man who she bit pulled his shashka out of its inverted scabbard.

"I'll teach you a lesson, you privileged Kulak."

Johann bent forward with hands up, preparing to defend himself. Gerhardt and other villagers moved forward to help but stopped when two soldiers cocked the machine gun on the tachanka and pointed it at them. David gasped and fell back into Johann. Johann looked over his shoulder and saw one of the three thugs pulling a rifle-mounted bayonet out of David's belly then thrusting it back in again. Out of the corner of his eye, Johann saw a flash and raised his arm to deflect the shashka.

The crowd gasped, and Susanna shrieked as David fell to the ground. The shashka slashed Johann's left forearm, and he tripped over David as he fell back. The other two assailants pulled their shaskas and started to swing at Johann. One hit him in the thigh, and one hit him in the lower leg. He rolled onto his hands and knees and struggled to get up. One of the shaskas struck him on the left side of his head.

Susanna held her hand over her mouth, tears cascading down her cheeks. She quivered in Maria's arms as Maria and Gerhardt held her back. Johann held his hands over his head to fend off the flashing shashkas. The attack stopped for a moment while the men caught their breath.

Johann struggled to his knees. Sitting back on his feet, he looked under the arm of the assailant between him and his wife. The world seemed to stand still for a while as his and Susanna's eyes locked. He swayed back and forth, both arms hanging useless. His right arm had been virtually severed below the elbow. Blood ran down his face from the gash on top of his head. A gash exposed his left eye and ran to the back of his head, showing his skull and removing the top half of his ear. Johann stared at Susanna with apologetic sorrow in his eyes. He knew that he would not grow old with her or help raise their child.

"Mine!" the lead assailant bellowed.

The other attackers stood back from the swaying Johann. Letting out a loud grunt, the thug spun completely around, shashka flashing in the cold January sun. Johann's head bounced off of David's body and rolled toward Susanna. His body remained upright for a moment until his assailant's boot shoved it onto its side. She fainted into Maria's arms, and Gerhardt caught them both before they fell to the ground.

The village minister came from behind and urged them, "Get her out of here! Get her out of here!"

Another villager quickly grabbed Susanna's feet. He and Gerhardt carried her behind the church and hid her in a carriage. Maria and the villager took Susanna to Gerhardt's parents' house while he went back to the street to retrieve his brother's body.

Looking down at the bodies, the soldiers laughed. The leader cockily strutted around in a circle, taunting the villagers. Pointing his shashka at the corpses, he yelled at the onlookers, "Where is the witch? See what she caused?" He swaggered out of the circle of soldiers and pointed back at the bodies with the saber. "No one touches them. They will stay where they are until the dogs eat them!"

Sitting around drinking for the rest of the day, the soldiers roughed up anyone straying too close. Every now and then, one of them would walk across the street to urinate on a tree in the church's front lawn. Invariably, on the way back, he'd detour and kick Johann's head like a soccer ball.

His head traveled up and down the street, collecting mud into the open wounds until it could barely be recognized as human. Gerhardt and his brothers waited stoically in the shadows, biding their time until the bodies could be retrieved. Letting the savages know the men they'd just butchered had close relatives in the vicinity would be certain suicide.

After sunset, the soldiers staggered to the inn and took it over. The village minister guided the evicted travelers in their nightclothes inside of the church for shelter. Gerhardt and others waited, out of sight in the dark recesses, until midnight when they were sure that the soldiers had passed out and the sentries posted at the inn's doors were asleep.

The men crept out of the shadows and spirited the corpses into the darkness on stretchers. Carefully, they followed well-traveled routes so they wouldn't leave any traceable tracks. Carrying the litters behind a barn, the men hid the bodies under a haystack until they could later be buried safely.

Slipping up to his parent's house in the wee hours of the morning, he heard a rifle's safety clicking off by the barn. He hissed, "It's me, Gerhardt."

His brother, Heinrich, stepped out of the shadows. "I was just making sure."

"Where are Maria and Susanna?"

Heinrich nodded toward the main house and said sadly, "In there. It doesn't look good."

Gerhardt quietly entered the house, but he needn't have bothered. All of the adults were wide awake, sitting in the dark. His sister Helena hugged him; her tear-stained face could barely be seen in the dim candlelight.

"Where's Maria?" he asked

"She's upstairs in my room with Susanna."

Gerhardt quietly went up the stairs. Maria was sitting on the bed monitoring Susanna.

"How's she doing?"

"Not good. She miscarried the baby and is bleeding heavily."

He looked sadly at Susanna, "That's too bad. They both wanted the child so badly."

"She's been staring blankly at the ceiling all day. I think she's just lost the will to live. She finally went to sleep a little while ago."

"Has the doctor been here?"

"Yes, but he couldn't stop the bleeding. He said that her fate is in divine hands now."

Gerhardt hugged Maria and sadly went back to the parlor.

The next day, the locals gave the hungover soldiers milling around in the street a very wide berth. Makhno's men resumed raiding household larders for provisions and forcing the farmers to supply oats for their horses. An armored car with an escort cadre motored into town at noon, obviously carrying the men's immediate commanding officer. Their demeanor changed instantly as the car stopped beside the tachanka. When the sergeant of the unit started to give his report on provision gathering to his superior, the officer stopped him and pointed at the bloodstained mud and snow in the center of the road.

"What happened there?"

The sergeant glanced over at the bully who murdered Johann, leaning against the tachanka smoking a cigarette, and replied, "Oh, nothing. The locals offered some resistance which had to be restrained."

The officer looked at the blood for a moment, then at the soldier leaning against the tachanka before he addressed the sergeant, "That better be all, Sergeant. You know how headquarters does not want us alienating the locals. We need the peasants to support our cause."

The sergeant snapped to attention. "Yes, sir."

Frowning, the officer waved the car into motion. The armored car and entourage motored out of town toward the next village, leaving the sergeant watching down the road behind it. Johann's murderer sucked down the last of his cigarette, threw it on the ground, and laughed as he brushed past the sergeant with his two accomplices.

The soldiers stopped when they saw some local women watching from the church windows. The thug leader grinned and made sure he was facing them as he urinated on the church lawn. Shocked, the women pulled back from the windows as his accomplices laughed.

Finished gathering provisions mid-afternoon, Saturday the 11th, the soldiers mounted up and headed off in the same direction as the armored car. Johann's murderer paused and looked at the small group of men Gerhardt was standing with. He patted his shashka, smiled broadly, and spurred his horse into action, catching up with his unit.

The villagers nervously watched the roads into town until dark. When Johann's brothers and David's cousin thought that it was as safe as it was likely to get, they went into the cemetery behind the school and dug two graves in the frozen ground. At nine o'clock that night, the bodies were retrieved from under the haystack and buried.

Afterward, Gerhardt went into Susanna's room to see how she was doing. The doctor was leaving, sadly shaking his head as he chatted with the family women down the hall. Gerhardt sat on the bed and patted Susanna's hand. "When you're up to it, we'll go to the grave and put flowers on it."

She stared blankly back at him, not saying a word. Then, she turned her head and looked out the frosty winter window at the moonlit night. Gerhardt and his brothers were worn out from lack of sleep. The women had been taking care of Susanna in shifts. When he came shuffling sadly out of her room, Maria took him by the arm and led him across the street to their house where he collapsed into sleep.

The next morning, Gerhardt awoke alone in bed. He wandered around an empty house, even his children were gone. Having not seen them since Friday morning, he surmised they had stayed at his parents' house. When he walked into their house, the children were sitting quietly in the parlor while the rest of the family were in the kitchen.

The women were preparing breakfast, and the men, who had just finished the morning chores, were sitting at the table sipping coffee. The atmosphere was subdued. Gerhardt didn't even get a chance to ask before his sister, Eva, came over and hugged him.

"She's gone. She died after midnight."

Church services that day were sad. Four of the congregation had died in the last three days—David Block, Johann, Susanna, and the baby. After services, they buried Susanna beside Johann, their tiny baby in her arms.

CHAPTER TWENTY

CONSCRIPTED INTO REVOLUTION

In March 1919, a group of horsemen showed up at the family home. Brother Heinrich, the only male at home, was in the barn caring for the few animals still remaining when he heard them ride up. Coming out of the barn carrying a hunting rifle, he saw the men heading into the house.

"Hey there, what are you doing?"

Heinrich didn't make it four steps out of the barn when one of the horsemen hit him from behind with the butt of a rifle. The men ransacked the house, shoving the women aside, taking clothing and food. Then, they took the three best horses from the barn. After loading up their booty, they threw the unconscious Heinrich over the back of a horse and rode toward town. By the time the family patriarch came in from the field with sons Daniel, Peter, and David in the wagon, the raiders were gone. The family searched all over town. Nobody saw where he'd been taken.

Gerhardt was north of town helping on another family's farm, unaware of what had happened. On his way back into town for the evening, he was waved down by a local Russian boy. Gerhardt had grown up with the boy's older brother and knew the family.

The young man ran up to the carriage. "There's a man in the brush by the side of the road. I'm not sure if he's alive."

Gerhardt charged into the brush and found his severely beaten brother. It took a few moments for him to even recognize Heinrich. Gerhardt checked to see if he was breathing. He was, just barely.

Gerhardt and the youth loaded Heinrich into the back of the carriage. Whipping the horse into a gallop, they headed into town. He didn't let up as the carriage flew down the village's main street. Shouting and waving pedestrians out of the way, the boy fought to stay in the carriage. Reigning the horse to a halt in front of his parents' house, Gerhardt yelled for help. His brothers carried Heinrich into the house, and Gerhardt wheeled the carriage around, heading back into town to fetch the doctor.

Heinrich would live, but it would take a while for him to recover. When spring planting time came, he wasn't well enough for the hard manual labor. Buying a wagon and a team of horses, he procured a job hauling freight and mail.

Gerhardt took odd jobs and worked part-time at the mill. It was becoming obvious that, with the lack of rain, the harvest would not be enough for the whole clan to survive the winter. He and Maria made plans to relocate to Franzthal in the Molotschna colony as soon as it was safer to travel.

The village's summer fruit crop was bountiful although the grain crop was meager. Thanks to the militaries' confiscating the best horses, there were few left to do the draft work needed in plowing fields and harvesting.

Late July, the front shifted again, and the White Army occupied the village. Over one thousand men camped in and around the town. Isaac Derksen, the village Dorfschulze, was summoned and ordered to collect rations for the army. Before evening, each family was to hand over underwear for the troops, a pud of oats for the horses, and two hams.

Soldiers ransacked the houses for supplies, but this time didn't harm villagers, probably because higher ranking officers were present. Mid-afternoon, the soldiers drug two of the family's Russian workers out into the street. The town watched from a distance as soldiers pointed at the two men, yelling that they were Bolsheviks. Shouting back, the workers denied the claims vehemently. A command car pulled into the family's farmyard, and three officers went into the barn.

The workers were dragged into the barn and the doors closed. The family watched from the house as shouting and screaming came from the barn. At dusk, the barn doors opened, and the two Russian workers were led out, beaten and half naked. Soldiers pulled them through the family's orchard to the river behind the farm. Shots rang out.

In the middle of town, a band started playing. Soldiers sang and danced all night. At dawn the next day, the army pulled out, leaving the village to pick up the pieces. The two executed men's families came with a wagon to pick up their bodies. Gerhardt's sisters hugged them while the men loaded up the bodies. A third Russian man had been executed on the far side of town.

The front moved farther north, and Makhno's Black Army was driven west, away from the area. Gerhardt decided it was a good time to move closer to Maria's parents. They heard there possibly could be work for him there. He had no inheritance rights left in Karpovka. His share of the family inheritance was invested in the Terek settlement homestead. Therefore, he reasoned, he had no compelling reason to stay in Karpovka. He and Maria packed up and headed south to the Molotschna colony.

While convalescing from his beating, Heinrich started courting Aganetha Siemens. Stopping by after finishing his daily deliveries, they'd sit and talk on a bench in her parents' garden. Both their families had given up on either of them finding mates. He was now thirty-three years old, and Aganetha an ancient twenty-seven. Both had been through enough in life that neither one placed much significance in traditional mating rituals.

Even if they had chosen to indulge in frivolous flirtations and ceremonial wooing, regional conditions were too precarious to have private picnics, moonlight carriage rides, and delegations of intermediaries. No, they just sat and discussed their compatibilities and visions of their futures.

Black Army bandit elements roamed freely while the White Army was occupied elsewhere. Frequent skirmishes cropped up randomly whenever the two factions stumbled upon each other. More than once, Karpovka became the front line in their confrontations, and several houses were destroyed in the shelling. When the armies moved on, the villagers came out of hiding like ground squirrels after a hawk flew away.

Amidst the chaos, the couple became closer and, in November 1919, were married by Reverend Peter Warkentin in a small ceremony. No one wanted to have an ostentatious display while beggars roamed the streets and neighbors were dying of typhus. Moving into a small house in Karpovka, the couple started their life together.

In March 1920, the Red Army attacked toward the Black Sea, splitting the White Army, trapping parts of it in the Don River area. The main White Army force in the south-central area of Ukraine consolidated. General Anton Denikin was forced to resign, and General Pyotr Wrangel came back from a short exile to take command. The front moved inexorably back toward the Memrick colony.

When the Don River pocket collapsed, that part of the White Army had to be rescued by ship from Novorossiysk. During the evacuation, all the horses and a third of the men trapped in the pocket were lost. The White Army was desperate to replace them.

When Heinrich was returning to the village with his team after a freight delivery, he was flagged over by a White Army soldier. Security checkpoints were now a fact of life, so he wasn't overly concerned. There was always the possibility that interaction with troops could go awry.

"Where are you heading, brother?"

"I'm just returning from delivering machinery, and I'm carrying mail to my village," Heinrich replied.

"That's a fine team and wagon you have."

"Thank you. It's my only possession and my family's income. I try to take good care of them."

"That's too bad, because the army needs them. We're authorized to confiscate them and give you a voucher for reimbursement."

Heinrich bristled. Without the team and wagon, his family was reduced to pauper status. "Just where do I present this voucher for payment? Which government?"

"The one that wins. Listen, brother, the only option you have is to stay with the wagon and maybe you can keep it when it's no longer needed."

Heinrich had no choice. He had seen men shot for refusing the vouchers. "At least let me deliver the mail to the village right over there." He pointed down the road. "I'll mull over my options on the way."

The leader thought for a moment and replied, "Why not? We could use a meal, anyway."

One of the men climbed onto the wagon beside Heinrich, and they headed toward the village. He considered his options as he guided the team to make his delivery. The soldier was right. He'd never see any money for the team. There was at least a minimal amount of hope he could keep his family's income if he went with the team. Aganetha could move back in with her parents while he was gone. By the time he had entered the village, his mind was set. He packed a bag, kissed Aganetha goodbye, and left with the soldiers.

Heinrich quickly fell back into the rhythm of military life. It hadn't been that long since he had left the carnage of WWI. He'd thought when he left the military that he would be able to settle back into the bucolic existence he'd grown up with. Unfortunately, revolutionary Russia was no less violent than the war. In WWI, the violence was mass scale impersonal carnage. During the Revolution, the violence was neighbor against neighbor, worker against employer. Raiding militias killed families for no other reason than they had too nice of a house or the wrong last name.

In the White Army, Heinrich's Germanic background wasn't held with as much suspicion as it was during the war. The Black Army's soldiers hated the German landowners' apparent affluence, and the impression that their wealth was gained by the sweat on the backs of Russian peasants. As a result, the German colonists formed protection militias—Selbstschutz—which eventually coordinated with the White Army.

There was also a substantial amount of German settlers who volunteered or were conscripted into the White Army. Even though some of his fellow settlers had picked up rifles, Heinrich did his best to maintain his nonviolent beliefs. The Revolution caused him to modify his community's creed of not killing out of anger. He now allowed for self-defense of his family.

Almost immediately upon his conscription, the White Army was driven south. Makhno was attacking from the west, and the Red Army was sending overwhelming numbers from the north. Heinrich kept busy moving munitions and supplies.

As the summer wore on, he wondered how his wife, parents, and siblings were doing back in Karpovka. He had no way of communicating with them. Even if he did, sending messages across the front lines would put everyone concerned in jeopardy.

He had only been married to Aganetha for six months when he'd been torn from her. Now, she was pregnant, and their child was due in late January. He took some solace knowing that she'd learned to live on her own long before they'd gotten together. She was far from being a helpless woman who needed others to protect her.

What concerned Heinrich most was the rest of his family. Three more of his younger brothers were now of military age and were subject to being forcibly conscripted at the whim of whichever army happened to be in the neighborhood. Seeing his own family members on the other side of a battlefield was a very likely scenario. One of them would have to die. They would have to die, not by their brother's hand, but by the hand of their own side for refusing to engage.

As the White Army was pushed back toward Crimea, Heinrich wondered how his brother Gerhardt was doing. He'd heard Gerhardt and some other families had been planning a new venture in Crimea but didn't know where.

In early September, Heinrich stopped to water his horses in a small, almost dry stream next to a shelled-out homestead. As he warily looked around for signs of danger, the odd shape of a tree caught his attention. Suffering a direct hit by an artillery round, it was split vertically down the middle.

Hanging off the branches of the mangled still upright half, were less than a dozen dry leaves and one lone, almost ripe apple. He pulled the wagon's whip out of its holder and held the handle up to dislodge the apple. He had to jump three times to swing the whip handle high enough to bring the apple down. It bounced off of a broken branch and rolled into the stream.

Wiping the mud off the apple with his sleeve, Heinrich used his knife to carve out the grit left when the branch put a triangular puncture wound in the skin. Amazingly, the apple had no wormhole. Sitting in the shade of the wagon next to the stream, he carved off one crisp slice at a time. It had just enough tartness left to give him the slightest pucker as he chewed. It was the best apple he'd eaten in a long, long time.

After carving off as much of the apple as possible, he laid the knife on his lap and nibbled on it like an ear of corn. He nibbled around the stem and then the flower. He chewed in between the seed pockets until there was absolutely no flesh left to savor. Staring at the core for a few moments, he wondered how, in such a horrible place, something which brought so much pleasure could possibly exist.

Walking up the bank of the stream, Heinrich found a place with good topsoil. He dug a hole with his boot heel, dropped the core in, and buried it with the side of his shoe. Maybe, just maybe, it would grow and offer another traveler some temporary pleasure. Pausing for a contemplative moment, he sighed, climbed onto the wagon, and resumed his grim task of delivering life-destroying munitions.

Ever so steadily, the front kept contracting toward Crimea. Red Army secret police, known as the Cheka, had spies in all of the villages. Heinrich had to be careful which villagers he interacted with. Local bands of bandits would happily slit his throat without a second thought just to get his wagon. During the Revolution, there was no safe place to relax his guard.

The British and Americans withdrew their Tsarist-regime-supporting forces in northern Russia. The French and Greeks pulled their expeditionary forces from Odessa and Crimea. Although the western Allies still offered material support, the White Army fought on alone in southern and eastern Russia. Britain still had its fleets in the Baltic and Black Seas. The French and Italians had fleets in the Black Sea.

After the Novorossiysk evacuation, the Allies' interest in supporting the southern Russian White Army waned. However, Poland's separate war with Russia was helping ease the pressure on General Wrangel. He decided to take advantage of the Polish conflict and attacked north toward Poland.

Heinrich's wagon headed northwest. Every time his team encountered an armored car on the road, they became unruly. He understood the attraction of surrounding yourself in a mobile fortress cocoon. But he considered them too cumbersome and almost useless in snow and mud. He'd heard a few British tanks were very useful in the White Army's attack toward Moscow the previous year, but he still hadn't seen one.

Most commonly what Heinrich encountered was armored trains and other heavy machinery left behind by Germany when it pulled back out of Ukraine at the end of WWI. All sides of the Revolution found the abandoned hardware useful.

Wrangel's attack toward Poland ran aground when the Bolshevik government made the tactical decision to put the Polish war on hold and momentarily ignore the Siberian White Army in order to concentrate on Ukraine. The Red Army entered into a peace treaty with Nestor Mahkno's Black Army and started coordinating their efforts.

Wrangel's attack, and therefore Heinrich's wagon, did a U-turn. He and his team headed south again. It wasn't long before the White Army was surrounded in southern Ukraine just north of Crimea.

CHAPTER TWENTY-ONE
MOVE TO CRIMEA

For Gerhardt's family, conditions in Franztal were no better than Karpovka. He found work with George Becker's relatives who lived next door to Maria's parents. The war front had remained far to the north during the winter and, in the spring, the White Army had taken Crimea from the Black Army. However, Makhno and his Black Army were starting to make gains from the west again.

With the front closing back in, George Becker decided the safe thing to do was to move into Crimea where there was more stability. He asked Gerhardt if he'd be willing to help. Having already seen what would happen if the Black Army took over, Gerhardt was willing. Becker traded his property for a herd of two dozen cattle.

"So, how are we going to get the cattle to Crimea?" Gerhardt asked. "Load them on a train and ship them?"

"I don't think that's advisable," George replied. "The cost is prohibitive, and I don't trust the rail route. It's a big target for the militaries. I think we'll be better off to herd them and take our household possessions by wagon. There's usually plenty of grazing along the way."

Before leaving, Maria's father took young Henry and Martin into his orchard. He led them to the tallest cherry tree, standing by itself on the edge of the orchard. Kneeling down, he hugged the boys.

Solemnly, he looked at them and said, "If something happens, the family's wealth will be buried under this tree. Do you understand, boys?"

The wide-eyed brothers looked up at their grandfather's creased face and nodded sincerely. He gave them both a hug and led them back to the house.

Setting out in their wagons, the families herded the cows southwest across Ukraine to Crimea. Gerhardt and Maria still had just the four children: Henry, Martin, Helen, and Katherine. George also had four children of the same general ages: George, Jake, David, and Katherine. Accompanying the Beckers and Wiens were George's brother, John Becker, and his family of all girls. Peter Kroeker's family, Maria's widowed great aunt, and her young daughter, Annie Dirks, filled out the caravan.

Gerhardt only owned a little bay gelding to ride while herding the cattle. It was a poor horse, prone to getting equine scurvy and constantly had saddle sores. Maria's father gave them a healthy mare to pull their wagon, which the children promptly named Kukla. While the men herded the Becker cattle and Gerhardt's lone dairy cow when they left Franzthal, Maria and the other women drove the wagons.

Following the Juschanlee River for two days, they crossed to the western bank of the Molotschna River near Altonau. The group traveled beside the Molotschna River until they neared Melitopol, then headed west cross country to the Isthmus of Perekop.

With the lack of rain leaving little forage for grazing, the cattle weren't doing well. There wasn't much more food for the families, but the caravan plodded along. Once across the isthmus, they drove the herd almost due south across the broad Crimean prairie lands. Finally, the travelers reached their sharecropping destination. Bek Bulatschi was part of the Schroeder Estate on the Salgir River, about forty miles north of Simferopol. The three-hundred-twenty-mile journey took the group a month and a half.

Gerhardt lamented, "The village is only a few miles from Station Kurman Kimiltschi on the main railroad between Melitopol and Simferopol. We'd have saved ourselves a lot of grief if we could have afforded the fare to transport the herd and ourselves by rail."

The trip had been hard on both the animals and families. The long, dry summer killed the vegetation, and the cattle were starving. Gerhardt did his best to favor the two milk cows when feeding. Milk was an absolute necessity for almost one dozen children.

By fall, there was only Gerhardt's milk cow left. Reports from the war front were just as grim. General Denikin had been forced to resign in March 1920 as head of the White Army, and General Nikolayevich Wrangel had taken his place. The Red Army had signed a treaty with the Makhno's Black Army and was doubling the pressure on the Loyalists.

The White Army was being pushed back toward Crimea. Everyone knew what that would mean. Armies lived off of the land. The villagers' land. Gerhardt had already seen what that meant. Back in Karpovka, a neighboring farmer had fed all of his remaining grain to his cow because he knew the army would take the grain when it passed through. The army took the cow.

With the battlefront nearing, Gerhardt, George, John, and Peter slaughtered the last cow and divided the meat to be hidden from the foragers. Their families were now reduced to gleaning barren fields on their knees, searching for remaining kernels of grain. After the fruit was gone from the trees and the tubers had all been dug from the ground, they'd be in dire straits. Maria, due to deliver another child in January 1921, was already frail from lack of nutrition.

White Army foragers started to roam through the villages. Usually, they were followed closely by confiscated wagons filled with wounded soldiers being evacuated from the front. The village men set about hiding the remaining livestock, as well of themselves, from the foragers. Fighting age men were just as likely to be conscripted as the animals.

Returning to the barn to retrieve Kukla and move her to safety, Gerhardt stopped when, in the distant line of evacuation wagons, he thought he recognized a familiar figure driving one of the teams. He could swear it was his older brother, Heinrich. He led Kukla to the edge of the village, trying to get a better vantage point of the convoy. As he strained to make out the driver, he failed to notice a squad of soldiers coming up behind him.

"You there! Surrender that horse to the cause."

Startled, Gerhardt was ashamed he'd let himself be caught in the open. "But, sir, this is the only animal we have left to farm with."

"Too bad, it belongs to the army now."

Gerhardt looked around and saw his family watching from a distance. Not wanting to give the soldiers any reason to escalate the situation, he reluctantly handed the halter lead to the nearest soldier and turned to walk away.

"Hear now, where do you think *you're* going?"

Cautiously, Gerhardt turned, looked at the squad leader, and said, "I've nothing left to contribute to the army."

"That's where you're wrong, citizen. We need more teamsters for the evacuation wagons. Take this horse and hitch it to the wagon you tried to hide in the barn."

Gerhardt knew he had no chance to escape, so he sadly led the horse to his neighbor's barn and hitched it to the wagon. Martin, never the shy one, ran over to help his father as Maria futilely called out to stop him.

"What are you doing, Papa?" Martin asked.

"These men need me to help win the war, son."

"Are you leaving with them?"

"Yes, Martin, please run and fetch a bag with some clothes for me. I won't be gone too long." Gerhardt hoped he wasn't lying.

He stalled as long as he could hitching the wagon and loading the pillaged food. Maria came out of the house with the bag. Martin had just enough time to run up and throw the bag into the wagon as the soldiers forced Gerhardt to whip the mare into motion. Gerhardt looked back at Maria as she stood stoically with her apron sheltering their two young daughters. Henry glared at the soldiers from her side. Martin ran alongside the wagon for as long as he could, urging his father to win the war soon. Finally, he fell to the ground, exhausted.

The squad leader ordered Gerhardt to turn the wagonload of supplies north toward the front when they reached the main road. It was tough, slow going against the flow of the ambulance wagons and army units moving to set up fallback positions. Even though it was October, all of the moisture was gone from the drought-stricken area.

Heavy traffic had pounded the desiccated road into boot-top-deep fine powder. With each step, dust flowed back into the depression left by the horse's plodding hoofs. Dust rode the wagon wheel spokes to the apogee of their rotation, then cascaded back down over the wheel's center hub. Even at such a slow pace, the fine particles of dust rose above the soldier's heads and wafted into the roadside field, coating everything with an inedible tan flour.

Gerhardt mused, "Any miller would be envious of how uniformly fine these particles are ground."

He picked the crust of hardened dust away from his tear ducts with the tip of an index finger. Then, he brushed the crust off of his eyelashes with the side of the same finger. Flicking the handkerchief tied over his nose with the back of his hand sent up a plume of dust.

Every now and then, when the wagon was forced to stop for passing traffic on a narrow bridge, Gerhardt would rinse and retie the shirt he had fastened around Kukla's nose. It was a trick he learned during the war's gas attacks. Sullenly, he mostly just stared ahead through parched eyes and trudged along. Finally, the party reached a rear marshaling area in the northern part of the Isthmus of Perekop to unload their supplies.

The scene was all too familiar. He'd spent the majority of his war years in such places. Luckily, the wagon was light duty and unsuitable for packing heavy ammunition or weaponry. Sent to the field hospital, he was loaded up with walking wounded to be evacuated. They weren't very badly injured but still unsuitable for fighting. He was impressed that the White Army command valued their sacrifice and refused to leave them behind to fend for themselves. In this war, to be captured by the opposition meant almost certain execution. Rations couldn't be spared for prisoners.

Gerhardt helped one soldier up on the seat beside him and arraigned the rest on top of their duffels in the back. Pulling the wagon into a small convoy, he headed south toward the local railroad spur. There, the wounded would be loaded onto cars for their journey through Dzhankoi on their way to Simferopol. At the railhead, he loaded up light munitions supplied by the French and English for his return trip.

By mid-October 1920, the White Army was driven back and trapped in Crimea. But, at the same time, its positions were very defensible. The Isthmus of Perekop was narrow, easily barricaded and, most importantly, the only land access to Crimea. In all but the coldest times, the Syvash, a wide saltwater swamp, insulated Crimea from attack all the way to the Sea of Azov.

The only other possible accesses were the easily defended Chongar crossing where peninsulas from both Crimea and the mainland were close enough for a bridge, the Syvash crossing a few miles to the west of Chongar and, further east, the Arabat Spit. The Arabat Spit was a long, narrow, offshore sandbar extending from the mainland all of the way down the eastern seaboard of Crimea to the Kerch Peninsula. It formed the boundary between the Sea of Azov and the Syvash.

Even though it appeared to the troops that they were relatively safe behind their fortifications, the leadership knew they were also trapped there. Since they were impotent to conduct offensive operations against the Red Army, the Western European Powers lost interest in supplying active support.

Brutally cold weather hit in late October. Before long, the frost layer made the ground rock hard. It was unusual for the freeze to hit this early. Since he'd been conscripted in March, Heinrich didn't have winter clothes. Because of his upbringing and experiences with looters during the Revolution, he refused to take from others to bolster his own comfort. Wearing almost every piece of tattered clothing he had, he layered up to fend off late fall frigid winds. His current posting was relaying supplies to the garrisons around the Chongar Crossing and the Taganash railway station.

Not native to the area, Heinrich looked out across the Syvash and pondered. As cold as it was, he wondered just how long it would be before the brackish swamp would freeze solid enough to support heavy wagons. Growing up, he'd spent many winter days on nearby lakes with a wagon, cutting ice blocks for summer cold storage. A fellow soldier, native to the region, walked up and shared the panorama. The man sighed with resignation and looked at Heinrich.

"It won't be long now. The Syvash is only a couple of yards deep during high tides, and we've been having unusually low tides. The Bolsheviks will be able to drag whatever piece of equipment across that they want."

Heinrich looked puzzled. "Surely the commanders know this and are making preparations."

"They're either too snug in their warm rail cars to realize how cold it is, or they just don't believe the Bolsheviks would make their troops wade across a frozen swamp."

Heinrich nodded. "My brother was at Lake Naroch. The generals have never been reticent about sending thousands of men wading across a freezing swamp into the sights of machine guns. I fully expect that soon the morning fog will raise and we'll see Bolsheviks wading ashore with bayonets fixed."

Nodding, the soldier walked away. Heinrich climbed up onto his empty wagon and urged the team into action across the frozen ground. He wondered how much longer the wagon could hold up against the unforgiving ruts' punishment. His injuries from the previous year still hadn't healed completely, and his body ached in the frigid temperature. Every time a wheel dropped into a frozen rut, it felt like he was being struck with a scythe handle. Heinrich adjusted his ragged woolen scarf and resolutely forged ahead.

CHAPTER TWENTY-TWO

THE BEGINNING OF THE END

Gerhardt, never one to shy away from formulating a hasty opinion on a matter, grumbled to himself as he guided Kukla up the Litovskii Peninsula. The weather was grim but, since it was the sixth of November, he expected it and bundled up against the cold. Mostly, he was dour about his wagon's cargo. There was a war being fought, and soldiers survived on minimal survival rations. His wagon was loaded with wine, vodka, and other luxuries for the officers in General Barbovich's headquarters.

He'd been raised in an upper-middle-class family and was used to seeing workers live a more spartan lifestyle than their employers. But those were employees, and they were always free to work elsewhere if they became unhappy. Here, officers were supposed to command loyalty and inspire the troops to fight for the cause. It's hard to be fervent in the cause with moldy bread in your rucksack while your leader's breath smells of wine and there are bits of meat in his beard.

Gerhardt's attention snapped back to the present when he saw a work crew repairing the roadside telegraph line. One of the uniformed workers flagged him to a stop.

"Have you seen any suspicious groups in your travels today?"

Gerhardt half wished he'd be waylaid of his decadent cargo, yet relieved he wasn't. Being robbed held a high likelihood of getting shot or skewered.

"No, I haven't seen anyone other than the usual traffic. Why? What is going on?"

"Oh, there's been a lot of sabotage to the communication lines. There's got to be a band of Bolsheviks in the neighborhood. Be careful."

"Thanks, I will."

Renewing his trip, Gerhardt's mindset changed. He was no longer as concerned about the inequities of rank as he was with ending the day with the same number of holes in his clothing he'd started with that morning. These days, he thought, new holes in your shirt were often accompanied by unwanted leakage of bodily fluids. He'd become attached to the amount of fluids his body contained, and he wanted to maintain that level. Nervously shifting around on the wagon seat, he frequently looked over his shoulder until reaching the officers' field kitchen.

The next morning, Gerhardt loaded up some rations to deliver to a company mess on the shores of the Syvash. It was a miserable trip in worsening weather, but he managed to make it back to the headquarters by evening. Surrounded by frantic confusion, he couldn't locate his commanding officer, so he headed Kukla to the stables.

The horse was uneasy and difficult to control. He was starting to lose his temper with her when, during a break in the wind and a lull in the background camp noises, he heard the faint sound of cannon fire in the distance. *Here they come*, he thought grimly.

Throughout the night, the cannon fire only got louder. Gerhardt found it hard to believe that soldiers could even see what they were shooting at in the dark and miserable weather. At first light, he knew the fighting would increase with better visibility. An hour before morning twilight, his lieutenant ordered him north to pick up casualties on the Litovskii Peninsula. It was slow going with Kuban and Don Cossack cavalry units continually forcing him to pull to the side of the road so they could pass.

In the distance, Gerhardt saw a group of General Fostikov's command staff gathered on a small rise. Automobiles were parked in the frosted, windblown grass just below the hill's crest on the near side. At a fork on the south side of the rise, he was directed to take the eastern road around the base of the promontory.

Gerhardt should have pulled up Kukla on the southern protected slope, but his curiosity got the best of him. He allowed the horse to round the incline just far enough to have a good view of the battlefield. In the distance, barely visible in the low-lying coastal mist, was a long line of cavalry advancing over the frozen plain.

Cossack cavalry were lined up at the foot of the hill in front of him, steam rising from hundreds of nervous horses' nostrils. With their mounts stomping back and forth, the riders' inversely curved shashka scabbards clanked against the tack of the horse beside them. The stomping and snorting of the steeds and the rattle of the soldier's gear was loud, even at this distance.

It had barely sunk in to Gerhardt that he was about to witness a large cavalry conflict when the line of horses in front of him started off, heading north at a brisk walk. Artillery shells from both sides exploded all around the opposing riders. In unison, the horses broke into a trot, then a gallop.

Fascinated, Gerhardt watched the lines near each other. He could see the glint off of the soldiers' raised shaskas. He smiled when the opposing cavalry split and headed off the battlefield to the left and right. *They're running*, he thought. The jubilation was short lived when he realized that the divide exposed hundreds of tachankas—carriage mounted machine guns—hidden behind the front-line enemy cavalry.

Before the Cossacks could react, the machine guns opened up. Rows and rows of horses collapsed to the ground, crushing their riders. The guns kept firing. Riders who survived the initial barrage tried in vain to use their fallen steeds as cover and return fire. The Bolshevik cavalry flanked the fallen White Army soldiers and cut them to pieces. Gerhardt couldn't believe the carnage—on a scale he hadn't seen since the Great War.

He glanced up to the top of the rise just in time to see the staff running to their cars and fleeing. Looking back toward the battle, Gerhardt saw White Army infantry abandoning their emplacements and falling back, attempting to regroup. He realized there was no way he could move forward to retrieve casualties without certain capture. Even his current position was quickly becoming at risk.

Just as he was turning the wagon around to move farther back, a Bolshevik artillery shell made a direct hit on the top of the hill where the staff had been gathered a few moments before. Gerhardt covered his head as chunks of frozen dirt rained down on him and Kukla. Another shell landed near a White Army gun emplacement below him.

Gerhardt wheeled the reluctant horse around and forced her toward the wounded soldiers crawling out from the debris. Quickly dismounting, he began helping the wounded into the wagon. The sergeant in charge staggered around, dazed, still yelling orders at the top of his lungs. Gerhardt grabbed the man's arm to get his attention. He'd been in the sergeant's place and knew the shell-shocked man couldn't hear himself.

Once eye contact had been established, the sergeant calmed and they managed to communicate with hand signals the need to get the wounded loaded and evacuate the area. The Bolshevik artillery obviously had found its range. The sergeant and Gerhardt loaded as many wounded into the wagon as possible. Gerhardt urged Kukla into action and pointed the wagon south, away from the front. The sergeant and the rest of the platoon who could walk followed behind.

Turning to look back, Gerhardt realized the sergeant was trying to keep up and administer first aid to one of the wounded on the wagon. He slowed so that the man could be tended to more efficiently. The man's leg was almost severed at the knee and was bleeding profusely. The tourniquet wasn't working. Every time the leg was stabilized, the wagon would jolt and the leg would fall out, causing the man to scream and the bleeding to resume.

Finally, out of grim resolve to save the soldier, the sergeant pulled out his bayonet and sawed through the remaining tendons holding the leg on. It fell to the ground behind the wagon. The rest of the platoon stepped around the leg, each man giving it a momentary glance of numb curiosity before moving on.

Once he'd stopped the bleeding, the sergeant slapped the side of the wagon and motioned to speed up and leave the walking men behind. Gerhardt looked at the man and couldn't tell if the leg had stopped bleeding because the tourniquet was working or because the man had died. He whipped Kukla into a canter and headed toward the field hospital's last location.

Every jolt from the frozen road brought gasps, moans, or wails from the wounded men. Gerhardt had conditioned himself during the Great War to tune out the sounds. It was important the men be delivered to care before the initial shock of their injuries wore off and they started to feel real pain—or died from blood loss.

As he pulled into camp, the area was in a state of chaotic desperation. No one seemed to be in charge. His lieutenant looked in the wagon and said, "Just keep going, Wiens. Take them to the railhead. All of the doctors have evacuated there. Saboteurs have cut all the communication wires. We've absolutely no idea what the status of the front lines are. There's no control of the situation."

"Okay."

Gerhardt turned Kukla toward the railway. As his wagon neared where the Litovskii Peninsula attaches to the main Isthmus of Perekop, he looked over his shoulder. A large cavalry unit accompanied by tachankas was crossing behind him.

He recognized the uniforms. He'd seen them many times before. They were Nestor Makhno's anarchist Black Army. They hated German settlers and, in his opinion, had even less of a disciplined command structure than either the White or Red armies. They were responsible for his brother Johann's death. Gerhardt's fear spiked. Then, he realized they were ignoring his lone wagon of wounded.

Momentarily puzzled by the cavalry not molesting him, it dawned on Gerhardt what was happening. They were turning west toward the Isthmus of Perekop and moving behind the White Army's front-line defenses.

He thought, *This isn't going to be a good day for General Wrangel.*

An artillery shell shrieked over his head and exploded near the line of cavalry behind him. Looking south, Gerhardt saw White Army Cossacks charging at a full gallop.

"Schiet! Dat is nich goot!"

He realized he was about to be smack dab in the middle of a cavalry engagement. Gerhardt had just begun to think his overcoat might make it through the day with no new holes. He did the only thing he could think of. Turning Kukla south, he whipped the tired horse into a full gallop toward the onrushing Cossacks, hoping that the wagon might pass through the line unmolested.

To his amazement, the line of Cossacks parted with just enough room for the wagon to pass. Gerhardt didn't bother looking back. He knew the scene would be gruesome. As he neared the line of cavalry held back in reserve, an officer flagged him through an opening, motioning him to hurry.

"Keep going! Keep going! We can only stall them so long before they outflank us again."

Gerhardt kept going. Every small village he went past had heard the news and was making preparations for the battle to engulf them. He was now sharing the road with other troops heading south. A few miles south of where he was caught in the middle of the cavalry skirmish, he passed through a line of fortified positions hurriedly being prepared.

Finally, after dusk in Ishun, Gerhardt found someone to take the wounded from the back of his wagon. He was directed to the rail yard where the casualties were loaded into a railcar. Two men had died, but the man whose leg had been amputated was still alive.

Later, he found a quiet spot to rest and feed Kukla. She'd performed well and deserved more oats than he had. The next morning, Gerhardt heard fighting at the fortified fallback positions he'd passed through the evening before. Order had been restored somewhat, and he found the lieutenant he'd been assigned to marshaling the surviving teams near the rail yard.

"The Bolsheviks have taken the Isthmus. If they move us off of these positions, there's no geographic aid behind us to help hold them back. We're the cork in the neck of the bottle. Do your jobs, and maybe we can drive them back when we get reinforcements."

Gerhardt and the others kept busy on November 9, ferrying supplies to the front and returning with wounded. While guiding Kukla down the road, he wondered just where the reinforcements the lieutenant referred to were coming from.

Having survived the Great War, he was used to the sounds of artillery. He couldn't help but notice that there were a lot less outgoing barrages than incoming. In a slow moment, while reloading cargo, he asked a soldier what had happened to the artillery.

"We were outflanked and overrun so quickly. We had to pull back. It was left behind."

It didn't take too long for the Bolsheviks, with Makhno's assistance, to push through the last defenses on the Isthmus of Perekop. For two days, Gerhardt drove Kukla down the western flank of the main road between the Isthmus and Simferopol. Makhno's troops spearheaded the attack along the road while the Bolsheviks spread out the assault behind them. Gerhardt desperately wanted to cross over to the eastern side of the road, hoping to check on his family at Station Kurman Kimiltschi south of Dzhankoi, but he was constantly foiled. He didn't know if he would ever see Maria and his children again.

By noon on November 8, the men assigned to the supply depot at the Taganash railway station heard there was an assault taking place at both the Chongar and Syvash crossings. Heinrich had been expecting the assaults. The shallow Syvash was of little use defensively when frozen. His commander ordered as many munitions as possible to be loaded in his wagon for evacuation before the station was overrun.

By evening, Heinrich was well on his way to Dzhankoi. The next morning, they heard the Isthmus of Perekop was probably going to fall, and there was a rumor that Bolsheviks were moving down the Arabat Spit. They were about to be surrounded with no room to maneuver. He was attached to a demolition platoon and ordered to follow the railroad tracks south toward Simferopol with his wagonload of explosives.

His team was being pushed hard. He complained about the pace his horses were forced to maintain, but his platoon leader gave him a cold look and told him to keep them moving. At dark, the night of the eleventh, the convoy made camp under a trestle near the small highway intersection town of Station Kurman Kimiltschi. A courier pulled up to the small convoy in a command car and talked for a few minutes to Heinrich's lieutenant.

The lieutenant divided his platoon. He ordered all but one squad and Heinrich's wagon to fall in behind the courier. After the courier left, the lieutenant made his way over to the remaining men, lost in grim concentration. After a few moments of contemplation, he addressed them.

"There are going to be two trains coming through after midnight. The second will stop just past us. We are to destroy the tracks and get on that train."

Following the curt orders, the men set about unloading the explosives from the wagon and placing them around the trestle pilings. As soon as he saw the lieutenant off by himself, Heinrich approached him and said, "If it's all the same to you, sir, I'd like to stay with my team. They're my family's source of income, and I'd like to try to get them home."

Looking Heinrich in the eyes for a moment, the officer turned and walked over to the horses. He pulled his pistol and unceremoniously shot both of them in the head. Heinrich's knees went weak, and he had to lean against a bridge piling in disbelief. The lieutenant walked back, holstering his pistol.

"You won't have to worry about your horses anymore. If you don't get on that train, the Bolsheviks will do the same to you. Get back to work."

While the men were sitting in little groups gossiping over current events and speculating over strategy, the first train rumbled through just after midnight. Moving faster than usual, the men watched the train's approach curiously. One of them jumped to his feet in recognition and stood at attention.

"It's General Wrangel!"

The rest of the unit vaulted to their feet and stood at attention as the flag-draped, armored, train sped by. The command car was followed by two flatcars laden with guards manning machine guns. Heinrich turned and watched the train disappear south. In his present dour mood, he didn't much care who it was. He'd never been much interested in this political war. And, now that his team lay dead in the gully below the tracks, his incentive to stay had evaporated.

Unfortunately, his only options were to either walk away or stay. If he was caught walking away, he'd be shot. If he managed to get away and was caught by the Bolsheviks, he'd be shot. According to his math, he had twice the chance of getting shot if he walked off than he did getting on the next train—at least for tonight.

It was almost dawn when the second train stopped beyond the trestle. The passenger cars were standing room only. The boxcars were full, and men were sitting in the doorways. Shepherded by the lieutenant, the men climbed into a coal car while one of the men stayed behind to light the fuse. The train slowly started to move as the man ran up behind, waving his arms to go. It had only moved a hundred yards when the trestle went up, raining debris down on the men in the open cars. Heinrich thought for a moment that the rear of the train would derail with the concussion, but it didn't.

Settling down into the coal dust on the floor, he ruminated that the last time he was in such a place, he'd been heading home. This time, he was headed toward Simferopol—the opposite direction. Each day that went by, it seemed that he found himself farther away from the quiet, bucolic existence and family he'd always thought would be his lot in life.

Wedged between other exhausted soldiers, he drifted off to sleep in the clacking, jostling coal car. He didn't know where the train was going nor what was going to be expected of him next. Maybe the dawning of the next day would bring with it a renewed drive in him to make it home.

CHAPTER TWENTY-THREE
BROTHERS RECONNECT

Since the breakthrough at Ishun, Gerhardt's unit had been driven steadily south by the combined Red and Black armies. By November 11, they were over halfway to Simferopol. After dark, his lieutenant came over and ordered him to the command tent with his wagon. The colonel came out and had his orderlies load his luggage into the wagon. The colonel's aide climbed up beside Gerhardt and pointed to the road south.

As Gerhardt pulled out toward the road, the colonel yelled at his aide, "You get that to the station. My family will meet you there. Don't fail me!"

The aide looked back and saluted. Gerhardt whipped Kukla into her best distance-covering gait and headed south down the road. After a few moments, Gerhardt asked the aide, "Where are we going, sir?"

"The main train station in Simferopol."

"Simferopol?"

"Yes. Our situation in Crimea is hopeless. We've been ordered to the ports for evacuation. All soldiers have the option of either loading on the ships to seek foreign refuge or take their chances with the Bolsheviks. I'm getting on the ship."

Gerhardt stared straight ahead in thought. If he were a single man, there would be no question. He'd get on the ship and get out of the God-forsaken place his homeland had become. He had been to America as a child. Even with the violent railroad strike which scared the family, it was still exponentially better than here. It was a tempting thought. He could evacuate safely and send for his family.

Scenarios bounced inside his head and, one by one, were discarded. Yes, he would be safe, but how would he get word to his family? How would the Bolsheviks treat his family if they got wind of his involvement with the White Army? How would his family survive without him providing for them? Would his wife stay where she was, or would she try to get to Franzthal? Would Maria try to get to Karpovka?

The aide had been studying Gerhardt's face while Gerhardt mulled his options. "Have you decided to evacuate?"

"I don't know if I can. I have to worry about my family."

"Once you get out, you can always send for them. They can take a train to Romania or Bulgaria where you can meet them."

"That would be a possibility if they still lived north of Melitopol. Unfortunately, they live near Station Kurman Kimiltschi."

The aide looked sympathetically at Gerhardt. "Oh, I'm sorry. The whole of Crimea will now probably be the center of the Bolshevik's attention. They probably won't let anyone in or out without being thoroughly examined."

"That's what I'm afraid of. I'm going to have to stay and care for my family."

"I guess if my family was here, I'd have to stay also. I'm glad I don't have to make your decision."

By the time they arrived at the passenger station in Simferopol, it was late in the evening of the 12th. Gerhardt had made up his mind to stay. He took the aide to the station and pulled up to the loading dock. Amid mass confusion, officers and their families fought to board the train. The military weren't the only ones trying to evacuate. He'd never seen well-to-do people indulge in such uncivilized activities as pushing and shoving. The crowd bordered on panicked uncontrollability.

After unloading his passenger and cargo, Gerhardt turned the wagon toward the northeast corner of town. Not having much money, he figured he might find some pasture there for Kukla to feed and rest. He needed time to plan how to get home. He had a tentative plan to follow the Salgir River, but he needed to do some research on where the Bolsheviks were before striking out blindly cross country.

"Gerhardt! Gerhardt!"

Hearing a familiar voice over the railyard's din, he saw a hand waving above the pushing crowd. Shoving his way into the open, Gerhardt's older brother came toward the wagon in a limping run with a satchel slung over his shoulder.

"Heinrich!" Gerhardt leaped off of the wagon and ran to help his brother. "What are you doing here?"

Heinrich hugged his brother and replied, "I was conscripted by the Whites along with my team. What are you doing here?"

"The same." Gerhardt looked around. "Where's your team?"

"Station Kurman Kimiltschi. They shot my team and blew up my wagon when the Bolsheviks got too close."

"Station Kurman Kimiltschi?" Gerhardt's heart sank. "My family is only a couple of miles from there, in Bek Bulatschi."

"I'm sorry, Broder. If it helps, there was no fighting taking place. We just blew up the tracks to slow them down and evacuated by train."

Gerhardt threw his brother's bag into the wagon, and they headed out of town. Only this time, he pointed the wagon south to be farther away from the advancing army until they could figure out a plan. Camping on a grassy hillside south of town for the night, they fell asleep soon after unhitching the horse. It had been a long couple of days for both of them.

Rumbling artillery and flashes in the north woke them at dawn. Since Simferopol is on the edge of the northern foothills of the Crimean Mountains, the brothers could see military activity on three flanks of the town. They agreed on what their next move was not going to be. They couldn't go north, at least for the moment. That path was blocked. Behind them, the mountains sloped up gently but dropped off precipitously into the Black Sea on the south side. They weren't exactly trapped, but their north-south movements were restricted within those parameters. Still, they could move laterally east and west without too much difficulty.

For the moment, the brothers ventured farther south into the eastern foothills of Chatyr-Dag, finding a good campsite in a grove of yew trees on the side of the mountain's lower plateau. Since eating yew foliage could kill his horse, Gerhardt was apprehensive of the site.

He reluctantly agreed when Heinrich said, "The clearing is large enough that Kukla can be tied out of reach of the trees. Besides, the Bolsheviks would think it absurd to check here. After all, who'd be stupid enough to camp in such a place?"

Neither of the brothers had been issued military clothing when they were conscripted. Digging through all of their possessions, they made sure there was absolutely nothing which could tie them to the White Army. Any suspect items were burned or buried. Both having military identification from the Great War, they decided that the papers would be neutral if checked. It would be suspicious if they hadn't served. They reasoned that the volume of identifications in their possession showed they had nothing to hide.

Gerhardt also had papers showing that he lived in central Crimea. Unfortunately, Heinrich's papers stated that he lived in east central Ukraine, hundreds of miles away. They hoped they could explain away his lack of local residency by claiming that he'd been visiting on a property search and was trapped by the military activity. They still had a problem over what they were doing south of Simferopol instead of back at Bek Bulatschi.

They remained camped for a few more days on the frigid mountainside until they figured the battle in Simferopol would be over. During scouting walks, they'd seen troop movements on the road below. Running short of grazing for Kukla and supplies for themselves, they knew they had to relocate soon. The issue was decided when a band of Tatar partisans stumbled into the clearing.

After a few tense moments, both sides decided that neither group posed a threat. After inviting the partisans to share the campsite, the brothers soon appreciated the partisans' wealth of information. Tatars had long fought against any Russian rule. They had fought against the White Army, and now they vowed to fight the Bolsheviks.

Gerhardt did most of the speaking for the brothers because he'd interacted extensively with Muslims when he lived in the Dagestan Governorate. In fact, it was a Muslim friend of his, Semih, who had spirited his wife and children to safety when the Nogai tribesmen attacked out of the Chechen highlands.

With spies everywhere, the Tatars had a far-reaching information network in Crimea. Their leader said, "When the Communists took Sevastopol on the 15th, anyone wearing a White Army uniform was arrested. Officers or anyone whose uniform looked like an officer's insignia had been ripped off, were executed on the spot."

"Communists?" Gerhardt asked.

"Yes. They changed their name a while back. They get mad if you call them Bolsheviks now." The partisan leader continued, "On the same day, the Whites remaining in Feodosia surrendered without firing a shot. Immediately, the Communists executed hundreds of the wounded and imprisoned the rest. Everyone in Crimea was ordered to register by the twentieth. Cheka agents are everywhere checking papers."

As the two parties prepared to part ways the next morning, the brothers tried to buy some supplies from the partisans. Their leader laughed at them.

"The Communists have declared that the Don Ruble is no longer any good. You might as well use it for toilet paper."

Then, he waved at his men to hand over a few days' rations. After the brothers shook his hand, the partisans left in the direction of the mountain's upper plateau. From what they had told Gerhardt and Heinrich, the mountain had numerous caves to find refuge in. The brothers considered following suit but soon discarded the notion.

It was tactically impossible to get the wagon farther away from roads, and they only had one horse. From what they'd been told, the countryside below was still in a state of confusion. Now would be an optimal time to use the confusion and try to slip through.

Hitching up Kukla, they pointed the wagon toward the main road cutting through the mountains from Simferopol to the coastal town of Alushta. Descending, they worked on their cover story. A mistake would more than likely get them killed. They came up with the story that Heinrich had come south on the train to look for land and that the moving war front had prevented him from returning to Karpovka sooner. While he waited for the path to clear, he and his brother had decided to look at the land around Alushta with the possibility of starting a vineyard. The sudden collapse of the White Army and accompanying military actions had trapped them there until recently.

They recited the plan until almost convincing themselves on its veracity. Their main concern was not the story but the fact that they were German farmers. German farmers were considered Kulaks. Kulaks were wealthy landowners who subjugated peasants and were prime targets for Communist wrath. Being a Kulak was only marginally better than being ex-White Army in the eyes of the Cheka.

The brothers' clothing had become quite frayed in their time away from home, allowing them to downgrade their story. Gerhardt could show that he was a poor tenant farmer. They modified their story to one where Heinrich was looking for work in a vineyard instead of purchasing one.

A couple of miles after turning north on the main road, they were stopped by a Red Army patrol. The brothers' story held up with the cavalry officer since he didn't dig too deep. He wasn't Cheka. It was the mood of the rank and file troops which concerned Heinrich and Gerhardt the most during the interview.

Their impression was that the soldiers would just as soon shoot and move on, worrying about reason later. Luckily, the officer was more concerned with whether the brothers had seen any partisan activity in their travels, and kept the interview short. After being released to continue their journey, they knew that this was not going to be an easy trip.

Gerhardt and Heinrich decided it would look less conspicuous if they followed main routes as if they had nothing to hide. Every instinct told them to scurry from hiding spot to hiding spot while they worked their way north. Instead, mustering every ounce of bravado they possessed, they headed directly through the lion's den.

Simferopol was in turmoil. Working their way through town, they were repulsed by cadavers hanging from street lights. Residents hurried from place to place with heads down, not daring to look anyone in the eye. Soldiers patrolled every street looking for anything suspicious.

Soon after entering the city, the brothers were stopped by a command car and a transport truck pulling quickly up in front of them, blocking the street. Leather-overcoat-wearing Cheka police exited the car and back of the truck, storming into a nearby house.

Gerhardt and Heinrich watched nervously as a couple of Cheka operatives drug a man out of the house wearing civilian clothes, unceremoniously shooting him in the middle of the street. Another operative brought out a White Army officer's tunic and threw it on the corpse. One of the shooters went to the truck, retrieved a can of fuel, and doused the corpse while the third went back into the house.

The officer's wife and children were dragged out and forced to watch while the men lit her husband on fire. Then, they forced the hysterical family into the back of the truck. Leaving onlookers and the brothers stunned, the vehicles sped off in the direction of the city's center.

The whole episode only took a couple of minutes and was over. Gerhardt started to get off the wagon to extinguish the flames, but Heinrich grabbed his arm and shook his head. Looking around at the dispersing crowd, it became apparent that no one dared to interfere with the arbitrary sentence which had just been carried out. The brothers urged Kukla around the still-burning body's stench and continued upon their way.

If they were going to maintain their story, the brothers needed to stay on the main boulevard through the middle of the city. Thanks to a cruel trick of topography, the most logical path to Bek Bulatschi was along the road following the Salgir River. That was the very same road they had been on from Alushta. The road continued north of town all the way to Dzhankoi and the Chongar crossing.

When possible, Gerhardt kept Kukla in as brisk of a pace as was acceptable in town. Speed was of the essence, but they didn't want to raise the ire of any officials. Like all large cities of the time, Simferopol was having trouble with the convergence of traditional equine traffic and the newer automobiles. In the center of the city, traffic halted.

A crowd had gathered around a large, wooden gallows erected in front of the city hall. Twelve well-dressed men and four women stood on short stools with nooses around their necks. On the steps of the city hall, a group of official-looking Communist party members was gathered to witness the execution. A stern, middle-aged woman with pince-nez glasses and her hair in a bun walked back and forth in front of the condemned.

Puffing on a cigarette, she stopped in front of a sobbing woman and looked into her eyes. Caressing the woman's cheek as if to wipe her tears away, she instead held the woman's eyelid up with her thumb and ground out the glowing cigarette in the woman's eye. Laughing heartily at the wailing, she waved at the executioner to proceed as she strolled to the scaffold stairs.

One by one, the executioner slowly walked the full length of the scaffold, kicking the stools out from under the condemned. Some of the doomed closed their eyes, waiting for their turn. Others turned and looked in panic at the person next to them as their neighbor's stool was kicked away. One woman wailed loudly, looking at the sky, pleading for divine intervention. The executioner seemed to take pleasure in how long it took him to complete his task. The brothers couldn't hear what was said, but it appeared the man taunted each person before removing their stool.

As the bespectacled woman ascended the city hall stairs, most of the officials gave her tepid applause. Slapping her on the back, the man in the center heartily shook her hand. The officials turned and walked back into the building while the still-kicking condemned slowly strangled on the ends of their too-short ropes.

Gerhardt looked down at a man beside the wagon and asked, "Who were those people, and what were their offenses?"

The man looked up and replied, "They had the temerity to be bankers. The woman supervising the hanging was Rozalia Zemlyachka, herself. She's Lenin's favorite executioner. The man congratulating her on the steps was Bela Kun, the head of the Revolutionary Committee in Crimea."

Eying the brothers suspiciously as he turned to leave, he warned, "You'd be well advised not to have them put their sights on you."

Gerhardt urged Kukla into action again and picked his way through the thinning crowd. Heinrich looked one more time at the scaffold, all but one of the condemned now swaying limply on the end of their rope. One unfortunate man's feet still twitched.

Dusk was fast approaching as the brothers neared the northern end of town. Hoping to clear the city and camp somewhere the horse could graze, they were crestfallen when a checkpoint blocked the road. Everyone was being interviewed and searched before being allowed to leave Simferopol. The guard strolled up to the wagon and requested their documents. After examining the papers, he asked them to please dismount the wagon. As Gerhardt and Heinrich stood nervously, one soldier looked around in the wagon. Another soldier searched brusquely inside their overcoats.

The guard looked at the brothers then back at their papers a couple of times then asked, "Selbstschutz?"

Gerhardt shook his head. The guard asked more forcibly, "Selbstschutz?"

Heinrich replied, "No, sir, we're Mennonite farmers sworn to pacifism."

"So were the Selbstschutz until they weren't. It says here that you were both in the Imperial Army during the war. How does that make you pacifists?"

"We were both conscripted and were assigned to drive ambulances. Neither of us carried a weapon."

One of the soldiers walked up behind Gerhardt and knocked him to the ground with a rifle butt between the shoulders. As he struggled to get up, the guard watched Heinrich's face closely. When Heinrich failed to react, the guard huffed and walked off, waving for the brothers to leave.

"You're both too meek to have ever carried a weapon. Get out of my sight before I get sick."

The soldiers laughed as the brothers drove off. Gerhardt tensed up as his fiery temper started to get the best of him. Heinrich elbowed him and reminded, "It's better to be laughed at than shot."

Gerhardt sulked until they found a place to stop for the night. Heinrich managed to bring his brother out of his dour mood by punching him on the arm and telling him, "Hey, we managed not to get shot or hung today, didn't we? Of course, it was without any help from you, *Goaschthaumel*."

Gerhardt smiled as he remembered the name his grandmother called him as a child—troublemaker. It brought back fond memories of good times. But that was long ago in a more innocent era. He fell asleep remembering his grootmutta and how she would sneak him treats.

CHAPTER TWENTY-FOUR
REPERCUSSIONS OF DEFEAT

With her frightened girls shivering under her work apron's fringe, Maria watched conscripted Gerhardt disappear down the road with the military foraging party. Martin picked himself up from the dust and started to walk back to the cottage. On his way, he kicked furiously at every rock in the road while using language she hadn't heard since Gerhardt smashed his thumb with a hammer for the second time in less than five minutes. Nine-year-old Henry stood stoically off to the side, his brow furrowed, believing his childhood was over. He was now the adult male in the family.

As Maria led the children toward the house, she mulled over how she was going to put away the rest of the family's winter provisions without her husband. The rest of the villagers started coming out from hiding to check on their losses and console her. Smiling weakly, she thanked them for their concern, then purposely turned to take stock of her own house's condition.

Beside inventorying the foodstuffs and checking for damage, she needed to incorporate Martin's language lessons into her list of things to do. The family bible and spare razor strap needed to be located. There was no time like the present to commence his instructions on proper phraseology.

The next day, she sent Henry and Martin to the local railroad tracks to glean coal which fell off of passing trains' coal tender cars. Martin was still walking a little stilted after his language lesson the previous evening. Taking turns, they pushed the wheelbarrow containing a couple of buckets along the mile-and-a-half-trail to the tracks. Balancing the full-size wooden wheelbarrow on a dirt path was a considerable task for a nine-year-old boy and his eight-year-old brother. Their father and the family's best horse and wagon had been taken before winter fuel gathering was completed.

With the lack of commerce trains during the Revolution, pickings along the tracks were meager. After two hours of walking up one side of the tracks and back on the other, the boys only had a couple of lumps of coal to show for their efforts. They did manage to find a wooden shipping crate which had fallen off of a passing train. While breaking their prize into pieces small enough for the wheelbarrow, the tracks began sizzling with an approaching train.

Just pulling out of Station Kurman Kimiltschi and gaining speed, the fireman and engineer were having an uneventful trip south out of Dzhankoi. With the boiler up to pressure, the fireman had just sat down on the locomotive's left seat when he spied two ragged small boys scavenging firewood along the tracks. Standing back up, he scooped another shovel full of coal. Since the firebox was already well stoked, the engineer eyed him curiously.

Smiling, the engineer shook his head and looked back down the tracks. The fireman "tripped" and accidentally dropped the coal onto the tracks. As he sat back down, the fireman glanced at the other man to see if his accident had been witnessed. With no reaction from the engineer, the fireman looked back down the tracks, secure his hard-nosed reputation was intact.

At first, the boys were offended that something was thrown at them from a moving train. Their ire turned to jubilant gratitude when they saw a few days of fuel for the kitchen stove laying at their feet. Jumping up and down, they excitedly waved at the end of the train. Then, they made sure that not one crumb of the valuable commodity was left unclaimed in the gravel. Winter was coming, and scavenging would only get harder.

With the boys out gathering fuel, Maria used her five- and six-year-old daughters as kitchen help to finish preserving food for the winter. On laundry day, the girls actually were a great help doing things she'd otherwise have to bend over to accomplish with her six-month pregnant body. With the other villagers also in bad shape, she wanted her family to carry their own weight.

During the week, she made sure the children attended the school classes given by one of the Schroeder daughters. The village banded together and paid the girl to teach their children. The Schroeders were the wealthy family who actually owned the estate, Bek Bulatschi, the families lived on. She didn't need the money, and was perfectly happy to help the children for free, but the men didn't want charity. It was in her classes the children were introduced to Latin letters. Up until then, they'd only received instruction using Cyrillic script.

Toward the end of October, the weather turned bitterly cold, and the ground quickly froze hard. There was little Maria could have the children do outside in the way of work, except to care for a few chickens, fetch water, and look for more fuel. Gerhardt had been absent for about a month, and the family had settled into a routine.

Maria was thankful her two young sons stepped up and assumed most of their father's workload. She knew the old adage about idle hands but hadn't always been able to prevent her sons from tinkering in the devil's workshop. For the moment, Henry and Martin seemed willing to set aside their mental mechanisms of mischief.

War news wasn't good. It didn't matter which side you were on, if any. An approaching battlefront meant danger and hardship. Reports of the White Army being driven out of Ukraine and down into Crimea meant nearby fighting soon. General Wrangel had set up his headquarters in Dzhankoi, less than twenty miles away. That placed Station Kurman Kimiltschi and Bek Bulatschi in the bullseye.

The village didn't have long to wait. It was only a little over a week into November when the Red and Black armies crossed the Syvash. By the 11th, artillery flashes were seen across the full span of the northern horizon. Just like a tiny lap dog when there are large, raucous dogs roughhousing nearby, the community winced and hunkered down for the oncoming onslaught.

Before dawn on the 12th, there was a large explosion in the railroad's direction. With fighting so close, the Schroeders wouldn't let their daughter venture out to teach. Since it was Friday, that meant the children had three days without something to occupy their minds, interrupted only by Sunday service.

Maria warned Henry and Martin to stay nearby. But as soon as they were out of her sight, their boyhood curiosity overrode their obedience, and they circled around the village to investigate the explosion.

Unencumbered by the wheelbarrow, the mile-and-a-half-long walk to the railroad didn't take long for the boys. A few men were walking around surveying the damage when they arrived. Amazed at the smoldering exploded trestle, Henry and Martin's curiosity wouldn't let them stand back. So, they waded into the wreckage and began rummaging.

Soon, the men shrugged and left, leaving the boys to explore. Shattered timber girts and ties were strewn everywhere. Corkscrewed steel rails twisted down into the gully from both sides then diverged into four separate directions like twisted glistening ribbons on a present. Martin spied pieces of a freight wagon laying near the bottom of the wreckage.

"Look, Henry! Someone shot horses and left them still hitched to the wagon."

Henry glanced over to acknowledge his brother's find but was too busy surveying the bigger picture. Amazed at how much splintered wood there was lying about, he guessed there was enough wood to supply the small village for the winter. He wouldn't have to go on any more foraging trips.

"Come on, Martin. We have to go back to the village and get wagons before anyone else gets this wood!"

Interrupted from examining his find, Martin looked around and realized his brother was right. Running the entire way back to the village, the boys went past their own house and found George Becker working in his barn. Panting, they had trouble conveying what they'd seen but he soon understood the importance of their find. It didn't take the men long to hitch up their remaining teams and head for the destroyed trestle with every able-bodied boy along for labor. Henry and Martin had honored seats on the first wagon as guides.

Other salvagers were already at the trestle, but there still was enough wood left to fill the three wagons and maybe enough for a second trip. Martin was still fascinated why someone would shoot the team of horses and leave them there. As cold as it was, they still weren't frozen.

After his wagon was loaded, George Becker wandered over, amused at how much work Martin was putting into removing the harnesses from the team. After a few moments, George bent down and felt the closest horse. Realizing that they were fairly fresh, he motioned to the other men.

"Hey, let's butcher these horses. It may be horse, but it's still meat we don't have."

Without their normal butchering equipment, they used axes and pocket knives. It wasn't an exceptionally artistic slaughter job, but they managed to save enough meat to feed their families for quite some time. The tack and spare parts from the ruined wagon were also saved for future use. When the work crew arrived back at the village, the men unloaded the wagons while the women started cutting up the meat.

Exhausted, Henry and Martin collapsed into bed while the men and older boys went back for any remaining trestle wood. Even though they had disobeyed her, Maria was proud of her two little men. They were village heroes—for the moment. She knew all too well a camel couldn't disguise its hump for long.

Saturday the 13th was fairly quiet, and the community went about its normal routine, preparing for Sunday's day of rest. No one heard artillery, and no foragers were seen. It seemed to be almost a normal prewar day to the village. After a year of German occupation and then the Revolution, this was an unfamiliar and uneasy feeling for the adults. Things changed on Sunday.

As usual, most of the village gathered in the meeting hall for services. The congregation had just begun a moment of silent prayer and contemplation—always an uneasy time for Maria's boys. In the silence, the usual sounds of the boys' fidgeting echoed in the hall. Martin's boot clunked against the leg of the bench with rhythmic regularity as he burnt off excess energy swinging his legs. On Maria's other side—she had long ago learned to sit between the boys during services—Henry was busy irritating Helen by poking and pinching her. Hearing horses and automobiles, Martin leaped up and ran to a window before Maria could catch his arm.

"It's the Red Army!" he declared.

Abandoning the normally solemn moment, the rest of the congregation lined up at the windows to watch a column of soldiers moving through the village. Nearby Station Kurman Kimiltschi was a major crossroads where north-south, east-west roads and the railroad all intersected.

After the main convoy had cleared the village, the congregation started to filter away from the windows. A second, much smaller unit, stopped in front of the hall. These soldiers' uniforms were different from the first group.

One of the congregation asked, "Who are they?"

"Cheka," someone else muttered.

Apprehension in the hall elevated. The troops knew their objective. Their leader waved them in the direction of the building and, in a well-rehearsed manner, they quickly surrounded it. Opening the door, the leader walked in. Standing inside the open doorway, he surveyed the congregation for what seemed an eternity.

"We're looking for deserters and enemies of the Revolution," he unceremoniously declared. "Please line up to be interviewed."

When Martin started to confront the officer for interrupting the service, Maria's fingers dug into his shoulder, and she shook her head at him. Seeing how serious her face was, he stopped. The girls assumed their normal position under her apron corners while Henry stood to the side, exhibiting his usual stoic observation.

The men were separated to one side of the hall where a clerk took their names and conducted a quick interview with each of them. Obvious paupers and the very old received only minimal attention and were quickly released. Anyone well-dressed or military age was saved for deeper questioning. Sometimes, for no apparent reason, the officer would have someone set aside for special treatment.

The women were treated basically the same. Maria was one of the first to be interviewed. When she was called over, she gave Martin her stern "keep your mouth shut" expression. The interviewer looked at her obviously malnourished and pregnant condition, and was about to release her, when the officer stepped over and held her up.

"Where is your husband, Mother?"

Maria knew that everything depended on her answer. In Karpovka, she'd witnessed how the wrong answer could lead to bad endings. She also knew it was critical that everyone was on the same page. Maria gave her best helpless look to the officer and replied in a voice loud enough that everyone in the hall heard.

"The White Army took him away, and no one has seen him since."

Her answer was short and expressed in a way to give the impression that he was a prisoner. It was misleading but not a lie. The story might be accidentally contradicted by one of the other villagers. It was better to feign confusion than being caught up in deception. He bought her evasion and offered his condolences for how her family was treated by the criminal White Army. Martin started to protest, but Maria's grip tightened into his shoulder. After she had shepherded her family out of earshot of the meeting hall, she turned to the children and gave them a stern warning,

"Do *not* tell these people that your father is anything other than a prisoner. Do you understand?"

Martin protested, "But Mutta, he's off helping win the war!"

Maria hissed, "He's *not* helping to win the war! The war is lost. These are the men he was fighting against. They must never know he was on the other side. Do you understand?"

The children nodded solemnly except for Martin, who glowered. Maria shook him and repeated the warning. After he reluctantly nodded, she turned to take her family home.

Suddenly, a shot rang out behind them. The family turned and saw the wealthy head of one of the local estates lying dead in the street with the Cheka officer standing over him. The man's wife came screaming out of the hall and ran toward her husband. The officer hit her on the head with his pistol when she lunged at him, knocking her to her knees. Unceremoniously shooting her in the head, he walked back to the meeting hall, leaving two bleeding bodies in the frozen dust. The couple's hysterically screaming children were loaded into the back of a truck, and the convoy drove out of the village.

Maria grabbed her crying girls' hands and drug them away from the sight. Henry and Martin stood wide-eyed, pivoting to watch the Cheka patrol pull out of the village. Everything their mother had just told them about the soldiers would not need to be repeated. The sight of the couple, who had been community leaders a few hours before, being carried off the street back into the meeting hall drove home reality.

Seeing the man and his wife shot right in front of them removed any illusions about war that might have remained in the boys. It was all too clear this was no longer the childhood game most boys cavalierly played with wooden guns.

The White Army loaded onto ships and abandoned Crimea. Reports of the Communists summarily executing any wounded White Army soldiers they encountered shocked the village. Hundreds of soldiers and officers, which had been promised amnesty if they surrendered, were either shot en masse or loaded onto trains which disappeared north.

Only a few miles from the main transportation junction of Station Kurman Kimiltschi, rumors quickly arrived in the village. The Communists had set up headquarters in Simferopol, forty miles south of the village. Lenin personally sent the head of Cheka, Bela Kun, to oversee the "digestion" of enemies to the Revolution. Kun brought his right-hand woman Rozalia Zemlyachka who, by all accounts, was ruthless when ferreting out anyone she felt stood in the way of her agenda. Nikoli Bystrykh was put in charge of finding all individuals considered subversive to the Soviet government.

Cheka centers of operation were established in Simferopol and Sevastopol with many smaller outposts. If roving Cheka units discovered anyone who, in their opinion, was an obvious threat to the

State, they'd summarily execute them on the spot. If the unit was in doubt, they'd load the prisoners into a truck and send them to stand trial before a tribunal at one of the outposts. Then, the prisoners were usually immediately executed. Anyone who had high intelligence value was forwarded to an operation center for "special attention"—a euphemism for torture.

It wasn't uncommon for a Cheka truck, laden with prisoners, to pass through the village on its way to Station Kurman Kimiltschi, one of many such outposts. No one seemed exempt from the interrogations and torture, including women and a suspect's children.

Whenever a truck passed, Maria looked out her cottage window, straining to see if she recognized any of the prisoners. It had been weeks since the Communists had taken over, and she still had no word of her husband's fate. Winter was hard upon the area, and her due date was nearing. She needed to decide whether to stay put or take the children back to Franzthal.

In desperation, she summoned the boys and instructed them to go to Station Kurman Kimiltschi and see if any of the prisoners was their father. The boys put a bridle on the family's remaining horse, the sickly, little, bay gelding that just wouldn't die. Henry led the horse up to a low rock fence and climbed onto its bare back. Reaching down, he pulled Martin up behind him. Henry then urged the reluctant horse to turn and start the four-mile trip to the station. The frigid air held the breath of the boys and the horse in a lingering plume as Maria stood, watching them cut through the morning ice fog until out of sight.

When the bundled boys rode into Station Kurman Kimiltschi, Henry went to the mercantile first. His mother told them not to act like they were there solely to check on the prisoners. The boys spent time window shopping, always surreptitiously watching the administration building that the Cheka had taken over. At noon, a small crowd gathered outside the building. Curious, the boys joined a group watching through the windows.

Five men were led into the courtroom from the building's basement. Looking like they'd been severely beaten, their clothes were torn. After the prisoners stood in front of the tribunal for only a few minutes, they were taken from the courtroom and out the back of the building. The boys had strained to hear the proceedings, but the frost-coated windows muffled the voices and they couldn't tell what was going on.

Henry and Martin followed the crowd around the building where they watched the men being lined up against a wall. The boys were off to the side of the crowd and could only see the lined-up men just standing there. Henry and Martin looked at each other and shrugged in confusion—then the machine gun opened up.

The startled boys stared in disbelief as a work crew loaded the bodies into a wagon. Along with the crowd dissipating back into the town, the shocked boys walked to their horse silently. They led the horse to a high porch and used it to climb onto the gelding's back. Not a word was said until they left town and were well down the road back to Bek Bulatschi. Martin finally broke the silence.

He softly asked over Henry's shoulder, "Did you recognize any of those men?"

Henry shook his head.

Martin asked again, "What are we going to tell Mutta?"

Henry turned and looked back at Martin. "Nothing. We tell Mutta nothing. All we tell her is that they led the prisoners out and put them on a train, and we didn't know any of them. Do you get it? We tell Mutta nothing."

Martin nodded, and the boys rode the rest of the way home, quietly digesting what they had just witnessed.

When they rode into the family's small barn, Maria was waiting with warm broth for her little troopers. The boys recanted the story they'd agreed upon. Begging off any further questioning, they asked to be allowed to do their daily chores. As her boys went off, she watched after them. They seemed unusually quiet and worn out. She thought to herself that they must have had an adventurous day which burned off a lot of their usual destructive energy.

From what the boys had told her, there was a daily transfer of prisoners who had been detained while trying to return home from the war. Maria decided her boys had shown responsibility today. She would send them back tomorrow and every day until she learned of her husband's fate. It would be good for the boys to get out of the house.

CHAPTER TWENTY-FIVE
HOME

It took three more days for the brothers to traverse the forty-five miles between Simferopol and Bek Bulatschi. The morning of the first day, a storm descended upon the region, and frigid headwinds battered the wagon. Gerhardt joked between shivers that at least it kept the Communists inside and away from them. Kukla was wearing out and needed rest. They hadn't eaten since the morning. Their breakfast was the rest of the meager rations given to them by the Tartar partisans. As evening neared, the brothers approached a small village with familiar architecture and layout.

Shivering, Heinrich stammered, "It's German."

"It must be Spat," Gerhardt replied, barely able to hold Kukla's reins. "I've never been there, but I heard it was located somewhere along here."

The brothers pulled up in front of the first house, and Heinrich managed to dismount the wagon and make his way to the door with his stiff legs. He only could manage a weak knock with his shivering hand. The door opened tentatively, and a middle-aged woman peered out.

Heinrich managed to stammer, "We're German."

The woman opened the door farther, looked at Heinrich, and then out at Gerhardt in the wagon. She grabbed Heinrich and pulled him inside while barking guttural orders to unseen persons behind her. Two teenage boys rushed past and ran out to the wagon. One boy helped Gerhardt into the house while the other led the horse into the attached barn and unhitched the wagon.

The woman shoved the men into the winter living room and sat them down on the hearth. Taking their coats, a young girl hung them to dry. The mother returned with two steaming cups of coffee. As soon as their teeth started to chatter a little less, Heinrich tried to explain their plight.

The woman quickly held up her hand. "Ah! The less I know, the less I can say!"

Gerhardt tried to add, "But …"

The woman insisted, "The less I know, the less I can say. Drink your coffee."

The brothers took the hint. It wasn't a good thing these days to know too much. The Cheka did terrible things, even to children, if they thought there was information to be garnered. The conversation switched to more banal subjects such as the weather. Soon, the men were led into the kitchen for a hot bowl of borscht and zwieback. After eating, the woman brought out blankets and made the brothers comfortable in front of the hearth for the evening. It didn't take long before the exhausted men were hard asleep.

While still dark the next morning, the woman woke them with the clanking of pans in the kitchen and the smell of hot coffee. The wind had died down, but snow still fell. After a hearty breakfast, the brothers checked on their horse in the barn. Kukla had been curried, fed, and hitched back up to the wagon by the boys. Apparently, their welcome was over. The woman came into the barn and handed them a sack of toasted zwieback. Looking around, the brothers could see her family didn't have much in the way of rations to spare.

Gerhardt looked at her sadly. "We don't have anything to offer you in payment."

The woman just smiled. "If you happen upon my husband, do the same for him. Now go before someone sees you."

Heading down the main street on their way north, the brothers quietly left the village. The town was larger than they had thought the night before. On the right side, next to the river, was a small factory area. In the village center was a school and a church. Not wanting to arouse suspicion, they did not tarry. Before morning light started to filter through the falling snow, the wagon was miles away.

The snow proved a mixed blessing. It made the footing for Kukla a little more treacherous but also kept road traffic minimal. By mid-day, the falling snow was tapering off as the brothers passed the half-way point between Simferopol and Bek Bulatschi. Traffic and military patrols would soon pick up. The halfway point was also when the Salgir River headed more easterly, away from the main road and railroad. Gerhardt turned Kukla onto a smaller road following the river.

He explained, "The river passes within a few miles of Bek Bulatschi, so our route will look completely normal. Hopefully, there'll be fewer patrols on back roads."

The day went well, but slowly. By dusk, the brothers made it to Karassan. Gerhardt pulled the wagon into a forested area next to the vineyard southeast of the village. With the lack of wind, the trees provided enough shelter to camp under the wagon for the night. Bek Bulatschi was only a few miles farther, but they thought it best to approach during daylight.

Mid-morning the next day, Gerhardt stopped the wagon in front of his Bek Bulatschi house. He was relieved to see smoke coming out of the chimney; maybe Maria hadn't left for her parents' house in his absence. Heinrich pointed at horse tracks in the snow exiting the barn and heading out of the village. The front door opened, and a little girl peered out cautiously. Six-year-old Helen stared seriously for a moment, then recognition flushed over her face.

"Foda! Foda!"

Leaving the front door swinging behind her, she ran out of the house and leaped into Gerhardt's arms. Katherine ran out of the house, followed by Maria, wiping her hands on her apron. Maria's great aunt, the widow Dirks, and her daughter Annie watched from the doorway. Maria gave Gerhardt a rare public kiss on the cheek while the girls hugged his legs. She then gave Heinrich an unprecedented hug while the girls watched suspiciously from beside their father.

Gerhardt looked around and asked, "Mame, where're the boys?"

"Oh, the boys are in Kurman Kimiltschi. I send them there every day to see if you're one of the prisoners transferred from the courthouse to the train."

Gerhardt paled as he and Heinrich exchanged a knowing look. "What do they say that they've seen?"

"Oh, nothing much. They say every day the detainees are led out and put on a train. The adventure is good for them. They're always so quiet and worn out when they get back, they don't get into much mischief."

"Oh, Mame." He hugged her again while sadly locking eyes with his brother.

With the girls' dubious help, Gerhardt put the wagon away and unhitched Kukla. The girls helped feed and put her in her stall while Maria took Heinrich into the house for coffee. There was a lot of catching up to do. Gerhardt mulled just how much to tell his wife about the true state of violence taking place.

She was a very strong woman and would find out eventually. He mainly worried about how she was going to take it when she found out what the boys probably were really witnessing in Kurman Kimiltschi. George Becker, his brother, John, along with Peter Kroeker came down the street to greet Gerhardt and exchange manly gossip.

The group of adults gathered around the kitchen table, discussing current events. Gerhardt and Heinrich were told about the neighbors killed in front of the meeting hall. Then, the brothers described the killings they had seen firsthand and the atrocities they were told about by the Tartar partisans.

Maria was reaching for the pot of coffee on the stove as she listened to the story of the hangings in front of the Simferopol administrative building. She suddenly realized just what the boys were really witnessing on her errands. Shocked, she turned to look at the table and missed the pot, placing her hand on top of the hot stove. She jumped back, crying out in pain—less for her hand than for her boys.

The future looked grim for the country these families had called home for generations. They discussed the importance of keeping their stories straight and what that story should be. The whole village had seen Gerhardt conscripted so Maria's story to the Cheka would seem quite defensible.

Explaining Heinrich was somewhat more problematic since most of the village hadn't seen him before. The families who had moved into Crimea with Gerhardt's family had met his brother previously, but the rest of the village would be at a loss to his identity. Village inhabitants' loyalty to each other would be tested. Hoping the village would remain cohesive, the scene outside the meeting hall reminded everyone what would happen if they fell apart.

Hearing the barn door opening, Gerhardt stood and went through the passageway between the conjoined barn and house. Henry and Martin were leading their decrepit horse to its stall and saw the wagon in the back of the barn. Hearing a snort of recognition of her fellow barn mate, the surprised boys turned to see Kukla leaning over her stall gate. Excitedly, they turned and saw their father standing in the doorway. Martin ran to his father, and Henry dropped the reins to follow.

"Mind the horse, boys," Gerhardt reprimanded.

Henry quickly picked up the reins before the horse could get into mischief. Gerhardt put his arm around Martin's shoulders and walked over to help Henry put the gelding away. Having been raised in a family where chores came before all else, Martin opened the gate while Henry led the horse into the stall. Once in the stall, Martin closed the gate from the outside, and Henry scaled the railings and removed the horse's bridle.

Gerhardt stood back, admiring how the small boys had figured out how to handle a horse so much larger than themselves. He was proud they'd stepped up for the family. While helping his sons complete their chores, he brought up their trips to Kurman Kimiltschi.

"I'm sorry for what you had to witness in the city, boys."

Henry looked at his father. "You know?"

Gerhardt nodded. "I saw the same things where I was."

He put his arms around the boys' shoulders and led them to the door to the house. None of them were comfortable with any further verbal showing of feelings.

"Come, I have a surprise for you inside." In the house, Gerhardt motioned to the table. "You boys recognize your uncle Heinrich?"

The boys walked over and stood respectfully at Heinrich's side. He laughed and rubbed the heads of his two oldest nephews. "You both have turned into quite the young men. We could have used more like you where I was."

Martin beamed, but Henry wasn't so sure it was really a compliment. When Maria hugged her boys in front of the guests, they uncomfortably squirmed from her embrace. The boys were allowed to sit in the corner of the kitchen and listen to the adult conversation for the rest of the afternoon. Henry and Martin both knew it was a rare exception, and they felt honored.

Heinrich listened for a while about the news of mandatory registration. He and Gerhardt had missed the deadline. He worried about the difficulties of explaining his presence in the village to the Cheka. He made up his mind to immediately start working his way home. When he announced his plans, George Becker gently told him that his plans were unworkable.

"You can't leave Crimea. The Communists have sealed it off and aren't letting anyone out. They're using the typhus outbreak as an excuse to quarantine the area."

Heinrich and Gerhardt exchanged a surprised look. They hadn't heard of an outbreak. With the shared, unsanitary close proximity of soldiers, typhus was a fact of life in military campaigns. But they'd been busy ducking bullets and hadn't paid attention to the civilian population around them. The brothers had avoided contact with people as they worked their way home. When around people, they'd been so concerned with not being captured they had become tunnel visioned.

Heinrich mulled quietly while the conversation continued around him. The more he thought about it, the more convinced he became that he was a dangerous burden on his hosts. In his opinion, the sooner he left, the sooner he could reduce their jeopardy. The sooner he left, the sooner he could get back to caring for his own family.

His mind was set. "I've decided that I'll still try to get home. It's only about sixty miles to the Chongar Crossing."

Gerhardt looked at him. "What'll you do then? They have guards at all crossings."

"I'll get out the same way the Communists got in. I'll walk across the frozen Syvash. Once across, I'll simply go from one friendly village to another until I get back to Karpovka."

George Becker joined in, "It's less than twenty miles to Dzhankoi, a day's trip with a wagon. If you really want to go, we could get you that far under the ruse that we're going to market with crops."

John Becker added, "That's right. When our neighbors were murdered by the Cheka, we'd just completed a deal for some of my potatoes. They were killed before I could deliver. I don't feel right in keeping the potatoes, even though we could use them. Maybe this way, something good can come from the deal."

Heinrich wasn't convinced. "Won't the Cheka question why we're going that far instead of selling them in Kurman Kimiltschi?"

"Oh, that's easy," John replied. "The only money around here had been issued by the White Army. The Communists declared it to be of no value, so we barter. The only way to get recognized currency is to go to a bigger city like Dzhankoi."

CHAPTER TWENTY-SIX
ACROSS THE FROZEN SYVASH

The plan came together. Heinrich and John would leave for Dzhankoi with the potatoes. Heinrich would be introduced as John's employee. Gerhardt would stay in Bek Bulatschi; his presence would only complicate the story. The next day was spent preparing John's wagon. After the wagon was serviced, it was loaded with potatoes blanketed with straw to prevent freezing or bruising. Heinrich was issued a bag of toasted zwieback, dried fruit, and dried horse meat to tide him over in emergencies. Carefully crafted to conceal that it originated in Crimea, Maria gave him a letter to her parents.

At dawn, the men left for Dzhankoi. Heinrich's brother wished he'd stay longer but, in the end, his reasoning won out. The longer he waited, the tighter the Cheka's grip on Crimea became. During the trip, they were checked twice at checkpoints maintained by soldiers of the regular army. Accepting the ruse, the men were only checked lightly when the soldiers saw the wagon's cargo.

Arriving in Dzhankoi, John drove the wagon directly to a produce exchange. Due to the shortage of food in the city, John was able to negotiate top prices for the potatoes. To save money, the men forewent getting a room for the night. Instead, they stayed at a livery, sleeping in the back of the wagon on the straw.

Parting ways the next morning, John tried to hand Heinrich the money made from the sale. He wouldn't take it, claiming the Becker family could find better use of it. When John would not take no for an answer, Heinrich finally accepted a fourth just so John would go home, away from the danger of his association.

Pausing thoughtfully for a moment, Heinrich looked at his new friend. "You know, there is one thing you can do for me."

"What is it?"

"Where I'm going, it's foggy most of the time. I have to travel cross country and stay away from roads. Would you go to the mercantile and get me a compass?"

John walked down the block and purchased a compass, spending more than he wanted. But a cheap one wouldn't have done after he told the clerk it was for his son's birthday. Mulling over the purchase on the way back to the livery, he chastised himself for needing to spin a tale at all. It was the times. Everyone felt guilty and continually looked over their shoulders. After shaking hands, John drove off satisfied that he'd done a good deed, relieved the threat of Heinrich's presence was gone.

Heinrich made his way out of town toward the railroad track. Having been stationed in the area just before the White Army loss, he knew the area around the Taganash railway station and the Syvash crossing better than he did the Chongar crossing. Rather than walk the next twenty miles, Heinrich decided to risk riding a cargo train. To avoid patrols, he walked cross country for a few miles before approaching the tracks. He knew about a siding north of Dzhankoi where he used to pick up supplies for outlying posts. The train would have to slow there to safely clear the switches.

He spent the afternoon watching the siding from a safe distance in a small grove of trees. The tracks crossed a small, dry drainage canal on a low trestle just beyond the siding area. The canal and trestle solved this leg of his trip. Heinrich was sure the train would still be going slow enough near the trestle for him to come out of concealment and make it on board.

Heinrich knew the area around the Taganash rail station by heart. While delivering freight to the front, he'd visited most areas of concealment between the station and the Syvash crossing at one time or another for nature calls. He knew where the White Army had set up their defensive positions along the Syvash and how the land lay. Surely, he thought, the Communists couldn't be that different in their troop positioning philosophy than the Whites had been. After all, if they had any military education, the officers on both sides trained at the same places.

Having the luxury of plenty of provisions, he could afford not to be in a hurry. With no one waiting for him at some rendezvous point, he had plenty of time to exercise caution. Heinrich had to stifle an audible laugh. How did his pacifist Mennonite farmer past allow him to know such things? He knew how to handle a rifle. In his youth, he hunted for family sustenance. That was a detail he'd kept carefully hidden from the military. Killing an animal for food was a far cry from killing a human in anger.

At evening twilight, he took one more look around for patrols, then slipped into the dry canal under the trestle, hoping a cargo train would pass by during the early evening. Because of Cheka guards, a passenger train wouldn't be acceptable. If a train came by too late, it wouldn't get to Taganash while it was still dark. Getting off the train undetected was just as vital as getting on unnoticed. Luckily, the night was going to be dark. It was an overcast evening and, with the new moon due on December 10, it was barely a sliver now.

His luck held when a train pulling empty coal cars slowed two hours after dark. He made it out of hiding and onto the train at the mid-train point, happy he'd refined his skill at boarding trains unseen. He managed to make it onto the train far enough back of the engine and far enough ahead of the possible guard car at the back to remain undetected. The only drawback, he thought, was how he managed to only get into empty coal cars when he was aboard a train.

Only about a two-hour trip to Taganash, Heinrich didn't bother sitting down in the car. Kneeling slightly to get out of the cold winter wind, he continually peered over the side of the car, looking for signs of danger. The trip went uneventfully until he neared the station. There were vehicle lights along the tracks. He'd have to get off sooner than planned, and the train would not be going as slowly as he'd wished.

Scrambling over the side of the car, he hung on the ladder with one hand while holding his satchel with the other, waiting for a chance to jump. It wasn't an optimal spot but, getting too close to the lights, he twisted the ankle slightly on his already bad leg. Overriding the pain, he rolled into the brush along the track before the end of the train passed. From behind a bush, he looked after the train.

His instinct was correct. The vehicles pulled onto a frontage road and followed the train into the station with their lights shining on the back of the cars. As the train slowed, a couple of figures jumped off and ran. Unfortunately for the running figures, the truck lights caught their every movement. Shots rang out. Heinrich was shaken. He hadn't seen other men getting on the train, and he hadn't anticipated a welcoming party that far from the station. The Cheka was intent on making sure no one escaped Crimea.

It was still before midnight when he jumped from the train. Taking advantage of the remaining dark night, he headed west, away from the tracks. It was so dark, he didn't bother walking in recesses. Instead, he limped along, following higher ground where the wind had blown away the snow, hoping he could keep his footprints to a minimum on the frozen ground.

After he'd traversed about a half mile, he saw the headlights going back along the tracks. Cheka agents were looking for anyone else who may have been on the train. Heinrich crouched until the lights passed. He was far out of their range, but with his confidence shaken, his crouching was almost instinctive.

At the salt lake west of Taganash, he turned north, fenced in between the shallow lake and the heavily patrolled railroad. He was glad the mining of salt in the lake still appeared to be shut down after the recent military activity. Making good time, he walked north along the lake, leaving no footprints on the bare and hard service roads. After being surprised by the lights along the tracks, Heinrich tried to ensure he was always within fast limping distance of concealment.

He snorted to himself. Concealment was overstating any nearby hiding place. In the salt flats along the shoreline, there were only some reeds. Portions of abandoned cofferdams used to mine salt remained in the water. He knew he'd have to find a hiding spot before daylight. Without trees, the land was just too flat. In fact, he could still see the lights from the train tracks. Heinrich was relieved when he arrived at the Syvash shoreline. With the gimp slowing him down, it was only about five miles from where he'd left the tracks.

Heinrich knew every gun placement that the White Army had abandoned along the shoreline. He turned west along the narrow spit dividing the Syvash from the marsh he'd been following. There was a fairly large emplacement near the outlet of the lake where the ground was normally too soft to approach with vehicles. Supplies usually had to be carried in by hand for the last hundred yards or so. Unfortunately, the ground was now frozen hard.

A dense fog formed over the Syvash. Morning fog was common during the time Heinrich had spent near there. He'd hoped the fog would come in and help hide him. The spit was so narrow, it made the emplacement almost impossible to miss. With an abundance of caution, he approached quietly. A lack of diligence had almost got him caught back at the station.

Unable to see signs of recent foot traffic as he neared the emplacement, he paused often to listen for unusual sounds. The occasional splashing of migratory birds resting along the shoreline momentarily stopped him while he looked around. Full daylight illuminated the fog when he slid into the emplacement.

It wasn't much more than an above ground foxhole, built with sandbags and a few timbers. Heinrich turned over a couple of the sandbags to have something not frost-coated to sit on. Curling up in the corner, he tried to get some rest. The fog would probably last until midday and he'd be able to hear approaching patrols. For the moment, he was safe.

Early afternoon when the fog lifted, Heinrich watched the trestle in the distance. There was far too much activity alongside the tracks for his comfort. Once, he caught a glint from another emplacement halfway between the tracks and his position. He quickly ducked back below the top of the sandbags. The emplacement was manned, and the glint was from binoculars. He'd been in the same site and had used one of the soldier's binoculars to look across the Syvash before the White Army's collapse. Now, soldiers weren't looking across the water for invaders, they were looking along the shoreline and inland for potential escapees.

Deciding that getting to the tracks and crossing by train was very improbable, he crawled to the other side of his hiding spot and examined the shoreline to his northwest. The narrowest spot where he could cross the Syvash was about ten miles away. There was no cover in that direction in case he ran into patrols. Basically, he was frozen in position.

Directly in front of him, Heinrich knew, was the widest spot for him to attempt a crossing. He guessed it was about seven miles. The distance didn't bother him too much because he knew there was a long sandbar-like island in the middle which covered more than half of the distance. He would only have to wade through the muck for a short distance on both ends.

It would be cold and wet. He reasoned that if the Communists could do it while being shot at, he could do it while sneaking. Heinrich saw old footprints frozen in the muck, leftovers from when the Red Army crossed a month before.

With the night bringing a new moon and probably foggy, he could get easily misdirected. Now appreciating John buying the compass for him, he took many readings with it to etch the vectors of travel into his mind. Settling in, he waited for dark.

Heinrich looked at his watch. It was an hour after dark. Even though it was almost the winter solstice, which meant a long night, he didn't want to wait too long. He didn't know how fast he could move without making excessive noise, and he definitely didn't want to get caught away from shore in the daylight. With a low fog setting in, and stiff from crouching behind the sandbags all day in below freezing temperatures, he slid over the sandbags and set out across the Syvash.

Soldiers' voices, manning the lookout post, resonated through the cold night air. Hearing their flatware on metal plates while eating supper urged Heinrich onward. He soon perfected a gait which made the least noise in the frozen mud and still allowed him to move along at a brisk pace. He heard a train crossing to his right, but the fog was so dense the train's light couldn't penetrate.

Barely able to see his feet in the blackness, he tripped and fell, making a loud grunt. Scrambling back into a crouching position, Heinrich listened for sounds of alarm. He heard nothing but the normal activity around the railroad in the distance. While wiping the mud from his coat, he searched for what he'd tripped on.

His hand touched what he thought was a branch. Turning to see what kind of a log could possibly be out here in the middle of a salt swamp, he found himself staring into the vacant, mud-caked eyes of a frozen White Army officer's corpse. A quick check of the body revealed an exit wound in the man's chest.

Assuming the officer was shot trying to cross the Syvash, Heinrich shook his head. The body had just been left where it fell, without a proper burial, stripped of any valuables. Even though he felt guilty, he couldn't do anything for the man either. Back to his own needs, he checked himself over and didn't seem to have lost anything. Taking a compass bearing, he resumed traversing the tidal expanse.

Seemingly, the crossing was taking forever, and Heinrich worried he'd missed the island. Finally making it to the island's shoreline, he looked at his watch. He'd actually made good time. Sitting down, he pulled some food out of his pack for a snack. Shots rang out in the dark. Heinrich jumped even though the shots were far away. Unable to tell for sure which direction in the dark, he assumed they came from near the station.

After eating, he stood up and adjusted his compass to take him a few more degrees to the west. The spit paralleled the Chongar Peninsula with a bay in between them. The closest point between the two was where the peninsula hooked around the spit to the northwest. He'd heard somewhere that the area was being considered for a wildlife refuge. To him, it would normally be just a useless piece of sand and swamp. At this particular moment, it was an excellent highway to freedom.

The water crossing at the northern end of the spit, only about two thirds the length of the one he'd already made, was even easier due to a string of short islands. Since the tide was coming back in, the shorter distance was helpful. Through thinning fog on his right, he saw the lights from a couple of villages as residents rose to do their morning chores. Nothing but darkness lay ahead of him. Heinrich looked at his watch. It was about an hour before morning twilight.

He walked north into an area of low-lying brush to hide in for the day. Breaking off branches, he made a minimal mat to keep him off of the ground while resting. He removed his boots to dry and put on a spare pair of dry socks. Not having slept much for two days, Heinrich curled up and blacked out.

Barking dogs woke him late in the morning. Fearing a patrol, he carefully peered up over the edge of the brush. Instead, he saw a rifle-carrying farmer surveying his land. He considered the farmer only marginally less of a threat. He wouldn't be shot on sight, but the farmer could inform the authorities. Once reported, the Cheka wouldn't rest until he was hunted down. The dogs jumped a deer and chased it across the field with the man close behind.

Taking the opportunity, Heinrich scrutinized the area better. If he had reckoned correctly, the railroad should now be about seven to eight miles east of where he was. Permeated with reed-filled marshes on the Syvash side, there were farm plots and a couple of small villages on the railroad side. He decided to travel during daytime light through the unfamiliar terrain. The marshy area appeared to have enough vegetative cover to keep him out of sight of the villages. He soon felt justified.

An inlet from the Syvash fed a large swamp to his right and blocked his path. If he had walked into the area in the dark, he would have had to backtrack and feel his way around the swamp. Instead, he picked his way across the shallow inlet, conserving many miles of walking. Even though walking in the open was risky, he made good time across the frozen fields. As a farmer himself, he couldn't see a reason the locals would be in their fields this late on a December day.

With dusk approaching, Heinrich found himself on a long outcropping of land with the Syvash on his left side and a bay on his right.

The bay was a frozen marsh just like the one he had walked across to get out of Crimea. He didn't want to cross it in the waning daylight, and he didn't want to waste time waiting. Letting out an audible sigh, he turned to walk around the bay.

It was now a total new moon, and there weren't many landmarks available as he rounded the end of the bay in complete darkness. Heinrich checked his compass and tried to stay on course. From what he'd seen in the waning daylight, the shoreline went in a northeasterly direction. Hearing a passing train, he guessed it was about five miles away. That meant the railroad was also generally headed northeasterly.

Crushed when yet another body of water blocked his path, Heinrich stood on a point of land. With the bay he'd just walked around on his left, the swamp in front of him appeared about a half mile wide. To his right, another salt swamp looked at least three times farther across than what was in front of him. Unable to see how far behind it extended, he checked his watch—a little after midnight— not enough darkness left to walk around another bay.

Passing on the other side of his latest roadblock, a northbound passenger train engine's light's reflection on the frozen swamp reinforced his fears. The bay extended at least two miles behind him and probably six miles in front of him. Even worse, the tracks looked to be almost on the shoreline, leaving him no room to maneuver if he made it to that side. He was just about to sit down in despair when a glint from the disappearing train showed a shadow in front of him.

Barely believing his luck, he made out the outline of a still-in-use salt mine cofferdam. He carefully made his way onto the dam, watching for guards. Even though worn out from a long day of walking and disappointing detours, Heinrich made good time crossing the dam. Slowing slightly near the far side, he couldn't see or hear workers. Exhausted, he walked past the mine's infrastructure and onto a road heading north.

Heinrich forced himself to push through the pain of his sprained ankle, bad leg, and now sore, wet feet. He managed to make it another half mile before seeing the lights of a village in the distance. Limping into another dry irrigation canal, he crawled under the dam gate's catwalk and pushed as far out of sight as he could.

Once again, he mulled over his luck and choices. He'd only been able to hitch rides in coal cars, and now it seemed that his daytime hiding options were heavily tilted toward canals. He thought, *I really need to expand my repertoire.* Taking off his boots and hanging them under the catwalk to dry, he didn't have the strength to eat.

A passing salt company truck woke Heinrich. Stretching his legs out, he gnawed on toasted zwieback for breakfast. The land was still too open, and he was still too close to Crimea to travel in daylight. Able to see changing terrain, he was coming out of the salt swamplands and into dryer farmland. Farms meant orchards and more irrigation ditches to hide in during daylight and roads to walk on at night.

Tonight, he'd hike toward Melitopol, which he estimated was about seventy miles. A few days' walk would get him near enough he could afford a train ticket. And, more importantly, far enough from Crimea he'd feel safe enough to buy one. He had relatives near Melitopol in the Molotschna colony. He'd be as safe as anyone could be in the aftermath of the Revolution. Today, Heinrich would nap and rest his feet.

CHAPTER TWENTY-SEVEN
COLLECTIVIZATION

Gerhardt watched his brother and John Becker disappear into the winter fog, then turned back into the barn to do chores. There was no cow to milk, no pigs to feed, and few chickens to give eggs. His family only owned the two horses. Stores in the pantry were slim. It wouldn't be long before his family would run out of food. Other families in the group offered help, but they weren't in much better shape.

Maria's baby was due in a few weeks, and they were almost out of money. Gerhardt heard of a minor opportunity which might become available. The estate of the couple who'd been executed had been collectivized. Local authorities were looking for someone who was literate to supervise the workers. Since his family's outlook was the most tenuous, he applied.

He moved his family from Bek Bulatschi into the foreman's cottage of the estate-turned-collective-farm just before Palm Sunday. They took Maria's great aunt and her daughter, Anna Dirks, with them.

Even though her due date was any day, the government's collective representative designated Maria as the cook. When her day finally came, Anna and her elderly mother helped with the delivery. Gerhardt now had a fifth child—Frieda. With the Dirks' help, Maria's duties in the collective were lightened.

When the Schroeders deemed it safe enough for their daughter to teach again, the village's informal school started back up. Gerhardt, Martin, and now Helen commuted from the collective to school on the old gelding.

During spring planting, Gerhardt could see that interference from government agents was going to be problematic. A young, wire-rim-spectacle-wearing agent came with documents dictating what crops were needed and how much of each to plant. When Gerhardt shook his hand, there were no calluses.

Looking over the plan, he asked the agent, "Who came up with this?"

"This is the latest science we've developed at the university. We found this is the best way to farm at our test plots near Petrograd."

"Ahh . . .I see. Umm, Petrograd is almost two thousand miles north of here, and growing conditions are different," Gerhardt said. "Besides, the fields where winter wheat was planted last fall can't be changed."

The agent insisted, "The amount of land committed to wheat needs to be modified to reflect your quota of barley and oats."

Gerhardt did his best to not scoff at the inexperienced youth. It was obvious the agent had never worked on an actual farm. Nevertheless, the boy didn't get his position from achievement. Gerhardt assumed the agent had been a fervent party worker during the Revolution and had high-level party contacts. He mulled over the most diplomatic way to express how this plan had an identical odor to the stall floors in the livery before the workers cleaned them.

"Da."

"Excellent, I knew you'd agree. This is the future of farming in the new republic."

Gerhardt watched the young man get into his car and drive off. Going back into the barn to resume preparing the machinery for spring, he was sure what the agent said was true. This *was* how farming was going to be in future Russia. He wondered just how those like him would fit in with the coming times.

Summer came, but conditions didn't improve. The drought, which started the previous year, settled in for another. Crops withered in the fields. Fruit on the trees was sparse. The young agent came by weekly to check on the farm's progress. In early July, he handed Gerhardt an invoice for the percentage of the expected crop yield to be sent to the government. It took only a perfunctory glance at the document for Gerhardt to realize it was complete fantasy with absolutely no consideration of actual conditions.

"There's no way the farm can yield this much grain during this drought. If we send this much to the State, there won't be anything left for workers to eat or seed to plant next spring. I'm not even sure the gross harvest will be able to meet the government's projected share."

The agent brusquely answered, "That's how much our planning models have projected for a farm of this size, so that's how much we will produce."

Gerhardt watched the car disappear into the summer dust. There was barely enough food to feed the farm's families now. If the total harvest was confiscated, they and the livestock would starve during the upcoming winter. If the seed stock was depleted, there'd be nothing to plant for the next year, and matters would be even worse, regardless of weather. The situation in Crimea was becoming untenable.

Late July, a traveling Tartar trader pulled into the farmyard with a large wagon behind his four-horse team. Henry and Martin abandoned their chores to admire the pony and large camel tied behind the wagon. Since their sickly bay gelding had finally died from old age and stress from the drought, the pony behind the wagon really interested them. The boys' pleadings fell on deaf ears. Gerhardt was focused on the camel, far superior draft animals in poor conditions than horses.

The boys were crushed when the trader left with Kukla behind the wagon, leaving a camel in the barn. Maria watched the transaction from the cottage door. She stepped aside as Gerhardt came in for a cup of coffee and followed him into the kitchen. Quietly pouring him a cup, she stood behind him for a few minutes, watching him stare into the liquid.

Finally becoming impatient, waiting for an explanation, she asked, "And? What was that? Kukla was a good horse."

"We have to leave," he answered.

Frieda started to cry. Maria picked her up and sat across the table from Gerhardt to feed the baby. "What do you mean, we have to leave?"

"The crops are failing. The government is going to take whatever harvest that we do get. There's no future here."

"The camel?" she questioned.

"The camel can pull more than a horse. We need it to take all of our possessions with us."

"Where will we go?"

"I don't know yet. West. The Balkans or Germany? I'd like to go back to America. It was nice there. All I know is we cannot stay in Russia."

Maria nodded. She rarely let Gerhardt make such a major decision without giving her input—a lot of input. "I'll start gathering the household together."

"Thank you. I fear we're about to go on another trek that'll be even worse than when we came here from Franzthal. We'll need to be well prepared."

Quietly, with the help of her cousin and great aunt, Maria set about getting the household ready. Gerhardt met with George Becker, John Becker, and Peter Kroeker. There was consensus. The situation had degraded so far that they had no choice but to leave if they wanted to survive. However, Gerhardt was the only one who thought they could get out through the Balkans.

John pointed out, "It's almost impossible to get through the Isthmus of Perekop without attracting the Cheka's attention. The trip would take months and stretch into winter if we left this late in the year."

George agreed, "Maybe a better choice would be if we went to Yalta and took a ship to Turkey. There, we'd be free of the Communist government and can go wherever the best prospects are."

Making it to Turkey was the lynchpin of the plan. Gerhardt returned home. The families quietly started selling off everything that couldn't be easily carried with them. Traveling finances were more important now than trinkets with emotional attachment. When at all possible, the items were bartered in exchange for gold. They had already felt the sting of paper money being rendered useless by the capriciousness of a government. The families who had crops took the risk of not storing any of their harvest for winter consumption. There was no fallback position. Everything was sold.

Just as Gerhardt feared, the collective's total harvest didn't even meet the quota the agent had mandated be turned over to the government. The agent strutted around the farm, demanding to know where the rest of the harvest was hidden. He accused Gerhardt of selling the crop on the black market. Since they sold all of their crops and had none to give the government for tax, the other families were also in jeopardy. Promising an investigation, the fuming agent got into his car.

Before he left to check on the other collectives, the agent turned to Gerhardt and said, "School is starting soon. It has been decided that it would be more efficient for the children to attend a government boarding school where they'll be properly educated. It'll give the parents more time to work for the good of the nation."

Stunned, Gerhardt watched the agent's car drive away. The government was blaming him for missing crops, and they also were going to take his children. He wasn't sure if the agent was telling the truth about the children or if he was simply using them for leverage to find the phantom crops. Gerhardt turned and walked into the cottage.

"Load the wagon. We leave tonight."

CHAPTER TWENTY-EIGHT
HALBSTADT

By Christmas 1920, Aganeta was pregnant with her first child. She had absorbed a lot of her oldest sister, Maria's, strong-willed drive. Being less than five foot tall, she learned to speak up or be overlooked. Aganeta made sure she was never overlooked.

Not having seen Maria and Gerhardt since they left for Crimea the previous spring, she missed her oldest sister's advice and company. Maria was unable to attend when Aganeta married Heinrich Unrau in March 1919. The Black Army had just killed Gerhardt's brother and sister-in-law. Travel was dangerous and very unadvisable. The front had moved through her present city of Halbstadt several times since then. Now, the area was in total Bolshevik control and in terror of the Cheka.

Late evening, she heard a knock on the door. Just in case it was the Cheka, it had become customary for the woman of the house to answer the door. When political police came to a house at night, they invariably wanted to detain the adult males. Aganeta cautiously peered out of the partially opened door. A gaunt man dressed in rags stood there.

"Can I help you?"

"Aganeta? It's me, Heinrich. Gerhardt's brother."

She stared into the man's face intently for a few moments. He was so dirty and thin but, behind an unkempt beard, she recognized

Maria's oldest brother-in-law. Looking behind him to make sure he was alone, she opened the door.

"Hurry, come in before someone sees you."

Aganeta introduced her husband and led their ragged guest into the kitchen. Heinrich immediately started wolfing down the ham slices and bread she put on the table. While interrogating him on her sister's whereabouts and condition, she put a kettle of water on the stove to warm. He took time between bites to discourage her from fawning over him too much.

"It's so late, coffee isn't really necessary."

"Coffee? No, this is bathwater," she replied.

Heinrich looked at his hostess blankly, then down at his frayed garb, still caked with swamp mud. He hadn't bathed since leaving Bek Bulatschi and had been sleeping in ditches, barns, and orchards for weeks. Aganeta's husband was maintaining a respectful distance across the room.

He broke into a broad grin. "Yes, I suppose that a bath might be in order."

After eating, he did his hosts a huge favor and retreated behind a curtain to scrub his journey off. Aganeta washed his clothes and hung them over the stove to dry. Since he was considerably taller than her husband, she handed a blanket through the curtain for him to wear until his clothes dried. Making Heinrich a bed in front of the hearth, the conversation could continue in the morning.

The next day, while letting their guest sleep, Aganeta and her husband quietly discussed the situation over coffee in the kitchen. She'd always found Maria's brother-in-law quite a pleasant person and was ecstatic to receive news about her older sister.

However, with the country's changing political climate, anything arousing even the slightest suspicion from a neighbor could bring the Cheka to your door. Just your ethnicity might get you arrested if the officials were in the right mood. The couple decided that no matter what the danger was, they could not turn out someone in need.

Heinrich finally walked into the kitchen wrapped in his blanket and apologized sheepishly for sleeping so long. It just wasn't like him, but it was the first time he'd had a warm, dry place to sleep in a couple of weeks. Retrieving his dry clothes from behind the stove, he went into the other room to dress. She set a place at the table and started preparing breakfast. When he returned, Heinrich profusely thanked Aganeta and her husband for taking him in.

"Somehow, I'll find a way to return the favor. When we get a chance, I have to introduce you to my wife. We were married a year ago." He offered up one caveat, "Although, we'll have to find a way to talk to each other without using names. My wife's name is Aganetha Siemens."

Aganeta's husband laughed. "That *would* be a difficult conversation between four people with only two names to share."

"Yes, it would've been nice if our people hadn't been so frugal naming their children."

While Heinrich ate, the three caught up on what had been going on in the country. He filled them in on the atrocities he'd witnessed in Crimea. He told them that the previous growing season drought made it bleak for the farmers there and that next year was going to be a tough one without any livestock or draft animals. Crimea's future didn't look good.

Aganeta and her husband exchanged a knowing look. Her husband told Heinrich of events in Halbstadt, "The conditions in Ukraine proper aren't much better than in Crimea. Drought's hit here hard also. The Revolution has depleted most of the livestock. Although the atrocities haven't been so openly committed, they're still taking place. Just last year," he continued, "the local government's head official was a lowly print shop typesetter. Because of his Communist Party affiliation, he's now in charge. The newfound power has gone to his head, and he's become dictatorial and cruel. He's not even native to the area. He's Latvian and came to Halbstadt looking for work."

Aganeta added, "Just a couple of weeks ago, some men from our church were detained and interrogated. One of the group, Clayton Kratz, was an American aid worker in his early twenties trying to set up a relief operation in the region. They were kept for a night and let loose. But after two weeks, the aid worker and his host were called back in. They were roughed up, and the local man released. Clayton hasn't been heard of since."

Heinrich knew that, even though he was closer to home, he was still out of place, bringing possible danger to his hosts. He said, "I appreciate you letting me rest here, but I should be going."

They would hear none of it. Agneta's husband stood up and said, "I have an idea."

Grabbing his overcoat, he disappeared out the door. As Heinrich watched her husband leave, he remembered Maria's letter. Rummaging through his duffle, he handed it to her.

"I almost forgot. Maria sent this with me to give to her family. I'm sorry it's so crumpled, but it's had a tough journey."

Aganeta sat at the table reading the letter and daubing her eyes with a napkin while he quietly sipped coffee. When she finished, he tried to answer her questions on any details which couldn't be put in writing. Her husband came back a couple of hours later with a train ticket to Zhelannaya Station via Donetsk.

"Here," he said. "We got together at the church and bought you a ticket home. You should get through with no problem if you look like you belong."

Heinrich stared at the ticket. "I don't know how to accept such charity. It's more than I could have imagined."

"Don't think about it as charity," Aganeta added. "Someday you'll have the chance to return the favor."

"I have enough money left from Crimea. Let me pay you back for the ticket."

"No, you keep your money," Agateta's husband insisted. "You'll need it to survive when you get home."

The next morning, one of the men from the couple's church showed up with clothes more suitable for travel. The shirt sleeves were a little too short, and the trouser waistband was loose, but they were infinitely better than Heinrich's. The young couple took him to the station and watched the train leave. As they made their way home, a Cheka agent wearing a leather overcoat watched them from the shadows. The agent wrote some notes in his book then left for headquarters.

CHAPTER TWENTY-NINE
YALTA

Gerhardt rode one of the collective's draft horses to George Becker's house and told them he was leaving that night. The other three families weren't quite ready but would be in a few days. Drawing on the time he and Heinrich had spent hiding in the hills south of Simferopol, Gerhardt described a spot where his family would camp while they waited. The plan was agreed upon, and he left for home.

With the camel hitched to the wagon, the family, including Anna and her mother, left just after dark. With virtually no food to take with them, their rations had to be divided between nine people. It took three days for the wagon to make its way south of Simferopol. Everywhere the family looked, others were in the same shape. It had been a hard summer, and governmental degrees left little to live on. No one had any food they were willing to part with.

Camping halfway between Simferopol and Alushta, the other three families caught up with them in a couple of days. The caravan moved on through Alushta and down the coast to Yalta. There, the men discreetly searched for someone they could barter their livestock and wagons to in exchange for gold. Going to a public market, they walked amongst the crowd looking for someone who appeared honest enough to trade with but shady enough to conduct the type of transaction they needed.

Gerhardt spied a Tartar man standing off to the side of the market. He was sure the man was a member of the partisan band he'd shared a campsite with the previous winter. Looking at his companions, he said, "I think I see someone who we just might be able to negotiate with."

George replied, "Fine, let's go talk to him."

"I don't think that'd be wise. If it's the man I think it is, he's also in a delicate situation and probably won't talk to more than one of us."

"I see. In that case, you go, and we'll check on our chances of finding a ship."

"I'll see you back in camp."

Leaving his companions, Gerhardt slowly worked his way through the market toward the shadowy figure. Finally, he was able to saunter up beside the man and look like he was examining the same items displayed on the table in front of them.

"I see that you've decided to come down off of Chatyr-Dag," he said.

The startled man instantly reached inside of his coat for a weapon. Gerhardt barely had time to continue before his shirt would develope a bodily fluid leaking hole.

"I mean you no harm. We met last winter when you camped with me and my brother in a yew grove."

"I remember you." Looking around, still suspicious, the Tatar asked, "Where's your brother?"

"The last time I saw him, he was heading toward the mainland. I don't know if he made it, though."

"What do you want from me?"

"Well, if you remember, we both have, umm . . .similar issues with the authorities."

"Maybe we do, maybe we don't," the partisan said. "That still doesn't answer my question of what you want."

"I'll take that as a yes." Gerhardt smiled. "I have some merchandise your leader may be interested in. I'd like to propose a beneficial trade for both of us."

"I see. Are you alone?"

"Yes. I sent my companions away."

The man looked around the market. "Come with me."

He led Gerhardt down an alley then stopped just around the next corner. After waiting for a bit, he looked back to make sure they hadn't been followed. Satisfied, the partisan walked to a tea house in a less desirable part of town. Gerhardt recognized two men sitting at a table as more of the group from the mountain.

"Wait here." The Tartar went in the back for a minute then returned. "Come on."

Gerhardt was led into an office in the back where the partisan leader sat at a desk.

"What brings you here?" the leader asked.

"I'm glad I found you. I've realized that the outlook for my long-term health in Crimea has become tenuous."

The partisan grimly smiled. "You're not the only one."

"Yes, but now I fear the government has placed an asterisk beside my name and is actively searching for me," Gerhardt said.

"That's not a real good thing if one desires longevity. What can I do for you?"

"My companions and I have some livestock and wagons we'd like to barter for some universal currency."

"You still haven't disposed of those Don Rubles? I told you what they could be used for."

Gerhardt laughed. "They didn't get used for that particular purpose, but they made a fine fire starter."

The Tartar smiled. "What kind of livestock?"

Gerhardt did a quick mental tabulation. "One large, harness-broken camel, three teams of horses, and four utility wagons with canvases."

"That's quite a bit of trading stock. I'll see what I can do."

"Thank you."

"Where can I examine the merchandise?" the man asked.

Gerhardt described where his group was camped and made arrangements for a time and place to meet. They agreed on a general price range of money expected. The final negotiations would take place after the Tartar had examined the quality of the merchandise. Gerhardt left the café, and his original partisan contact led him back to the market.

The next day, a mediary showed up at the families' camp and checked their trading stock. When he was satisfied there were no disqualifying defects, and most importantly no prying eyes nearby, he left, returning shortly with the partisan leader. Hard bartering continued for an hour. Both sides had advantages and failings.

The families' animals and wagons were top quality but needed to be disposed of quickly. The Tartars had the gold but, because of the lack of quality steeds after the Revolution, they needed the horses badly. Each side recognized the equality of their positions, and a fair trade was finally made. Disliking intruders in their land, the Tartars were glad to barter so a few German settlers would leave. The partisans drove the wagons away, leaving the families camped in an abandoned industrial area near the port.

Changing their focus, the men searched for a ship to take them away. They'd only been in Yalta a few days when a goateed German man with thinning hair discreetly sought them out. He nervously walked into their encampment, carefully looking around for inquisitive eyes. It was obvious he was also on the run.

"Are you the group from Bek Bulatschi?"

Gerhardt looked at him suspiciously. "Why do you want to know?"

"I heard through some friends that you're trying to get out of Crimea."

"That may or may not be true. Who are you to ask?"

"You people look like you might be in the same situation that I'm in, so I'm going to trust you. My name is Abraham Kroeker."

George Becker spoke up. "I've heard of you. Aren't you the newspaper publisher from Halbstadt? I've read your paper, Friedensstimme."

"Yes, that's me," the stranger answered.

John Becker entered into the conversation. "What can we do for you?"

"The government has become unhappy with my editorial opinions. They've been trying to arrest me for months."

"How've you been avoiding them?" George asked.

"I've been living in the shadows, going from one friendly enclave to another. I never stay in one spot for more than a few days. I don't want to place my protectors in danger."

"So, what can we do for you?" Gerhardt asked.

"I heard you're trying to get out of the country. If you'd let me, I'd like to join you."

"Won't your presence bring even more scrutiny upon us?" Gerhardt wasn't sure if he liked the guy.

Abraham started to tear up. "I wouldn't ask, but the Cheka have arrested my son and are trying to get him to tell them where I am. If I get it out of the country and make my whereabouts known, maybe they'll let him go. I fear for his wellbeing with the tactics they're using now."

"We've been out of the loop for a little while; what are they doing now?" John asked.

"My contacts have told me that they don't want to waste ammunition, so Rosalia Zemlyachka had an old barge loaded with tied up White Army prisoners and sank it in the Black Sea to drown all the men."

"That's horrible," John said.

Abraham continued, "The woman seems to have no limit to her depravity. I was told she had two officers at a time tied to opposite sides of a plank and then fed them slowly into a furnace, burning them alive. I don't want my son to have such a fate."

"Yes. I've heard that there have been even worse atrocities, but they are too fantastic for us to believe a human could do such things," George said.

Gerhardt softened a little. "Believe it. I don't think there's any depraved act these people aren't capable of."

The group looked at each other and thought for a few minutes. Agreeing that he couldn't really put them in much more peril than they were already in, they invited him to join their expedition. Once it was decided, Abraham Kroeker left to find a hiding spot elsewhere. He didn't want to bring more attention to the group than they were already receiving.

The families were running out of food, and they were afraid to use the gold to buy more. All they had was flour and water. Maria's milk dried up from malnutrition, and little Frieda was getting very frail, barely having the strength to cry. She sent Henry and Martin to find a goat or a cow to steal milk from. The boys understood the importance of their task. They hadn't swallowed food in days.

Their mother insisted, "Chew each bite until it just isn't in your mouth anymore."

The boys set out to find Frieda some milk. A cow couldn't be found anywhere in the area—all had long ago been eaten. They had no luck finding a goat either. Despondent over letting his little sister down, Henry spotted an old mare in a field with a foal by her side.

Martin questioned, "Can Frieda drink horse milk?"

Henry insisted, "It's better than returning to camp with nothing."

Too old to put up much of a chase, Henry held the mare's head while Martin crawled underneath and got as much milk in a pail that she was capable of giving. On their way back to camp, the boys took great care not to spill a single drop of the precious fluid. Surprisingly, Frieda drank the milk. The boys went back the next day and every day until they left Yalta.

Russian ships came and went. The group didn't trust Russian captains out of fear of being turned in. Finally, when a Turkish passenger ship pulled into the port, the men approached the captain. At first, he refused to allow them to board because they had no exit paperwork. The sight of gold coin changed his mind. The ship was scheduled to leave in two days so Abraham Kroeker was notified to get ready. The day before the scheduled departure, Cheka agents boarded and searched the ship. They put the captain in a car and disappeared.

The men took turns watching the ship. Spotting the first mate, they asked when it would be okay to board for departure. He replied that the ship would probably cast off the next day when the captain returned—if he was released. When the captain finally returned late afternoon the next day, Gerhardt caught his eye as he walked past. The man discreetly signaled to wait. Gerhardt waited in the shadows as the captain paced the deck, looking down the wharf. After dark, the Turkish captain came down the gangplank and met him in the shadows.

"It's too dangerous with the Cheka watching. You cannot board my ship."

"We've already paid you a deposit in gold."

"That's part of the problem. If I get caught with your gold, we'll all go to prison." Reaching into an inside pocket of his woolen bridge coat, he pulled out a sack of coins. "Here's your deposit back. If they'd found it on the ship, I'd still be in jail. Now, get out of here before someone sees you."

The captain cautiously looked around and slipped back onto the ship. Gerhardt worked his way through the shadows back to camp.

The mood in the camp was dour. Abraham came to check on the situation, and the group discussed their options.

"When do we board the ship?" Abraham asked.

Gerhardt, still depressed, answered, "We don't. The captain's too nervous."

"What are we going to do now?" Abraham pressed.

Peter Kroeker spoke up. "We can't go back to Bek Bulatschi. We don't have any seed to plant for next year, and we can't get through the year without crops."

John Becker added, "My family doesn't have enough to get through the winter."

"I don't think I can come out of the shadows here in Yalta. The government Collective agent has probably reported me as a thief for the missing crops," Gerhardt lamented. "The Cheka is undoubtedly looking for me."

Abraham sympathized, "I'll be sent to prison if they catch me."

George Becker mulled aloud, "We're pinned up against the Black Sea. It's too bad the only way we can escape Russia is through Turkey."

No one had permission to leave for Turkey, and there was no way to get consent. Getting to Turkey was impossible. Gerhardt stared at the ground for a while, listening to the group. Henry and Martin sat behind him during the conference.

Bored, Martin leaned over to his brother and whispered, "Look out at the water, Henry. Doesn't it look like the Caspian's water when we went for a picnic back in Sulak?"

Gerhardt sat upright and stared back at the boys for a moment. Jumping up, he rummaged through his family's possessions furiously while the group watched. After a few moments, he straightened up with a folder of papers and returned, beaming.

"I have it! We still own land in the Terek colony."

George Becker looked at him and said, "So?"

"The Terek colony is in the Caucuses. To get to the Caucuses from here, we'd have to take a ship to Batumi and then take a train to the Caspian Sea."

"Again, so?"

"We go there by ship, claiming that we're returning to the Terek colony to farm. Batumi is about fifteen miles from the new Georgian border with Turkey. Once there, we simply walk to Turkey. There, we can catch a ship in Trabazon or take a train to Constantinople."

George added, "The last that I've heard, Georgia has declared itself to be an independent country so the Cheka shouldn't be so omnipresent."

The group looked back and forth. Peter Kroeker finally said, "I believe it'd work!"

Abraham Kroeker spoke sadly, "I'm afraid that I cannot go with you. I've run out of funds and cannot pay the fare."

The Beckers talked for a few minutes, then George said, "It's okay. My brother and I will share in your fare."

The group broke up and settled in for the night. They hoped their meager supplies would hold out until a ship heading for Batumi came into port.

The Beckers and Peter Kroeker went to the administration building and received travel releases to Batumi. Concerned about the Cheka, Gerhardt decided not to get the documents. He didn't want to take the chance his name was on a list. He hoped his property ownership documents would get him through a shallow check at the port. Abraham Kroeker would have to be spirited onto a ship. The fact that some of the group had dubious documentation meant a passenger ship would probably be out of the question. A cargo ship with some passenger capability would have to do.

A few more days passed with Gerhardt hiding during the day. Finally, a decrepit paddle wheel steamer pulled into the port. He caught the captain on the edge of the wharf.

"Where are you going next?"

"Oh, we're heading for Feodosiya."

"And then?" Gerhardt pushed.

"We're going to work our way around the Black Sea. We're scheduled to stop at Novorossiysk, Sochi, and then Batumi. At Batumi, my holds should be empty and I'll go back to Rostov-on-Don to fill them again."

"Do you have room for some passengers?"

"A few. How many are we talking about?" the captain asked.

Gerhardt did a quick mental count. "Ten adults and, ummm…twenty-two children."

"Thirty-two? That's a lot of people to wedge onto my ship." The captain looked around the wharf carefully. "I assume you're asking me because your options are limited."

Gerhardt reached into his pocket and pulled out a few gold coins. "Discretion is always important."

Somewhat hesitant with the amount of people he'd have to pile into his limited number of berths, the sight of gold coins reduced the captain's reluctance considerably. His desire for profit overriding his fear of the Cheka, the captain said, "The ship departs at midnight tomorrow night. The passengers had better be ready."

Boarding the ship just before the hawsers were cast off of the pier bollards, every adult or child getting on the ship carried or drug as much of their family's possessions as they could. What couldn't be carried was left behind for the increasing multitude of scavengers to divide. The group doubled and tripled up in the available berths not already occupied by other pilgrims.

Maria settled the girls in while Gerhardt took Henry and Martin up to the railing as the Yalta harbor slowly faded into the moonless but star-encrusted night. He watched the paddle wheel blades articulating on their trunnions. He never grew tired of watching water wheels work, either as power for a mill or churning through water propelling a boat. He let the tired boys enjoy the sight as long as they could stay awake. It was too cramped below deck for the excited boys if they had even a tiny bit of energy left.

It was September 1, 1921. Watching the Crimean coast disappear, Gerhardt and the boys didn't know they'd never set foot in Russia again.

CHAPTER THIRTY

BATUMI

The trip to Batumi took five days with little food. Pausing at Feodosiya just long enough to exchange passengers, the ship worked its way down the Caucasus shoreline. Judging by overheard conversations, the group had to be careful when around the rest of the crew and passengers. There wasn't much sympathy for anyone without Communist leanings.

Disembarking in Batumi, they quickly discovered that the sentiments among the city's residents were the antithesis of the ship's crew and other passengers. Georgia had declared itself independent during the Revolution. Under the guise of protecting Communist sympathizers, Russia retaliated and invaded in February 1921. Turkey then attacked Georgia's disputed southern border and occupied Batumi.

Russian-backed Georgian troops retook Batumi in March. Britain and France abandoned Georgia's government which fled into exile on an Italian ship, protected by French warships. Russia assumed control of their puppet Georgian army the day after it drove Turkey out of Batumi. Battles were still being fought south of the city.

"What do we do now?" John asked. "We can't go south, there's still fighting between here and the border."

"We could take a train to Baku, Azerbaijan," his brother George answered. "It's on the Caspian Sea. Then we could take a ship to Iran."

"I don't know about that. Crossing the mountains is pretty dangerous with the guerrilla attacks. Maria and the kids barely escaped the guerrillas when they fled Terek," Gerhardt said. "Besides, in Baku we'd have the same problem getting visas as in Yalta."

They decided to stay in Batumi and try to board a ship to Constantinople. Not allowed to leave the general port area, the immigrants tried to stay out of the almost constant rain in an open-sided lean-to. Out of food, the men tried to exchange their remaining gold for spendable money. Running into one bureaucratic roadblock after another, their misery drug on.

It became apparent there wasn't an embassy in Batumi which would issue them visas. They'd have to go to Tiflis to get proper paperwork. Abraham and Peter Kroeker left on a train to check out how to get the proper documentation. Gerhardt and the Becker brothers took a separate train. In Tiflis, they discovered it would take quite a while for the paperwork to be processed, if at all. Except for Abraham Kroeker, who stayed hidden in Tiflis, the men returned to Batumi.

While they were gone, the Russian government started exerting more control of the country, which meant the Cheka. With their money reserves dwindling again, they began selling personal possessions. Gerhardt sold his silver cigarette holder and watch. Maria sacrificed her prized fur coat and her mother's pearls. Whenever a woman's item was sold, she'd go along so it wouldn't look like it was stolen.

When Maria and the girls accompanied the men into the city, they were stopped. A policeman said, "Papers please." As George pulled out his documents, a gold coin fell to the ground.

"Get your hands up!" Immediately pointing his gun at the refugees, the policeman's sergeant demanded, "Search them." Two more gold coins were found. "You're under arrest."

Taken in for interrogation, the men were placed in a row of twenty-person cells filled with suspects while Maria waited on a bench. As the day crawled into nighttime, Gerhardt worried about his frail wife and sickly baby Frieda outside in the weather. Because of his diminutive size, he'd learned a few life lessons. Sometimes, it was best to fluff up like a Bantam rooster and bluff his way through.

He started calling loudly, "Guard! Guard!"

"What do you think you're doing, Gerhardt? Keep quiet, and keep your head down."

He looked back at his companions, then shouted again, "Guard! Guard!"

A peevish guard came to the cell. "Shut up, and sit down."

"No, I need to talk to the commanding officer."

"Are you nuts? Sit down and shut up!" George said.

The other cell occupants tried to look like they had no idea who this maniac was.

"I need to talk to the commanding officer," Gerhardt insisted.

The guard gave in and opened the door. "It's your funeral. Might as well be now."

He was led out of the basement incarceration area and up two flights of stairs. At the end of a long hall, the guard opened a door with an opaque glass insert and shoved Gerhardt inside. Sitting behind the desk, a young Jewish officer leaned back in his chair, pulled out a German Luger pistol, and pointed it at Gerhardt.

Speaking in an odd guttural manner interrupted by random vibrato squeaks, he said, "So, you're the troublemaker with the death wish."

Gerhardt summoned up every bit of inner Bantam rooster he could muster and, with a smile, replied, "You wouldn't want to ruin a good suit, would you?"

Taken aback, the officer stared for a moment then sat the pistol down, still pointing at Gerhardt. "What do you want?"

"You can shoot me if you want, but my wife and children are outside in the rain. Let me find them shelter first then I'll come back."

Completely surprised by Gerhardt, the officer had never interviewed a prisoner with such audacity. They usually groveled for mercy or denied everything. He leaned forward and examined the men's files. Silently, the officer filled out a charging document and held it out.

"You and your companions can go take care of your families. Return here tomorrow at nine o'clock for your court hearing."

Gerhardt almost couldn't breathe until they were blocks from the courthouse. Then, his knees became so wobbly, he could barely walk the rest of the way to the waterfront.

Leaving the camp the next morning, the men put on brave faces, reassuring their families they'd be back soon. They walked to the courthouse, convinced they wouldn't see their families again. In the courtroom, all of the court officials were drunkenly passed out on the benches. Confused, the men stood around, waiting. Gerhardt approached the bored Georgian guard and asked him what they should do.

The guard pointed at the bottom of the form. "See that line right there?"

Gerhardt nodded.

"Write 'dismissed' on that line and leave. No one will remember when they wake up tomorrow."

Gerhardt did as the guard instructed and placed the document in the wooden tray on the magistrate's desk. In disbelief, the men left the courthouse and hurried back to the port area.

On October 13, 1921, the Turkish Empire and Russia finally signed the Treaty of Kars. The families could try to walk out across northern Turkey in the winter with no food, transportation, or money. A group that large would have a tough time living off of the land in a strange country. It wasn't an attractive option.

"It's been a month since we've heard anything," George said. "We should return to Tiflis and check on our paperwork."

"It'll take the rest of our money to buy the round-trip tickets," Peter Kroeker said. "If the trip fails, our only option is walking into Turkey."

It was a bittersweet moment in Tiflis when the proper documentation was waiting for them. They had permission to leave with official exit visas but no money to purchase tickets. All of their valuables had been sold to buy food. The trip back to Batumi was silent, only interrupted by security checks from Cheka officers.

Shivering in the early November rain, the families huddled in the wharf district. Most of the group fell ill. Abraham Kroeker spent most nights with a nearby family, which was okay with Gerhardt. The man was starting to get under his skin. Trying to crack down on dissidents, the Cheka started making mass arrests again. Hundreds of men were being rounded up.

Gerhardt finally found a bit of daylight in their bleak existence. During one of his many rounds of the various embassies still open in Batumi, he met a German Attache at the Swedish embassy. "So, you're a group of ethnic Germans trying to get out of Russia?"

"Yes," Gerhardt said. "The place has turned into a quagmire of political intrigue. Some of the peasants who've always resented us now think they have implied governmental consent to kill us."

"Come back in a couple of days," the man answered. "Let me check into this."

"Thank you for spending your valuable time with me."

The diplomat was sympathetic toward the group of ethnic Germans. When Gerhardt returned a few days later, the Attache had arranged for tickets on a ship to Constantinople.

On November 18, the families finally boarded the Celio of the Lloyd Triestino line. During the initial boarding confusion, Henry and Martin broke free from the group and wandered undetected around the ship. The boys' exploration instinct obliged them to go higher in the ship for a better view. Managing to slip through the bustle of passengers, they snuck into the first-class dining room.

The boys stood, gawking around at the splendor. With linen-covered tables, the room had a raised panel ceiling and electric lights with no exposed knob and tube wiring. Flower-filled vases sat on each table. The room even had carpeting on the floor with a diamond-shaped pattern. They'd only seen such luxury in the homes of large estate owners. Making their way out of the dining area, they entered a room filled with dark leather chairs around small, ornate, wooden tables. In the center of each table was a silver ashtray.

Martin asked, "They have a whole room for just smoking?"

Henry shrugged and, as they were starting to leave the room, they overheard voices passing on the promenade. It was a steward proudly telling some passengers, "The Celio is a single screw, 356-foot-long ship with a forty-two-foot beam. She has a single funnel and twin masts, one forward and one aft with a speed of about thirteen knots."

The affluent couple were nodding with appreciation when the steward spied the two obviously out-of-place boys wearing ragged clothing.

"Hey, you! What are you doing up here?"

The boys bolted out of the room and ran down an interior passageway. Weaving between amused passengers, the steward gave chase. Ducking into another room, the boys hid in the corner behind a couple of lavishly upholstered fabric chairs but couldn't resist peeking out. Sitting between windows was a piano that's bench fabric matched the wall panels. A large oil painting hung above the piano. The vaulted skylight was surrounded by another raised panel ceiling.

"Aha, gotcha!"

The steward loomed over the startled boys. Grabbing each by their frayed collars, he led the boys down two flights of stairs into the second-class level where they were remanded into the custody of another steward. Escorted down more flights of stairs until they reached the steerage area, they were unceremoniously shoved into a large compartment crammed with people wearing clothing just as frayed as theirs. The room's stale air was already permeated with the stench of many unwashed travelers packed together. It was a stark contrast to the airy breezeways above deck.

A lot of the children were still sick. Maria's great aunt was so ill, she had to be carried onto the ship. Still, the group was happy as they watched Batumi and the Georgian coastline disappear from sight in stormy seas. In cramped conditions, refugees slept on metal floors within the sparse third-class accommodations.

The ship's rolling and heaving made the already sick passengers even more miserable. With salt water running down the inner hull—a product of spray finding its way through leaking portholes—bedding was constantly damp. The ship's doctor, who could speak passable German, tried to alleviate sick passengers' suffering.

The din in the compartment seemingly never contained a lull among the mostly Armenian immigrants fleeing from their own persecutions in northeastern Turkey. During the voyage, out of sheer boredom, Gerhardt conversed with an Armenian man who had difficulty walking.

With limited linguistic skills he'd developed from his time in the region, Gerhardt understood the man used to live near Kars—a region which had long been an area of conflict between Russia and Turkey. The Turks apparently hated Christian Armenians even more than the Bolshevist Russian peasants hated ethnic German settlers.

"So, you fought for the Ottomans during the war?" Gerhardt asked.

"Oh, no. We fought for Russia. We've been in conflict with the Turks for decades."

"Decades?"

"Yes. Christians and Muslims in northeastern Turkey have been at each other's throats for a long time."

"Oh, that's right. I remember reading about that," Gerhardt said.

"In fact, when Russia signed an armistice with Turkey, the Russian Army left all of their weapons for us to continue fighting."

"Oh yeah, my brother was stationed near here during the war. He told me all about that. When did the war end for you?"

"I don't know that it has completely ended."

"Really?"

"Yes. That's why we're on this ship. We don't want to leave our homeland, but if we don't, I fear none of us will survive."

"I know what you mean. What happened to your feet?" Gerhardt asked.

"The war. Well, really the purported end of the war. The fighting was supposed to be over and, on October 30, 1920, our unit was ordered to surrender our weapons to the Turks. The instant we were all disarmed, the Turks forced thousands of us to strip naked and pushed us out into over four inches of fresh snow to freeze to death."

"That's awful. How'd you survive?"

"A local Christian aid society found us and tried to help, but they couldn't do much. There just wasn't enough clothing to dress us. They finally found a local merchant who opened up his warehouse and passed out empty flour sacks as a substitute. That helped a little, but my feet have never recovered."

"I wish you well in finding somewhere peaceful to live."

"Thank you. I wish the same for you," the crippled man replied.

Gerhardt knew full well the capacity of a society's self-escalating mob cruelty to its perceived enemy. He'd seen and experienced it firsthand.

Taking turns tending to the ill, the group's women used infrequent breaks to brave a few moments of fresh air above deck. Maria sat beside her great aunt, wiping her forehead with a cool rag. On the fourth day at sea, her aunt died. The doctor was summoned, and the group asked that the body be kept in storage until the ship got to port. The captain denied the request.

After Abraham Kroeker officiated in German at the funeral, the ship's stewards dumped her body overboard. John Becker's wife kept Maria's cousin, Annie, below deck during the service and burial. This was the first person in their party to succumb to the hardships.

Entering the Bosphorus, Gerhardt took the children up to the ship's lower class fantail observation area. Enclosed on the first floor, the second level was open to the elements. The upper floor had bow assemblies stretching across the deck where canvas could be stretched in inclement weather. Often, the heavy oil smoke coming out of the funnel found its way down onto the rear deck observation area.

While Gerhardt watched the narrow Bosphorus Straight's scenery, the boys were more interested in the three winch booms attached near the base of the rear mast. On the port side, hanging from one of the winch booms, was the ship's motor launch. The boys ran over to explore the lifeboat davits. There wasn't much to explore with only one small lifeboat on each side of the lower-class stern area. The majority of lifeboats were on the upper deck in first class—one small lifeboat, similar to the one in third class, and two much larger ones on each side of the ship.

Henry noticed the disparity in the number of lifeboats. "Foda, why are there more lifeboats up there than down here? Shouldn't all of the lifeboats be near the water?"

Gerhardt smiled to himself. "Well, son, I think they believe rich people can't swim as well as poor people."

"Really? I wonder why that is."

"Probably because all the jewelry around their necks and coins in their pockets weighs them down."

Henry asked, "Why don't they get rid of that stuff?"

"It's hard to give up something you think you've worked so hard to get."

"I guess you're right. I worked hard doing my chores to get my pocket knife. I don't want to lose it either."

CHAPTER THIRTY-ONE
YENI KUEY

The families prepared to disembark with the other passengers when the ship finally slipped into its berth in Constantinople. However, they were stopped from leaving the ship. Algerian soldiers in the French Foreign Legion were guarding the docks. Seeing that the families had Germanic names, the soldiers who still remembered the Great War wouldn't allow them off the boat. Gerhardt, with the aid of a sailor to translate, tried to reason with them.

Because of his darker complexion, the Algerians were a little more accepting of Gerhardt over the rest of the group. He and the sailor went into a nearby tavern and negotiated over Turkish coffee poured from a copper cezve into a tiny cup. After a while of negotiating and Gerhardt showing them his papers from the Russian army, the soldiers were convinced that these Germans weren't the same as the ones they fought against in the war. They agreed to let the families through.

When Gerhardt returned to the ship, the sailor who had been his interpreter warned that the occupying forces in Constantinople had a habit of shanghaiing strangers and conscripting them. Talking it over, the group decided to send the sailor to the refugee center and have someone come to escort them. Gerhardt bristled when Abraham announced he would accompany the sailor into town, like he was the leader. The newspaper editor stated that he was well known and had a contact address. Peter Kroeker put his calming hand on Gerhardt's arm and volunteered to accompany Abraham and the translator. The three men left for town.

The next day, the families deboarded the ship with their meager possessions and were sitting on the wharf, when a truck driven by American aid workers pulled up. A couple of American men got out and walked up to the group. Abraham immediately started telling his story of persecution and deprivation accompanied by more than a few tears. Gerhardt rolled his eyes, thinking that the man had suffered no more than the rest of the group.

When the workers came close to survey the needs of the group, Maria, who was sitting on the ground with ten-month-old Frieda in her arms, warned the men, "Excuse me, sirs, but you probably don't want to get too close to us right now. The lice on us are probably hungry enough that they'll jump to you to get a decent meal."

The Americans backed up a safe distance to finish their interviews. Counting Abraham, there were thirty-one starving, ragged, lice-infested refugees sitting there—nine adults and twenty-two children under fourteen.

Frank Stoltzfus introduced himself as the head of the Mennonite Central Committee local relief operations. Even though he maintained a respectable buffer zone between himself and the refugees, Frank kept fidgeting and squirming under the suggestive influence of a phantom legion of lice marching across the fertile feeding grounds of his flesh.

Loaded into trucks, the families were taken about ten miles north of the city to Yeni Kuey. During the drive, they passed one Russian refugee camp after another. There were still tens of thousands of White Russians living in squalid conditions, unable to move on.

At the refugee home, Gerhardt got out of the truck and took little Frieda from Maria, who held the hands of Helen and Katherine. As they walked toward the compound, Frank Stoltzfus pumped Gerhardt for his family's story, wanting to know how they ended up in Constantinople. After making it as far as Batumi in the telling, Frank stopped Gerhardt with a hand on his arm.

He asked, "You mean to tell me that since your family was driven out of the Caucasus, you've basically been refugees for four years, looking for a safe place for your family?"

Gerhardt shrugged. "I hadn't thought of it that way. I always thought we were just searching for a home to raise our children in peace."

Frank replied, "That's the definition of a refugee."

After Frank thoughtfully walked off, Gerhardt turned to look around at the greeting committee. All seemingly Americans, there wasn't a person among them who appeared older than thirty. Enthusiastic, the aid workers exuded efficiency. Consisting of several buildings, the compound had been divided into living, medical, and administrative uses.

While the men were being introduced, a group of young women descended upon the wives and children. A well-dressed tall girl, only about thirty years old, wearing glasses with her hair pulled back, seemed to be in charge. She came up to Maria and caressed little Frieda's face between her hands, then looked down at Helen and Katherine.

"My, but aren't you just a little dear. My name is Vesta Zook. I'm in charge of the children's home. This lady over here is Venora Weaver. She's in charge of the young women's home. What are your names?"

The girls shyly hid behind Maria's skirt while their mother introduced them. An inventory of the families was taken. Little Annie Dirks was identified as an orphan but didn't want to be separated from the group. As she hid behind Peter Kroeker's wife, Catherine, John Becker came over and interceded, "We'll assume responsibility for her. She can join our family. Our daughters are the same age, and she won't be a problem."

After being checked out in an attached medical center, the refugees were given baths, haircuts, then assigned to the second story of the main building. Single men, mostly remnants of Wrangel's evacuation from Crimea, were on the first floor. After they settled in, the center's volunteers started documenting everyone in the group. The heads of each family signed a promissory note that they would attempt to pay back any money spent on room, board, and travel.

When Gerhardt sat down for his interview, Frank Stoltzfus looked at his name and asked, "Gerhardt Wiens, huh? We just had a Gerhardt Wiens pass through here. He and Detrich Wiens were part of the White Army evacuees. We just sent them and sixty others to America. The rest we're trying to find a destination for elsewhere."

Gerhardt nodded. "I don't remember meeting either man. But our last name is quite common in Russia. They're probably third or fourth cousins."

As the interview progressed, Gerhardt was informed that getting into the United States was problematic. Recently enforced quotas limited immigrants from Eastern and Southern Europe. Even if he could get in, it was probably going to require a sponsor family and hopefully someone to loan him the money for the fares. Some of the refugees had gone to Germany, Mexico, and South America. Canada was still a good option.

Gerhardt thought for a few moments, then said, "I was in the United States as a child. I have relatives in Minnesota and Kansas."

"That's a good thing," Frank said. "We'll try as much as possible to contact them and see if they're willing to fund you. Meanwhile, we'll try to find work for you here locally to help out."

"That's good. We want to pay our own way."

The men shook hands, and Gerhardt returned to his family. So poor and thin, he couldn't afford to support even one more of the lice which had come to call his body home. But, for the first time in years, he could see a horizon to walk toward. Visiting the single men on the first floor of the home, Gerhardt discovered the Mennonites had invited Baptists, Catholics, and Lutherans to find refuge there also. The Red Cross, which Gerhardt was familiar with from the war, and something called the American Relief Administration was also in Constantinople.

He was confused. "I've seen the Red Cross during the war. But what kind of charity is the American Relief Administration?"

One of the more knowledgeable single men explained the ARA. "It isn't a charity. It's an American government group. I heard some millionaire mining engineer by the name of Herbert Hoover is in charge."

"A mining engineer?" Gerhardt asked.

"Yep."

"The American government?"

"Yes. Now that the war is over, the Americans are throwing around millions of dollars all over Europe. But, of course, they want things done their way."

Gerhardt was used to charities helping out the needy, but a government? He wandered back to his family's quarters. He was going to have to mull that over for a while. A government getting involved in charity work outside of its own borders seemed to be a double-edged sword. The money was definitely useful, but what were the strings that would invariably be attached?

CHAPTER THIRTY-TWO
CHANGES AT HOME

Gerhardt's sister, Helena, stood looking out of her parent's kitchen window and watched the 1921 spring planting in the distant fields. For the last couple of years, etching out a living on their land had been hard for the family. With the Revolution depleting their livestock and grain reserves, what remained was sickly and malnourished. Her siblings still living at home were out trying to plow, using the unlikely team of a swayback horse and the milk cow.

She'd be thirty-two in July. Still being single made her feel like a dead weight on the family. Up until recently, she felt useful helping raise her younger siblings. At 5'4", she was of average height and beautiful. She kept her wavy, brunette hair parted on the left and loosely combed down over her ears and back into a traditional bun. She had a small nose, full lips, pale skin, and a small familial cleft in her chin.

As the oldest daughter in a large family, she was strong, level headed, and confident, but had never learned to flirt. The local young men had all thought about courting her at one time or another but, believing they couldn't measure up, none made an attempt, and married others. Helena hadn't realized she was the object of so many men's thoughts. She assumed no one wanted her and had refused to put herself out on the openly available woman list.

Now, she just felt like another mouth for her parents to feed. Lately, a widower with two daughters had shown interest in her. He had a good job as a locksmith and had nice children. She would also be less of a drain on her parents' resources if she moved out. Helena snapped out of her mental wanderings, back to the present, when she heard the field crew coming in for lunch.

That summer in Karpovka was long and hot. The previous year's drought showed no sign of letting up. Field crops withered. Fruit on the trees had to be guarded or it would be stolen by roving beggars. It was always a difficult decision to offer food to the beggars because you might not have enough left for your own family. Helena watched as a steady stream of starving refugees from the north paraded by looking for food.

In August, her younger sister Eva married Peter Neufeld, the son of a large estate owner. Eva's wedding and the crop failure made up her mind. She would say yes to Johann, leaving two fewer mouths to feed under her parents' roof.

In a small and unpretentious September ceremony, Helena married Johann Wiebe. No one wanted to take the time off from harvest to plan and put on anything larger. Besides, Johann had already been previously married, and Helena, being an older child, was too practical to waste time and money.

A good man, Johann hired Helena's younger brother, Peter, as an apprentice to work in his shop. The money Peter made helped get her parents and siblings through the coming winter. Her father managed to hide some grain reserves from government confiscation by burying it. Still, it might not be enough to feed the family and have any left for spring planting.

Then a hard winter set in. By mid-winter, some of the less fortunate had eaten their dogs. Beggars came by daily trying to barter their meager possessions for food. Helena received a letter from Gerhardt's sister-in-law, Aganeta. Conditions were so poor near the Molotschna colony, that Russian peasants ground up thistle-stalks for flour.

Aganeta wrote, "I saw a widow removing thatch from her house's roof to feed their milk cow. The cow is the only source of sustenance left for her children. She's down to having only one small corner of her house they can still huddle under. It won't be long before the cow starves."

No one wanted to go near a train station. With restaurants becoming a rarity, travelers carried food bags with them. Beggars congregated on the platforms, beseeching passerby for spare morsels.

Helena heard rumors of relief organizations trying to get food into the area, but red tape and winter weather was tying up shipments. She thought it a macabre irony that Huliaipole was one of the worst hit areas. Huliaipole sat halfway between where the two women lived and was the hometown of Nestor Makhno. His Black Army had killed many of their family and friends. Russian peasants and ex-Black Army fighters living near there were dying in droves.

In March, 1922, Aganeta wrote, "Relief kitchens have been set up nearby, and the relief organization is hiring workers. They are only giving out one meal a day, and you had to prove you really need it. If you have two horses on your farm, you have to sell one to buy food. If you only have one horse left to farm with, the kitchen will feed you. When you register, they'll give you a ration card and mark it every time you eat. The meals are only 800 calories a day, but it's still better than starving."

Helena read the letters to her family, and they all waited. Since the Memrik colony fared marginally better through the winter, it was May before a sorely needed kitchen was set up. Even though most of the cats in town had been eaten by starving peasants, the rat population didn't increase. They'd been eaten also.

Helena's father had little grain left to plant in the spring of 1922. He began making chairs in his shop to build up cash reserves for the next winter, when he would again have few crops. Her brothers and one sister who were still at home ran the farm. It was a good thing her father thought ahead. The harvest in the area was still poor, and the famine would endure for at least another year.

Helena watched the poorer families with no livestock left pull a harrow through the fields themselves. Someone would follow, sowing the seeds in a desperate attempt to have something to eat the next winter. Beggars gleaned between the train station's rails for grain dropped when a relief car had been unloaded. Future prospects looked grim.

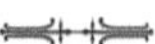

Heinrich sat, mulling his future in Russia. All of the military-aged boys, both native Russian and German settlers, in the village had been conscripted. Close to forty young men from the village, including his younger brother Peter, had recently boarded trains and were sent to the Don River town, Novocherkask. During the Revolution, it had been the headquarters of the Don Cossack Army.

Once the western White Army was defeated, the Communists took over the facilities. The Revolution was still ongoing in the far reaches of Siberia. Heinrich worried that his brother and the others would now have to endure the horrors of war he had just escaped from.

Heinrich reminded himself that he had to start being more careful how he referred to others in public. He'd always thought of anyone not of his ethnicity as Russian. The Revolution exposed many raw ethnic sensitivities. Ukraine and the Caucasus regions were a buffer zone between Russia and the Ottoman Empire. Katherine the Great had just taken most of southern Ukraine from the Ottoman Empire when she invited the German settlers in to cement her hold on the area. Later rulers added Crimea and the Caucuses into Russia.

Revolution scraped the scab off old wounds. Local Tartars, Nogai, and Cossacks considered Russians to be as much interlopers as were German settlers. That tension was one of the driving factors behind the Black Army's creation—the other being that the Communists wanted a large centralized government until equality was achieved and Makhno's group wanted to proceed directly into anarchist equality.

The perception of the Red Army representing Russia proper was one of the reasons the separatist Ukrainian Black Army originally fought the Red Army as hard as it fought against the White Army. A tentative alliance combined the Red and Black armies to defeat the White Army. Then, when the Communists showed their true colors and arrested the Black Army leadership, the various ethnicities coagulated with the common bond of resenting their Russian overlords.

The still ongoing famine didn't help matters. A drought combined with the Revolution started the famine. The new Communist government exacerbated the famine exponentially when it confiscated the harvest for dispersal in areas it thought were in worse shape. The problem was, the bureaucrats were thousands of miles away with absolutely no concept of the actual conditions in affected regions.

The Ukraine region was bristling under the heavy thumb of the new government. Cheka agents were everywhere trying to ferret out Tsarist loyalists, Ukrainian separatists, and wealthy landowners unwilling to convert their holdings into cooperatives.

Watching his brother Gerhardt, Heinrich had learned some of what not to do. In smuggled letters, he heard his brother had accidentally placed himself under the government microscope when he assumed the management of a coop farm. When Gerhardt couldn't magically pull the mandated harvest out of thin air, he was labeled as a criminal of the state and would have been imprisoned if he hadn't escaped.

Heinrich loved his family's adopted homeland, homesick when he was torn away from it. Russia wasn't perfect by any means, but it was his home. It was slowly dawning on him that his brother might be right—it was time to move on. Their father expressed privately that he was second-guessing his decision to come back from America.

Heinrich decided to go slow with his deliberations. His father told him many years ago that mistakes are spawned in the whirlpools of haste. He'd always tried to live by those words. Now that he was married, it wasn't his decision alone to make. What he did know was that he had to keep his head down and stay anonymous to the State.

He no longer wanted to risk becoming a landowner. In the current political climate, that would place a target on his back. Technically, as the oldest son in the family, he'd be the rightful heir of his parents' land. Heinrich was uncertain he wanted to claim that right.

CHAPTER THIRTY-THREE
ONE MORE LOSS

Life in Yeni Kuey was infinitely better than it had been in Crimea or Batumi. Gerhardt's family was being fed, and no one was threatening to imprison or shoot them. Gerhardt was put to work by the refugee center to offset some of his family's costs. In December, the immigration committee paid the embassy back for his family's tickets from Batumi and got them visas. Inquiries had been sent to every American relative Gerhardt could think of who might loan the money for his family's travel to America.

The refugees settled into a routine. During the day, the children would play along the bluff overlooking the Bosphorus with the children from the orphanage. On Sundays, Abraham Kroeker would lead a service in the chapel. With Abraham still getting under his skin, Gerhardt tried to maintain a buffering distance between them when at all possible.

He couldn't identify why, but the man just irritated him. Gerhardt settled on the comparison of a burr getting under a saddle. For some reason, even though the burr had been removed, the area would remain sensitive for a long time. Days seemed to pass slower in the close confines of the home.

Finally, on January 17, 1922 a cablegram arrived. A distant cousin of Gerhardt's, Peter Pankratz of Hillsboro, Kansas, agreed to pay for the family's fare to America. A few days later, Peter Kroeker was notified that his family was also funded. Gerhardt winced when he heard Abraham might make it onto the same ship.

Gerhardt noticed Frank Stoltzfus was spending more time with Vesta Zook, head of the orphanage, and Vinora Weaver, the manager of the single women's home. According to gossip, plans were being laid to shut down the refugee center. Gerhardt wondered just how the Americans thought it was proper for single people of their age to meet without a chaperone. He doubted if they would get away with such conduct back in Karpovka.

The young women's home would close soon, and the British had arranged to take over the orphanage. Frank Stoltzfus had been trying to transfer Russian orphans to an old embassy in Bulgaria. The organization was having trouble evicting the Russian refugee squatters in the embassy. The ordeal was dragging on.

Reports of the families' escape had made it back home to others hoping to flee Russia. There were now hundreds of ethnic German refugees flooding into Georgia by sea and land. With the survival prospects of the new batch of Batumi refugees looking just as bleak as it was for Gerhardt's group, the managers of the relief effort were scrambling to handle the situation before it degraded further.

At the same time in Yeni Kuey, the cramped quarters made it easy to transmit disease. Typhus hit the first-floor single men's quarters, and the sick were taken to the clinic. Soon, it infected the family area. At least having a healthier diet helped the inflicted withstand the disease better.

George Becker came down with typhus in February. Maria and Gerhardt had known George for most of their lives. It was through George's family that their wedding had been arranged. Gerhardt visited George a couple of times a day, pretending that all was well. They would reminisce about the good old days and what they'd been through. Finally, too weak to carry on the charade, George reached out and feebly grasped Gerhardt's hand.

"Listen, old friend, we can't avoid the subject forever. You and I both know I'm not going to make it."

Gerhardt looked sadly at George. "Don't say that. You'll be back bossing the rest of us around in just a few days."

"Don't try to humor me. We both know it isn't true."

"What do you want me to do?" Gerhardt asked.

"My family. I need to know that my family will be alright without me."

"They will. You have a strong family."

George pleaded, "I need you to promise me that you'll look after them."

"I will. I'll make sure that they get out of here safely." Gerhardt was having a hard time controlling his emotions.

"Thank you. You've been a good friend, and I'm asking a lot of you."

"It is nothing compared to what we've already been through together."

"Thank you, my friend."

George weakly squeezed Gerhardt's hand, then drifted off to sleep. He would never regain full consciousness after that exchange, and soon died.

It was hard on all of the families. George was the second member of the close-knit group which had left Franzthal almost two years before, to die in their odyssey. What made the occasion even sadder was that the two Becker families had not yet received funding, and the party would be split up. The home would be closed soon, and the remaining families would be transferred to another facility until they could also leave.

Gerhardt faced a moral dilemma. He had promised he would look after George's family. If he waited and missed his own family's assigned sailing date, the funding may fall through or the immigration quotas may be filled. If he left, he would be letting the Becker family down. John Becker, seeing Gerhardt suffering with the decision, came up and put his arm around him.

"You go with your family. We'll get funding. If we don't get the money soon, I trust you'll do your best to find someone who'll come to our rescue. What can be the worst outcome? These people are stuck with us now. We're in their hands."

"I made him a promise," Gerhardt answered.

"He was my blood. I'll take his family to America. Just because you received your funding first doesn't mean that we'll not join you soon."

"Are you sure?" Gerhardt asked.

"Yes. We've received preliminary notices that funding might be on its way. It's just taking a little longer."

Gerhardt grasped John's hand. "We'll get you out."

After the funeral, Gerhardt and his boys walked along the bluff overlooking the Bosphorus. They sat down on a rock outcropping and stared at the ships in the channel below. After a long period of silence, Henry looked up at his father and asked, "Why did God kill George? He was a good man. God has let all of those bad men around us go free."

Gerhardt didn't know what to say. His boys had seen a lot of bad men in their short lives. They had seen war. They had witnessed beatings and murders. They had seen people starving to death. The boys had endured starvation themselves. How was he going to explain God's rationale to them? He finally pointed at the blue water below.

"See the beauty of the water? It was put here by God. The water harbors fish for us to eat. It quenches the thirst of crops we grow. It can also flood and destroy all that it covers."

He picked up a handful of dirt. "See this dirt? It nourishes the crops we grow. The right dirt can make bricks to build houses. If you mistreat the dirt, it will dry up and blow away, leaving you with no way to grow food."

Gerhardt pointed at the mountains. "See the mountains? They store water as snow until we need it for the crops. Everything around you, God created to help us have a good life.

"God created nature, but he allows nature to have its own free will. That's what makes nature so wonderful yet fickle, and sometimes dangerous.

"God gave men free will to make their own decisions. Everything bad men do to each other is their doing, not God's will. Lately, nature has been fickle at the same time men have decided to take it upon themselves to kill each other. When that happens, people starve and get sick and die.

"God never promised us an easy life. He never promised we would live long or those we love would live long. What God has promised is that if we remain faithful, he will help us endure our suffering. He has promised us that if we remain faithful, our real reward comes after we die."

The boys mulled it over for a while, then got up to explore. Gerhardt hoped he'd helped explain life to the boys even though he did not understand it fully himself. He sat in the late winter sun on the bluff, staring off across the expanse toward Turkey proper. Updraft winds coming off the Bosphorus buffeted Gerhardt and kept the seagulls effortlessly suspended in front of him. Were the gulls there to taunt him, or were they showing that properly navigated head-winds could also help buoy him? Brought back into the moment by the boys returning from their wanderings, he strolled beside them to the compound.

Gerhardt didn't remember the walk back. His mind was tortured with guilt over breaking his promise to George, receiving immigration money before the rest of his group and leaving his own siblings and parents behind. He had fear of what unknown challenges and dangers lay ahead for his family.

Always so sure of his path forward, Gerhardt now second guessed his every step. He knew that he had to forge ahead on this path of unsure footing. Otherwise, he would surrender what little control he had over his family's fate. They would be doomed to become more faceless victims of the blackness enveloping Russia.

CHAPTER THIRTY-FOUR
THE ACROPOLIS

March 8, 1922, Gerhardt and Maria packed one change of clothes for themselves and each of their five children into a couple of flour sacks. The family loaded onto one of the center's trucks. Twenty-eight-year-old Nicholas Unger and his twenty-six-year-old wife, Nadine, rode with them to the wharf.

Thirty-seven-year-old Peter Kroeker, his thirty-eight-year-old wife, Catherine, and their five children, ranging from nineteen months to thirteen years old, were in a second truck. Fifty-nine-year-old newspaper editor, Abraham Kroeker, and nineteen-year-old Martin Toews rode with the Kroekers.

For ten miles, the trucks wound their way through the marginally smaller remaining refugee camps into Constantinople. The Red Cross and various religious relief organizations had been busy relocating the refugees to Germany, Bulgaria, South America, and even Palestine.

A substantial percentage of the refugees had been retrained and joined the local workforce. It was always difficult to see a former member of the Russian aristocracy working in a shoe repair shop. A few White Russian refugees had managed to carry a small amount of their previous wealth with them and had started up restaurants. Russian culture was changing the area. The locals had taken to emulating the more modern customs and attire of the immigrants.

As usual, it was tough restraining the boys when the trucks pulled onto the wharf. There was so much surrounding activity, it was hard for them to concentrate on any one thing. Conveyors were almost finished loading the last of the coal for the ship's boilers. Turkish police stood around the perimeter, watching for trouble.

Herded off to the side so first- and second-class passengers wouldn't be bothered, third-class riff-raff waited impatiently. Baggage and freight were being loaded by one set of cranes while, on the other end of the ship, another crane loaded food into the refrigerated hold. Black smoke billowed out of the rear funnel as the boiler built up steam.

Gerhardt had been told that the Acropolis was twenty feet longer than the Celio, but he couldn't tell the difference. It did have two funnels, with four horizontal stripes on the top of each one. In comparison, the Celio only had one funnel. The Acropolis was all white which only amplified the rust patches and grime streaking down the sides. An American flag flew on the stern of the ship. Behind the pilothouse, there were four large lifeboats hanging from davits on the boat deck. It was apparent the Acropolis was a much older ship than the Celio.

The families, along with the ethnic Russians and Turks boarding with them, made their way down to their assigned berths in third class. Joining passengers who had boarded in previous ports, they barely had time to store their meager possessions before the ship could be felt leaving the dock.

Gerhardt decided to help Henry and Martin burn off some excess energy by taking them for a walk around the ship. As they made their way around the promenade deck, the boys almost had to be physically restrained to keep from running. They'd almost circumnavigated the ship before it had crept out of the Bosphorus into the Sea of Marmara.

The Acropolis didn't seem to be going very fast. Only seeing coal smoke coming out of the rear stack, Gerhardt stopped a passing steward and asked when the other boilers would fire up so the ship could make full speed.

The steward laughed. "There *are* no other boilers, the second funnel is a dummy. This is as fast as she goes—eleven knots."

Gerhardt was shocked. "Why would anyone waste money installing a dummy funnel that does nothing?"

"It was installed to disguise an old cattle boat so that investors would give money and passengers would want to ride on it."

"A cattle boat?" Gerhardt asked.

"Yes, the Acropolis was built by Harland and Wolf in 1890 as a cargo ship with some room for a few passengers. The American government bought it in 1898, named it the Kilpatrick, and converted it to haul troops and horses in the Spanish-American War. It would haul 800 troops, forty officers and 800 horses. This company bought her in 1920 and refitted it again to have 250 cabins and carry 600 third-class passengers. It's been on this route for about a year now."

Gerhardt looked around at the other immigrants on the deck and thought out loud, "It appears like it's still being used as a cattle boat."

The steward laughed again. "When you've been doing this job as long as I have, you realize there isn't much of a difference between a cattle boat and the lower decks of a passenger ship."

Gerhardt glanced again at his fellow passengers and joined in the laugh. "I can see your point."

Quickly looking around to see if anyone had overheard their conversation, the steward said, "Don't tell anyone that I said that."

"Your secret is safe with me."

"Just let me know if you need anything else."

Gerhardt and the steward exchanged a handshake. Patting the man on the upper arm, he led his boys off for more exploration.

As Henry and Martin explored, Gerhardt chatted with a group of Russians who told him they had boarded in Constanta, Romania on March 4. One of the men pointed to another small group and said they had come aboard in Varna, Bulgaria on the 1ˢᵗ. Gerhardt and the Russians compared stories on how they happened to all be ex-Russian citizens headed for the United States. The stories all had one common thread: Communism.

After passing through the Dardanelles, the Acropolis added more passengers in Piraeus, Greece on March 11 and Patras, Greece on March 14. Each time, Henry and Martin would get off of the ship and explore the docks. Maria sat along the railing to watch, hoping they wouldn't stray too far. It wouldn't have mattered if they did. The din surrounding the ship would have drowned out any restraining shout she could have uttered. It was a relief when the Acropolis pulled away from the last port with both of her boys still on board.

Crossing the Mediterranean was rough but nothing compared to the weather on the Atlantic Ocean. Abraham Kroeker developed an infected lung. Nadine Unger had taken ill. Maria and baby Freida were still fragile, suffering from lingering effects of the famine. Catherine Kroeker and her youngest toddler were both sick the whole way. Thankfully, the time spent on the Celio had acclimated the family to life on a ship. Little time was spent with seasickness. Even though the Acropolis was older, at least the portholes didn't leak and the family possessions stayed dry.

The ship's surgeon, Dr. Paul C. Lybyer, stopped by now and then to check on ailing passengers. Gerhardt was amazed the shipping company worried so much about passenger health. On the Celio, the main concern was ensuring other passengers did not also become infected. Gerhardt asked the candid steward he'd taken a liking to why the special concern over passenger health.

"It's awfully nice of the ship's owners to furnish such nice medical care."

The steward snorted. "It's not that altruistic. Once the ship gets to New York, all sick passengers will be held in the Ellis Island hospital until they're well."

"That's very nice of the Americans."

"Not so very nice. If a passenger can't pay the hospital bill, the company whose ship brought them is billed."

"Really?" Gerhardt asked.

"I've heard there are patients at Ellis Island who are chronically ill and will never be allowed to leave the hospital."

That last piece of information made Gerhardt nervous. If Maria didn't get stronger, would the Americans keep them on the island like prisoners?

The steward continued, "Not only that, but there are always people with the wrong disease who get rejected at the port outright. They are loaded right back onto the ship and sent back to where they came from. We take a few back every trip."

"Someone is sent back every trip?"

"That's what I've heard."

Now, Gerhardt was really worried. "Even children?"

"Yep, even children. If the child is over twelve, they're sent back alone. If they're under twelve, one of their parents is sent back with them."

Thirty-four days after leaving Constantinople, the ship navigated the Hudson River. Having never seen such tall buildings as New York City loomed in front of them, the immigrants jockeyed for a place along the ship's railing. Gerhardt had been there before as a child, and he knew to stand on the ship's Port side while entering the channel. The ship slowed to a crawl when it passed the Statue of Liberty.

The children asked why anyone would build such a large statue of a green woman holding a flame. He explained the torch and why the statue ended up being green. The statue was only a few years old when he first came to America as a child. Tugboats shoved the Acropolis into her Port of New York berth on April 12, 1922.

Instead of being thrilled with his family's arrival in America, Gerhardt was filled with trepidation. Would the family be rejected? Even though they had been declared healthy in Constantinople, what about now? The steward said that any passengers immediately rejected at Ellis Island would be loaded back onto the ship and sent back where they came from.

If they sent his wife and child back, would he be allowed by the shipping company to go with them? Or would the family be forcibly split up? He'd been told that there were almost always some passengers rejected and sent back every trip.

The Russian government was rescinding the citizenship of anyone who had fled the country after the Revolution. Gerhardt's family had nowhere to go if they were denied admission into America. With the weight of the world on his shoulders, Gerhardt looked across the harbor toward the Statue of Liberty.

www.ingramcontent.com/pod-product-compliance
Lightning Source LLC
Chambersburg PA
CBHW061238310726
48971CB00007B/2124